CRIME IN THE HIGH STREET

A fiercely addictive mystery

CATHERINE MOLONEY

Detective Markham Mystery Book 19

JOFFE BOOKS

Joffe Books, London
www.joffebooks.com

First published in Great Britain in 2023

Cover art by Dee Dee Book Covers

ISBN: 978-1-80405-881-7

PROLOGUE

Summertime and the livin' is easy . . .

Monday 1 August looked likely to be a scorcher, Rosemary Blake thought, humming under her breath as she locked up at Number 16, the Copse before checking to see she had all her cleaning paraphernalia with her. Stella Fanshaw had raised merry hell the one time she had left her mop and bucket inside by mistake, so nowadays she was ultra-careful. At least the old sourpuss didn't stand over her the whole time, since Monday morning's hairdressing appointment was set in stone and she invariably met up with her friends from the bridge club afterwards. And it was relatively easy money, seeing as the place was always pretty much immaculate to start with. Rosemary was willing to bet Stella Fanshaw regarded the acquisition of a 'woman who does' as a status symbol which set her apart from other residents of the cul-de-sac in one of Medway's more salubrious districts. Out of the seventeen households in the Copse, only Stella, Sheila Craven and Tricia Dent employed a cleaner, no doubt thoroughly enjoying the one-upmanship of being able to afford such a perk.

The houses themselves were nothing special, being merely neat modern residences with dormers and pocket-handkerchief gardens to front and rear. However, the close boasted a parking bay and nicely landscaped central island (Stella Fanshaw objected to hearing it called 'the mound'), and it was a peaceful little estate where nothing much ever happened, the most excitement in recent times being a rather half-hearted 'street party' (of the most genteel kind) on the occasion of the Queen's Platinum Jubilee the previous year.

Rosemary's next port of call was Sheila Craven's residence at number 12, which she always thought of as the doll's house on account of its dainty decor. Widowed eighteen months previously, Mrs Craven was gradually rediscovering her mojo, venturing out to bowls and the occasional lunch at Rossi's on the high street. Most likely, in line with her usual Monday morning routine, she would be comfortably installed in her little conservatory (or 'orangery' as she called it) contemplating the beautifully manicured back lawn and flower beds which her gardener (one in the eye to Mesdames Fanshaw and Dent!) kept in tiptop condition.

Rosemary had a few minutes before she was due at Sheila's, so she wandered across to her car and rooted around in the boot for a bottle of water and Kit Kat. Having consumed the al fresco snack, she leaned against her vehicle savouring the warmth of the day.

Mad Dogs and Englishmen, she reminded herself, aware that she should get indoors since her pale Celtic complexion was prone to take on an appearance of boiled lobster with too much exposure to the summer sun.

Nonetheless she couldn't help lingering, the buttery heat making her feel languorous and featherlight. The day had a white glare which seemed somehow vaguely ominous. A hosepipe ban was probably just round the corner, she told herself, no doubt followed by thunder before long. She knew Stella Fanshaw would keep a beady eye out for any family which had the temerity to produce a paddling pool. *Snitches 'R Us*.

Time to get on. Sheila Craven didn't crack the whip like La Fanshaw. Nevertheless, she was pernickety in her own way and what her old gran used to call 'hard on a penny'. If Rosemary didn't give full value for money, Mrs C wouldn't be slow to let her know.

Rubbing her back, she contemplated the doll's house. It was strange, because normally she tore through her jobs in the Copse, but today she felt a peculiar reluctance to enter number 12 whose pristine tilt-and-turn windows looked as though they were squinting at her . . . somehow baleful and unwelcoming.

Get out of it, Rosemary admonished herself firmly. She couldn't afford to have sunstroke. Not with Tricia Dent's still to do followed by a trip to Sainsbury's for Rob's tea.

With the cordless vacuum under her arm (she swore by her own equipment) and hefting the mop and bucket with assorted cleaning products, she went up the neat paved path to the front door. She had her own set of keys for when Mrs Craven was away, but normally the front porch and inner door were left unlocked for her.

Stepping into the hallway with its deep pile rose carpet, she felt a prickle of unease.

Something felt subtly different . . . *off*.

'Mrs C,' she called softly. 'It's only me.'

There was no answer.

She felt sweat pooling disagreeably in the small of her back and caught the sudden acrid tang of her own fear. Her heart was beating so fast, it felt as though it must jump out of her chest.

Leaving her things in the hall, Rosemary peered round the living room door.

Everything looked the same as usual, from the plumped-up cushions arranged with geometric precision on the cream three-piece suite to the tasteful arrangement of pink and white roses in the Waterford crystal vase adorning the lacquered chiffonier. The eau de nil carpet, which matched the anaglypta walls, was unsullied and the coffee table magazines were undisturbed.

And yet she had the sense of something badly wrong . . . something that hung like spoor in the Jo Malone-perfumed air.

She passed into the dining room where eau de nil again predominated. Renamed 'the garden room' by Mrs Craven, frosted glass doors at the far end divided it from the hex-agonal extension which brought the outdoors inside as per approved middle-class fashion. Again, nothing appeared out of place, the Chippendale dining set and corner cabinets with their fine collection of Wedgwood apparently undis-turbed. Unusually, the glass doors were firmly shut, though Sheila Craven normally left them open when Rosemary was expected.

'Mrs C,' she called again through dry lips. 'Are you there?'

There was no answer and in that instant, somehow she knew that there never would be.

Stumbling round the dining table, she pulled the double doors open.

Sheila Craven sat in her accustomed rattan armchair, eyes closed, for all the world as if she was just taking forty winks, the picture of prosperous placidity . . . but for a trickle of dried blood under her left nostril and the protruding tongue that would have left her aghast could she have beheld it. Livid bruising on her forearms was the only indication of violence, and it was clear death had come on her unawares. A cushion at her feet told its own story of homicidal smoth-ering, however, for she could never bear to have anything out of place, still less one of the Liberty 'Strawberries and Cream' matching set that, along with pouffe and footstool in matching fabric, were her pride and joy.

Do not store up for yourselves treasures on earth, where moth and decay destroy, and thieves break in and steal. But store up treasures in heaven, where neither moth nor decay destroys, nor thieves break in and steal.

Rosemary could not have said why these words from church came into her head as she stood there gaping stupidly at the dead woman. She supposed it had something to do with the shock of seeing Sheila Craven suddenly wrenched from all that she held dear. All the dainty fripperies . . . her Liberty prints and the Herend figurines ranged along the white-painted bay shelving that were always such a nightmare to dust . . .

Mrs C will be lost in heaven without all her things, was all Rosemary could think. It won't be what she's used to.

As she stood there, her fear receded. The conservatory's French doors were wide open, so it was clear Sheila Craven's attacker had left through the garden and then gone over the low wall which backed on to Derwent Lane.

Mrs C must've let her killer into the house in the first place, Rosemary thought. Which meant this was someone she knew.

It was the ideal time to strike, what with it being the holiday season and only the Copse's retirees usually around at this time of the morning.

The bottom suddenly dropped out of Rosemary's stomach as she realized that Sheila Craven had most likely been in her death throes while she was happily wielding her Pledge and dusters four doors down.

Catapulted from here to eternity in the blink of an eye, she thought, wondering how it was that the birds outside continued to chirrup merrily, oblivious of death . . . Surely now that the silence in Sheila Craven's ears was never more to be broken, nothing should stir and summer noises should be hushed.

She wanted to say a prayer, but the words wouldn't come. In her dazed state, the only quote she could remember was 'where the wicked cease from trouble and the weary are at rest', but that felt all wrong.

She knew she mustn't touch anything.

She knew she had to ring 999. Fingers slick with sweat, she fumbled for her mobile.

On the other side of the wall, a shadow glided along Derwent Lane. And Rosemary shivered as though someone had walked over her grave.

CHAPTER 1

On the morning of Tuesday 2 August, DI Gilbert ('Gil') Markham sat on his favourite bench in the quaint terraced graveyard of St Chad's Parish Church round the back of Bromgrove Police Station, it being his usual practice to take stock there before the start of any new investigation.

Mercifully, it was too early for there to be any chance of the Reverend Simon Duthie — a late recruit to the priesthood after a career with Lloyds Bank — swooping on him for one of those earnest little chats he considered indispensable to his mission of 'pastoral outreach' but that filled Markham with dread. In the days when he had been accompanied by his former wingman, the redoubtable Yorkshireman DS George Noakes, there had been little to fear from the vicar, since the clergyman took a distinctly dim view of Noakesian biblical exegesis such as the sergeant's enquiry whether Judas Iscariot would have cured the sick and cast out devils just as effectively as the other eleven apostles given that he was 'a wrong 'un'. Noakes's notorious propensity for malapropisms also went unappreciated, though Markham had privately relished the expression on Duthie's face when his friend had asked where the priest stood on eating meat during Lent and if you could still get 'condensation from the Bishop'.

As for Mrs Duthie, it had been outright warfare between that good lady and Noakes ever since he had commented with a wink on the fine show of 'salivas' in the rectory garden before telling her to plant a row of 'spitoonias' on the other side. Yes, Noakes's fabled linguistic quirks and undoubted expertise in the art of 'insinuendo' had not endeared him to the Duthies, both of whose countenances wound up distinctly 'ultra-violent' after any chance encounter with the philistine of CID.

Smiling ruefully at the memory, Markham gazed around the little cemetery, admiring the ancient yews and cypresses interspersed with clusters of Japanese azaleas, marigolds, zinnias and exuberant rhododendrons which always reminded him of the late Queen Mother's hats. There were no squirrels scampering about, but presumably they were taking it in easy in the heat, though wood pigeons were cooing softly and butterflies flitted amongst the flowers.

Savouring the shade and peace, Markham's thoughts turned to the previous day's gruesome discovery in Medway . . .

Sheila Craven maintained a delightful back garden, vibrant with poppies, dahlias, larkspur and hydrangea, with a honeysuckle-clad pergola on the patio that adjoined her conservatory. It had struck him as being a little oasis in the parched suburban estate.

The murder victim herself presented something of a riddle, the bruising and misplaced cushion pretty much the only signs that she had been smothered where she sat. Markham was inclined to agree with Rosemary Blake that Sheila had let her killer in and settled down for an innocuous chat before the visitor launched their attack. But no one on the estate appeared to have noticed a thing . . .

'A nice place to live,' was the verdict of Anish Patel, the handsome young pathologist who was covering for Dr Doug 'Dimples' Davidson over the summer. Although Markham missed Davidson, the bluff, tweedy countryman who everyone said was a dead ringer for vet Siegfried Farnon in the old

BBC *All Creatures Great And Small*, he found Patel both efficient and congenial, with a respectful, compassionate way of handling the sad detritus of victims' lives. It was an approach which the DI, known to be savage with subordinates who attempted anything resembling gallows humour, found eminently simpatico.

'It was over very quickly,' Dr Patel reassured the ashen-faced DS Doyle after the young detective, who had answered the call-out with Markham, stuttered that Sheila Craven was the dead spit of his nan before blushing painfully at his unfortunate choice of words. Kindly, the medic added, 'She'd have fallen unconscious after around a minute given her age . . . No time to register what was happening or even be afraid.'

The cleaner Rosemary Blake was a nice woman who, despite her shock, did her best to give them a picture of the Copse and its residents; four young families with children and the rest elderly or retired. She cleaned for Sheila Craven, Stella Fanshaw — retired teacher and Mrs Craven's fellow stalwart at Saint Michael the Archangel Parish Church — and Tricia Dent who owned the second-hand bookshop Bookworm on Medway High Street.

'Well, it's called the high street but these days there's only a few shops along there,' Rosemary told them. 'Just Londis for groceries, the hairdresser's, Rossi's — that's the Italian restaurant — and—' a certain constraint crept into her voice '—the Healing Centre at the bottom next to the Medway Inn.'

'Healing centre?' Doyle was momentarily diverted from the horror of the crime scene. 'What's that then?'

'A sort of spiritual retreat.' Rosemary was clearly uncomfortable with the whole subject. 'Meditation and holistic remedies, that kind of thing,' she said vaguely.

Markham was pretty sure he'd heard about the healing centre in some other faintly scandalous context but couldn't immediately recall the details. All of the high street establishments would need checking out, given their proximity to the murder site — literally around the corner, just a few hundred yards from Derwent Lane.

'Do you know if Mrs Craven got out much?' Doyle asked, clearly wondering about their victim's connections to the local community.

'Well, she wasn't so active right after her husband Tom passed. He was in the police . . . got pancreatic cancer, it was pretty horrible, but she was starting to pick up the threads . . . played bowls at Medway Park now and again, went out to Rossi's, that kind of thing. Plus she hobnobbed with the vicar.' Now it was Rosemary's turn to flush, as though she realized that 'hobnobbed' made Sheila Craven sound like some sort of social climber. 'Sorry, that came out wrong,' she said in a flustered tone. 'I meant church was important to her and she got on well with Norman Collins . . . he lives in the rectory behind Saint Michael's.'

'Don't worry,' was Markham's gentle response. 'You're doing just fine, Mrs Blake. Perhaps you could take a quick look around with my sergeant, check to see if anything's missing? Or if you notice something different in any of the rooms.' He turned to Doyle. 'Then I want you to take Mrs Blake round to Stella Fanshaw's please . . . I'm sure Ms Fanshaw will be happy to arrange a cup of tea with lots of sugar.'

Rosemary's expression suggested that Stella Fanshaw would normally baulk at the prospect of playing hostess to her charlady. But in Markham's experience, social boundaries were never proof against prurient curiosity and getting the inside track on murder.

The Copse having been cordoned off and uniforms posted, the admission of paramedics and forensics was straightforward, with no rubbernecking circus or scrum of the kind that all too often attended a violent death. Markham had no doubt that neighbours' curtains were twitching like mad at the sight of the police cars and ambulance, but so long as the residents stayed safely behind their own front doors the situation was manageable. No doubt the *Gazette*'s intrepid reporters would soon be on the trail like the bloodhounds they were, but in the meantime the perimeter of the estate was secure.

Eventually Dr Patel was ready to transport the body, and Sheila Craven left her home for the last time on a sheeted gurney, forensics and police personnel bowing their heads in respect during the removal. As he watched the sombre procession depart, Markham quietly vowed to secure justice for the elderly widow who was obviously so proud of her little gem of a house and its immaculate garden. She had been 'picking up the threads' after bereavement, which made her murder particularly cruel. And for a devout churchgoer to be wrenched from life with no chance to prepare her soul, struck him as an especial outrage. The fact that her husband Tom was ex-job would no doubt also strike a chord with his team back at CID . . .

Recalled to the present, Markham thought about his tight-knit unit, or the Gang of Four as envious colleagues called them.

Pre-eminent at his right hand now that Noakes had retired was DI Kate Burton. She had faced opposition from home when applying to join the force ('no job for a woman' her father had maintained) but in the end overcame all obstacles through sheer determination and hard work. A psychology graduate, she was addicted to anything that touched on behavioural analysis. Perhaps unsurprisingly, she was engaged to Professor Nathan Finlayson of Bromgrove University's criminal profiling department. Their relationship appeared recently to have hit a rocky patch, though they were still together and Markham had heard on the grapevine that they were attending 'couples therapy'. The DI was uneasily aware that Finlayson, like Noakes, harboured suspicions about the strength of his feelings for Burton. Certainly their slow-burn friendship had contributed to Markham's breakup with Olivia Mullen, an English teacher at Hope Academy (popularly known as 'Hopeless'), which had led to her moving out of their apartment in the Sweepstakes. On joining CID, Burton had initially felt excluded from Markham's special relationship with Noakes (the latter being the only one apart from Olivia who knew that Markham was a survivor of childhood abuse by a stepfather and had lost his brother Jonathan to drink and drugs). However, with the passage of time, she and her uncouth colleague grew closer, gradually bonding over a mutual addiction to true crime, dedication to the job and fierce loyalty to Markham.

For his part, Noakes harboured a strangely chivalrous devotion towards Markham's ex, despite the fact that this was deeply aggravating to his bossy social-climbing wife Muriel (whom he had met, unbelievably, on the ballroom dancing circuit). Muriel had been delighted when Noakes secured the job of security manager at the exclusive Rosemount Retirement Home and even more delighted to learn that Olivia was seeing Mathew Sullivan, the deputy head at Hope who had come out as gay during the Ashley Dean investigation (during which he was briefly a murder suspect) before identifying as bisexual and enjoying romances with women. Sullivan now showed every sign of being infatuated with his colleague. much to the bafflement of Noakes who schemed relentlessly for a reconciliation between Markham and the flame-haired English teacher, vastly irritating his wife in the process.

DCI Sidney ('Slimy Sid' to the troops) had been ecstatic when Noakes finally retired, though his portly nemesis had somehow wangled himself an unofficial position as police consultant. The antipathy between Noakes and the 'gold braid mob' was legendary, not least his infamous retirement bash during which he informed DCI McAllister that he was called "Thrombosis" behind his back on account of him being a bloody clot. In the circumstances, it was something of a miracle that Noakes had lasted so long, but he had somehow bluffed, blagged and bribed his way through successive appraisals until the time came for him to collect his carriage clock.

DS Roger Carruthers, Noakes's replacement on the team ('Roger the Dodger' as Noakes immediately christened him), hadn't known what to make of the weird connection between Markham and his former wingman. With his albino-like pallor, horn-rimmed spectacles and a kind of fishy coldness, Carruthers's supercilious fastidiousness and watchfulness (nephew of Superintendent 'Blithering' Bretherton, he was rumoured to be Sidney's plant) was initially off-putting to Burton and Doyle. In the end, however, the new team managed to gel and suspicion of Carruthers melted away so that he became 'one of Markham's lot' and was no longer suspected of spying for the enemy. DS Doyle had bonded with Carruthers over football since, as Noakes put it, no one who loved the Beautiful Game could be all bad. Furthermore, the young sergeant — lanky, freckled and ginger — plumed himself on being able to dispense romantic wisdom to his colleague now that he had put his own relationship disasters behind him and was currently going steady with teacher girlfriend Kelly.

With a sigh of satisfaction at the way his subordinates had bonded, Markham took a last look round the graveyard. He had a predilection for such places — even chose his apartment on account of its proximity to the municipal cemetery — and loved the sense of timeless tranquillity that they exuded. Out of the corner of his eye, he spotted an elderly lady carrying a modest bouquet further up in the newer section of the burial ground. He chuckled at the recollection of Noakes's favourite joke about the little girl who gave her teacher a bunch of flowers with a promise to bring her more the following day 'if the lodger wasn't buried'. Catching sight of the visitor's mildly reproachful expression — clearly she wondered what on earth this strange man was doing grinning inanely — the DI hastily rearranged his features, nodded politely and made his way back down towards the station.

* * *

CID felt stale and stuffy. Needless to say, the radiators were going full belt despite the heatwave; no doubt when the cold weather set in, they would promptly give up the ghost.

His colleagues were already waiting in his corner office with its unrivalled view of the car park. Thankfully, the central heating in his room was off and a fan was keeping it reasonably cool. No doubt he had Burton to thank for that.

Doyle and Carruthers were both dapper dressers, so in one area at least Sidney's long-standing grievances about 'standards in Markham's team' were laid to rest. Kate Burton, of course, was always irreproachable when it came to costume. In the old days, she had favoured frumpy trouser suits in endless shades of beige, but nowadays chose clinging midi dresses that flattered her curvy frame. Even the Joan of Arc chestnut bob had mutated to something shaggy and streaked, with eye-skimming side fringe, so she was altogether a different creature from yore. She still regularly resorted to the glasses that magnified her eyes to enormous brown lollipops, but nowadays the brightly coloured frames made it look like a fashion statement rather than armour to hide behind. Today she wore a fuchsia linen sheath dress while her colleagues sported well-cut lightweight suits and skinny ties.

The trio took provisioning very seriously, in the best Noakesian tradition (the former DS being famed as the man who never ate on an empty stomach). 'For God's sake, Inspector,' Sidney had once expostulated, 'there always seems to be some sort of *picnic* going on whenever I come in here.' To which Doyle had replied solemnly, 'It helps us work smarter, sir . . . kind of like a power breakfast.' Well, at least Burton's granola ('birdseed crap' according to Noakes) qualified as brain food, but Markham wasn't at all sure about the blueberry muffins and creamy Macchiatos. Still, he wasn't going to look a gift horse in the mouth and accepted his share with a smile.

'Right, Kate,' he said after a period of silent munching (presumably, according to Doyle's theory, while their synapses fired up), 'let's run through the cast list.'

She had her glasses on and notebook ready almost before the words were out of his mouth, causing Doyle and

Carruthers to exchange glances expressive of an inner eye roll. *School Swot*. But there was none so good as Burton when it came to a succinct roll call of suspects.

'Our victim Mrs Sheila Craven was seventy-eight, widowed, no family apart from a nephew, Desmond Pettifer; family liaison are trying to track him down. Mrs Craven lived at Number 12, the Copse in Medway. Fairly affluent locale. Uniform are doing house to house with the neighbours, but most of them are off on holiday and those who *were* around didn't see anything. It's the kind of estate where folk keep pretty much to themselves, so no surprise that we've drawn a blank . . . She lived fairly quietly, played bowls now and again when she felt up to it, otherwise just the odd trip to the high street . . . There's a little row of shops . . . convenience store, local Italian, bookshop, pub, hairdresser's, healing centre—'

'Ah yes,' Markham interrupted. 'I picked up some vibes from Mrs Craven's cleaner regarding the healing centre . . . as if there was something she didn't approve of.'

'It's run by that ex-priest, sir,' Carruthers volunteered. 'Not Anglican . . . RC.' He had nearly said 'one of your lot', given that Markham was known to be a Catholic (which explained a lot in his opinion), but corrected himself just in time. 'The *Gazette* did a piece a while back after some woman made a fuss about him supposedly coming on to her.'

'Oh yeah, *I* remember that,' Doyle joined in. 'Name of Henry Morland . . . looks like Rasputin, you know, the famous hypnotist . . . all flowing beard and piercing eyes, like one of those creepy icons.'

Despite the closeness of the office, Markham felt his skin prickle. *Rasputin*. Our Friend, as the ill-fated Romanovs had called him. A sinister Svengali whose legend had cast a shadow over their previous investigation at the Newman psychiatric hospital, rearing its head again during the notorious Confetti Club murders. Surely it was only a coincidence that Rasputin was cropping up again . . .

'Henry Morland,' Burton said brightly, scribbling briskly. 'Right, he needs checking out. Then there's Rossi's where Mrs Craven liked going for lunch. Francesco Rossi's the owner . . . his daughter Marina manages the restaurant with her fiancé Matteo Bianchi. I think there's a couple of other siblings knocking around . . .'

'It's mint,' Doyle said enthusiastically then, aware of Markham's quizzical expression, he amended, 'I mean it's a great place to eat. That presenter from Bromgrove Radio's always in there with his mates . . . George Parker . . . A noisy crowd but they give him the red-carpet treatment.'

'Mrs Craven's neighbour Tricia Dent owns the bookshop,' Burton continued. 'And there's another neighbour Stella Fanshaw who knew her from church, Saint Michael the Archangel in Cabot Road. The vicar, Norman Collins can help with that side of things, and there's his deacon too . . . Graham Thorpe.'

'Blimey, looks like we're going to have suspects coming out of our ears,' Doyle said, looking somewhat disconcerted as Burton worked through her list.

'That's pretty much it,' Burton reassured him crisply. 'There's also Emma and James Carnforth who manage the pub, the Medway Inn . . . and someone said Mrs Craven knew Frances Langton the headteacher at Medway High. Obviously Londis and the hairdressers will need a visit too but they're small outfits and the hair salon's closed for a refurb at the moment.'

'Bags I not do the bowls club,' Doyle grinned as Burton shot him a reproving frown.

'Let me know as soon as you've located the nephew, Kate.' Markham never shirked the condolence visits.

'Will do, sir.'

'Our priority now is to get an incident room up and running. Then tomorrow you and I will hit the high street and church, Kate, while Doyle and Carruthers follow up at the Copse,' Markham continued.

'Are you bringing sarge in for this one?' Doyle asked slyly.

Markham suppressed a smile. Like Banquo's ghost, George Noakes was ever-present even when he was supposedly ensconced in executive splendour at Rosemount.

'I'll swing by and catch up with Noakesy in the morning. I imagine he'll have his ear to the ground,' he replied wryly. To say nothing of Muriel. 'In the meantime, let's crack on. Dr Patel's putting a rush on the PM but it seems clear Sheila Craven was smothered yesterday morning . . . most likely by someone she knew.'

'Her old fella was ex-job,' Doyle said soberly. 'Could be a jailbird or someone with a grudge against him.'

'That's definitely one line of enquiry,' Markham nodded. 'Check with Bill Keegan in Records. He should be able to help.'

'Press bulletin, sir?' Carruthers asked.

'Yes, but keep it short and sweet.'

Murder in suburbia, the DI mused as his colleagues headed to their various tasks. A harmless old lady and no discernible motive.

But if there was one thing he had learned over the years, it was that seemingly quiet communities were often positive hotbeds of gossip, jealousies and resentments.

Summertime and the heat was on.

CHAPTER 2

The Rosemount Retirement Home looked resplendent as Markham drove up to Noakes's workplace on the morning of Wednesday 3 August. Even with a drought beckoning, the landscaped grounds of the Georgian mansion appeared to be in tiptop condition, verdant lawns undulating grace-fully down to the little lake with its island and willow oak in the middle. The red sandstone paths and perfectly clipped topiary were as pristine as ever, fully validating Rosemount's reputation as Bromgrove's number one private facility for those in the twilight of their years (a few publicly funded patients admitted via the NHS took care of the social con-science side). Even the home's recent role in one of CID's most challenging homicide investigations couldn't detract from its bucolic allure, Markham thought as he checked in with the cheery new clinical supervisor who directed him to Noakes's cubbyhole where tea and biscuits were waiting.

His former sergeant could not have presented a greater contrast to Doyle and Carruthers, with his pouch prize-fight-er's features, chunky physique, unruly salt and pepper thatch (which never lay flat) and penchant for hideous ganzies. Today, in a concession to the heat, he sported checked mus-tard flannels and a bright red shirt that matched his perspiring complexion. All very Rupert Bear-ish, but no doubt it went down well with the retired army home counties types who comprised the majority of Rosemount's clientele.

Indeed, Noakes's mind was running very much on military matters when Markham arrived. Having previously not been all that keen on the portrait of bemedaled and moustachioed General Charles Gordon in the home's staff room, Noakes — ex parachute regiment — had gradually warmed to the Victorian hero of Khartoum and his unique brand of muscular Christianity, not to mention the general's defiance of the odds (nothing being so seductive to the black sheep of Bromgrove CID as the legend of this indomitable soldier prepared to tackle all comers, whether Egypt's Madhi or the government back home).

Taking his nose out of various gilt-bound volumes from Rosemount's handsome library, he confided to Markham, 'I'm thinking of getting some prints of Gordon for the residents' lounge, with them all being dead *patriotic* here.' Noakes sniffed approvingly. 'I reckon they'd like that. We could make it a bit of a *theme* . . . the way they do with destination hotels . . . summat to bring everyone together . . . kind of a talking point.'

It amused Markham to think of Noakes in front of the CEO pitching his plans for making Rosemount a 'destination' facility, but he kept a straight face.

'Well, I know Bromgrove History Society arranges lectures here, Noakes, so that's in your favour.'

His friend's St Bernard's face split into a smile. 'Yeah, they're interested in doing talks on Gordon an' Kitchener an' Monty an' other military types in the autumn.' Self-consciously, he riffled through a stack of papers on his untidy desk. 'I've got other ideas too . . . true crime an' stuff like that.' He whistled. 'Honestly, you wouldn't believe how some of them sweet old dears can't get enough of serial killers, guv . . . Shipman an' Bundy an' Fred West an' all that crowd.' It struck Markham as comical the way Noakes spoke of these unholy demons as casually as if they were old acquaintances (which, now he thought about it, in a sense they were). 'The events woman wondered if I could do a talk on our old cases . . . providing you didn't object, guv,' he added anxiously.

'Of course not.' Personally, Markham couldn't imagine a combination of homicide and Horlicks making for a peaceful night's sleep, but there was no accounting for tastes. *De gustibus non est disputandum*, as his old Classics teacher used to say.

'If you're after nineteenth-century prints,' he continued, 'I gather there's a second-hand shop on Medway High Street which might have something in that line. Bookworm . . . the proprietor's a neighbour of that poor woman from the Copse.'

Noakes settled his hands comfortably over the overflowing paunch. 'Wondered when you'd get round to that, boss,' he said complacently. 'She was murdered, right.'

This was by way of statement rather than an enquiry, but of course the ex-sergeant still had his sources.

'What do you know of the Copse, Noakesy?' Markham enquired mildly.

'The missus knows a few of 'em in there.' She would of course. 'Reckons it's like *Midsommer*, without the blood an' gore. Well, up till now at any rate, the most exciting it ever gets is someone putting their bins out on the wrong day . . . Mainly WI types an' nice little families . . . two-point-four kids. Dead safe an' ordinary an' boring.'

'Not now it isn't,' Markham replied grimly. 'Mrs Craven most probably let her killer in, so we think it's got to be someone in her local circle.'

'Have a Bourbon,' the other said consolingly, pushing the plate across his desk. 'An' drink your tea before it gets cold.'

Markham did as he was bid before returning to the topic of the moment.

'How about Medway High Street, Noakesy. Do you ever get round there?'

'Dead as a dodo these days, guv . . . Jus' a few little poxy shops plus the pub an' that Italian.'

'And the healing centre,' Markham prompted. 'The proprietor Henry Morland is somewhat controversial by all accounts.'

'Ex sky pilot.' Knowing Markham's religious affiliation, Noakes was clearly anxious not to cause offence. 'Nowt to do with the RCs these days, though . . . more like meditation an' yoga an' all that mindfulness crap. Bit of a boffin, teaches part-time at the university.'

'Doyle compared Morland to Rasputin,' the DI said flatly.

'Oh aye . . . The Mad Monk,' was the rejoinder. 'Well, Morland's got the look all right.' Noakes visibly perked up. 'Our Nat's doing Rasputin at the moment . . . the Russian Revolution an' all that stuff. *Ackshually*,' with a gleam in his eye, 'she says he's an OK lecturer, so most likely he soft-pedals the mystical hocus pocus.'

Natalie was Noakes's perma-tanned beautician daughter and the apple of his eye. Like her mother, she was partial to Markham while considerably less enthusiastic about Olivia (something Noakes had never cottoned on to). She had unwittingly triggered a serious crisis for Markham and Noakes when the latter learned that he was not her biological father, a discovery that sent him off the rails and nearly derailed his career. The two men weathered the storm, however, drawn even closer by their shared experience of familial trauma.

Markham was touched by Noakes's transparent pride in his brassy loudmouthed daughter's recent decision to undertake a foundation course in History at Bromgrove University with a view to improving on her poor showing at A level. Privately, Markham suspected that Natalie's pursuit of some qualifications had been turbo-charged by her split from Rick Jordan, the highly eligible heir to a fitness empire whose mother was inclined to look down her nose at his pneumatic fiancée. Even though she and Rick were now back together, the prodigal daughter continued to attend the university, encouraged by Noakes who, Markham knew, secretly regretted his own misspent schooldays.

Prompted by a mischievous impulse, Markham said, 'Perhaps you should follow General Gordon with a talk on Rasputin, seeing as they were both religious fanatics.'

Noakes appeared to consider it then: '*Nah,*' he replied. 'Folk here wouldn't like the sex stuff.' *Whereas they had no problem with the likes of Ted Bundy or Ed Kemper!* Markham's lips twitched. Truly the human psyche was unfathomable.

Before Noakes could get started on Rasputin's role in the downfall of Imperial Russia, Markham said hastily, 'So, is this Henry Morland some kind of sexual reprobate?'

'Like I say, guv, he's got the look. Y'know, weirdy beardy with strange glittery eyes. Looks like he could do with a square meal too.'

'Wasn't there trouble over some woman claiming Morland groped her under hypnosis?' Markham asked, having now been briefed by Kate Burton.

Noakes grunted. 'I reckon the *Gazette* made most of it up. Any road, it fizzled out as soon as he made noises about suing 'em . . . I think they had to print an apology in the end.'

'Hmm . . . Anyone else on the high street likely to be of interest, would you say?'

'It ain't xactly Party Central, guv.'

'Well, what about Rossi's?'

'Mainly flash gits from out of town . . . DJ crowd an' hangers-on. The missus didn't care for all them Del Boy types giving it large.'

'What about Natalie?' Markham had a feeling *she* wouldn't necessarily be averse to the odd medallion man, having at one time been somewhat notorious as the doyenne of Bromgrove's seedier nightclubs, though her doting parents never believed the rumours thanks to Markham's discreet damage limitation.

'She an' Rick prefer dinner parties nowadays,' the other said with complacently. 'Nat says it's much more *civilized*.' And less chance of her ending the evening dancing on the table belting out Beyoncé's greatest hits.

'The pub's halfway decent,' Noakes conceded, his thoughts returning to the high street's amenities.

'The Medway Inn?'

'Yeah, though they lost a heap of custom to Rossi's, so it were touch an' go if they could hang on to the place.'

'Would Mrs Craven have gone in there, do you think?'

Noakes nodded vigorously. 'Bound to. They did a decent carvery back in the day . . . Me an' Tom Craven were on the darts team for a bit.'

'We're checking out ex-cons with a grudge,' Markham said slowly. 'But somehow it doesn't feel like that kind of revenge murder.'

'I'm with you there, guv,' Noakes agreed. 'Tom spent his last ten years doing the community beat, supervising PCSOs an' specials . . . the nicest bloke you could ever meet an' never wanted to be some shit-hot inspector or owt like that. They called him Dixon of Dock Green, but everybody liked him, even the scrotes didn't mind being nicked by him.'

'Did you see much of his wife?'

'Not that I remember . . . She were churchy, him not so much . . . more a Christmas an' Easter kind of fella.' With Muriel being a pillar of High-Churchery, Noakes recognized Sheila Craven's type.

'Was she the sort of lady to make enemies?' Markham pressed.

Noakes frowned. 'Don' see how,' he replied. 'I mean the worst you could say is she were mebbe a bit "up herself".' He stuck out his pinkie and mimed drinking tea. 'You know, one of the lace doily brigade.' Given Muriel's lady-of-the-manor affectations and dogged adherence to the values of what Olivia called 'the crumbling classes', Noakes also knew more about such genteel aspirations than most. 'She were a bit po-faced,' he expanded. 'There were this time me an' Tom an' some of the lads came in from the pub an' she asked if I wanted to go an' wash my hands. An' I said, "No thanks, I've just washed 'em on the wall outside." Kind of like an ice-breaker, see . . . jokey, so she knew she didn't have to impress me or lay on owt fancy.'

'I take it there was a sense of humour failure then.'

'Yeah, she gave me this look, like I were summat she'd stepped in . . . reckon Tom got it in the neck afterwards.'

Markham tried not to laugh at his friend's expression of injured merit.

'Ah well, when it comes to comedy, they say everything's in the timing, Noakesy.'

'Anyway, there were no great harm in the woman,' the other added charitably. 'An' Tom worshiped the ground she walked on.' Such uxoriousness definitely met with Noakes's approval. 'It were cowardly sneaking up on her like that in the middle of all her nice bits an' pieces.'

Strangely, that was pretty much how Rosemary Blake had reacted to the desecration of Sheila Craven's sanctum, repeating over and over that it shouldn't have happened in her lovely conservatory . . . as if murder was ever acceptable on any terms! But Markham knew allowances had to be made for shock and, as ever, Noakes was attuned to the underlying nuances.

'This one's got me stumped,' the DI sighed. 'An apparently harmless elderly lady smothered in her own home . . .'

'P'raps she had some kind of secret life nobody knew about,' Noakes offered half-heartedly. 'Mebbe she were up to all sorts behind that respectable exterior, like Rose West . . . Would you believe, that one's into flower arranging an' crafts these days, like all the torture an' chopping never happened. Jus' some tubby bird knitting cardigans an' outfits for kiddies . . . Thass why so many folk reckon she couldn't have been in on all that house of horrors stuff.'

'I take it you're not going to do a lecture on Rose West for the residents, Noakes. That really would be a step too far.'

'Well, they'd be up for it all right, guv. But it's too close to home . . . I'll go with Jo Naso or some American whackjob to start with.'

Happy days! Clearly Noakes's remit extended beyond the usual purlieu of a security manager. As though reading Markham's thoughts, the other said virtuously, 'All the risk assessments and security upgrades are sorted an' up to date, guv.

But,' with a shy hint of pride, 'management reckon I can help give "added value".'

The DI smiled. 'None better, Noakesy.'

Both of them knew that after the revelations which had emerged during a recent murder investigation, temporarily sullying Rosemount's good name, whatever could be done to rehabilitate the home was a bonus.

'Am I in on this case then, guv?' Noakes asked hopefully as they made their way out to the forecourt. 'I mean, all the plans for improvements here don' mean I can't help out.'

'You're my civilian consultant, Noakes.' So what if Sidney had apoplexy, he'd square it somehow and anyway it didn't matter who cavilled, Noakes was his wingman *always*. God knows, he'd earned the right. 'Why don't we have a meal at Rossi's on Friday,' he suggested. 'Then we can share intel.'

'With your Liv?'

Noakes's knight-errantry meant he wasn't going to give up on his efforts to bring Markham and Olivia back together. 'Bet she's well up to speed on Rasputin,' he added in an attempt to be less obvious about it.

'Why not,' the DI said helplessly, rewarded by his friend's beam of approval.

'An' then you two can come to us for your dinner on Sunday . . . after trying out the service at Mrs C's church.'

'St Michael the Archangel.'

'Thass the fella. Reckon it'll be all smells an' bells, guv. Jus' how you like it.'

Which made him sound like some sort of religious maniac obsessed with sanctuary choreography, the DI thought resignedly. Having once overheard Doyle holding forth about having a guvnor who spouted the bible at the drop of a hat 'with a thing about mouldy old churches and statues', he imagined that was pretty much his reputation amongst the station's rank and file.

'Sounds like a plan,' he concurred resignedly. Now Noakes had the bit between his teeth, he might as well fall in.

They went outside by way of the rose garden at the rear of the building.

'The flowers are looking good, Noakesy.'

'Yeah. We've got one named for Andrée Clark,' the other replied, referring to the celebrity ballerina whose murder had launched one of their most complex investigations ever.

'*Sweet rose, whose hue angry and brave bids the rash gazer wipe his eye; Thy root is ever in its grave, And thou must die,*' Markham murmured meditatively, his eyes resting appreciatively on the dark red blooms which gave the flowerbeds the appearance of a rich damask counterpane.

That was just it with the guvnor, Noakes thought, bowing his head respectfully. Sidney and the high-ups couldn't *stand* the way he broke into poetry and quotations and what have you all over the place. Granted, it was kind of a coded language that didn't suit everyone. But Noakes *liked* how the words sounded. Musical and lush and mysterious, like something from another world. And it was true, there *was* something fierce and defiant about the colour of those roses. A bit like Andrée Clark herself. He just hoped that stuff about roots and grave and dying didn't turn out to be some kind of *omen* . . .

Such a sympathetic response to what DCI Sidney denigrated as 'Markham's *fey* streak' was typical of Noakes who possessed an unusually sensitive nature beneath the shambling, frequently tactless exterior. It was a source of endless mystification to those in CID who struggled to understood 'what Markham saw in that fat slob'. But Markham set high store by Noakes's authenticity — the dogged refusal to toady and sympathy for the underdog which went hand in hand with an intuitiveness that cut through artifice and chicanery and was keenly responsive to beauty in all its forms. Kate Burton too had a sensitive side, but whereas she knew better than to give DCI Sidney an inkling that she was anything less than a hard-boiled pragmatist, well attuned to the slick politics of CID, Noakes never bothered to camouflage his true feelings. In a world of self-serving careerists, it was a trait that Markham knew how to value.

* * *

'At least with the Confetti Club investigation, there wasn't any shortage of people with a grudge,' Kate Burton lamented later that afternoon as she and Markham sat in the beer garden round the back of the Medway Inn, their jackets off, nursing Diet Cokes.

'True.' Markham thought back to their recent investigation of the bridalwear store where just about everyone they encountered seemed to have it in for the flamboyant proprietor. This one, on the other hand, appeared to be a case of 'motiveless malignity', but logic dictated there *had* to be skeletons in Sheila Craven's closet . . . or some kind of secret, if they just dug deep enough.

'By the look of it, she was just this perfectly inoffensive old lady, boss. Mostly kept herself to herself apart from church and pottering along here now and again.'

'She seems to have stuck to a few favourite places,' Markham ruminated. 'They all seemed fond of her in Rossi's.'

Francesco Rossi, a middle-aged Italian whose receding hairline in no way detracted from a charismatic flirtatiousness, and his gentle wife Serena, with a faded prettiness that suggested she had once been something of a blonde bombshell, had appeared genuinely distressed by the news of Sheila Craven's murder. Glamorous daughter Marina and her darkly handsome fiancé Matteo also seemed thunderstruck, though the detectives knew better than to take such reactions at face value.

'Yeah, they came across as really warm and caring,' Burton said. 'Francesco's youngest, Giulia . . . what a cutie. It's sweet, the way Italians always make a big fuss of their kids.'

'They seem to consider their staff part of the family too,' Markham observed. 'That personable red-haired waiter said most of them have been there for years.'

Burton had her notebook at the ready. 'Yes, Ed Frayling . . . not a patch on Matteo in the looks department, but seemed like a nice guy. Apparently his girlfriend Barbara Price used to work there too, but now she's training to be a social worker . . . still does the occasional shift at weekends.'

'They were all very simpatico,' Markham said thoughtfully.

'Bit of a contrast with that pair in there,' Burton commented, jerking a thumb at the pub. 'He doesn't crack a smile and *she's* like something out of *Prisoner Cell Block H*.'

It was true. James Carnforth had none of Francesco Rossi's charm, being a short taciturn man with a fish face and grey comb-over. His wife Emma was short and stocky with a pudding bowl hairdo, clumpy shoes and badly applied make-up that looked as if it had been slapped on in the dark.

'It's been a struggle for them to keep going,' Markham pointed out. 'Especially with Rossi's poaching all their customers.'

Burton glanced down at her notebook. 'They live on Derwent Lane at the back of the Copse, but it didn't sound like they mixed with Sheila, even though they're churchwardens at Saint Michael the Archangel.' She took a long draught of her drink while pondering this conundrum. 'You'd have thought being fellow parishioners meant they had quite a lot in common.'

'There may be no obvious motive, but alibi-wise, they're potentially *all* in the frame,' Markham said ruefully.

Burton did a recap. 'OK, Dr Patel estimates Sheila died around eleven o'clock or not long before Rosemary Blake rocked up at half past. The Carnforths say they were here doing a stock check. And according to Francesco Rossi, he and Serena were having a lie-in at home because the restaurant is closed on Monday with them doing the deep clean in the afternoon. Ditto Marina and Matteo who weren't due in till two . . . Ed was doing circuit training in Medway Park before he met Barbara for coffee in the town centre at midday and then got a lift into work to help with the cleaning.'

Burton frowned.

'The Rossis' alibis are pretty much worthless seeing as couples will always lie for each other,' she summarized. 'Ed was doing a solo workout and there's no one to vouch for him, which means he's in the frame too . . . plus he's young and athletic, so—'

'He could have fitted murder in before coffee without breaking sweat,' Markham finished drily.

His colleague looked sheepish. 'I know, I know . . . on paper he's the likeliest, but he came across as genuinely upset about Sheila and he has no motive. Francesco thinks the world of him, too . . . says he's in line to become assistant manager.'

'Ed's another one who knew Sheila from church,' Markham mused. 'He said something about her singing in the choir with him and Tricia Dent before her husband became ill.'

'What did you make of Ms Dent, sir?'

'She seemed rather tense and brittle,' he replied, thinking about the deeply tanned, curly-haired brunette from the bookshop who was fine-boned to the point of looking unwell.

'Reminded me of that woman from *The Hotel Inspector*,' Burton volunteered.

'Alex Polizzi?'

'Yep, that's the one . . . You'd almost imagine Dent was Italian,' Burton pulled a face as she recalled the Sloaney drawl, 'until she opens her mouth.'

She referred to the trusty notebook once more.

'Doyle found out she dated that DJ George Parker for a while before it all went sour.'

'Indeed?' Presumably the split partly accounted for the hard-bitten look. She had made all the right noises about Sheila Craven, but there was a lack of warmth that Markham found repellent.

'Rosemary Blake was due to clean for Dent after she'd finished at Sheila's,' Burton continued. 'And according to her, with it being the holidays she put the Closed sign up so she could reorganize the shop.' She grimaced. 'Which means once again no alibi.'

Markham's thoughts turned to the other members of the team. 'Have we got anything from Doyle and Carruthers about the Copse?'

'They've been able to rule out the families. Solid alibis all round. Same with three elderly couples . . . district nurse giving an injection at number 5 . . . decorator busy at number 7 . . . and the accountant round at number 9.'

'Well at least that narrows the field. Anything else?'

'Bossy old trout at number 16 name of Stella Fanshaw,' Burton grinned as she quoted Doyle verbatim. 'She bent their ear for ages about the lack of police patrols, rising crime yada yada yada . . . Alibi-wise, she had a hair appointment in the town centre — not *Jon James* on the high street due to the refurb.'

'When was she finished in town?'

'Ten, because she took the first appointment. She usually meets up with friends mid-morning, but one's in hospital and the other away on holiday, so she decided to head back home . . . Carruthers reckons she wanted to check Rosemary hadn't skived off early.' Clearly their colleagues hadn't warmed to the lady. 'Anyway, she got the taxi to drop her off at Saint Michael the Archangel so she could check the flower arranging rota.'

'What time was this?'

'Quarter past ten . . . apparently she hung around for a bit, said a few prayers, that kind of thing, and then walked home. Got back just before half eleven but there was no sign of anyone, so she figured Rosemary had already gone next door to Sheila's. Then the next thing she knew, there were police cars everywhere.'

'And no one clocked her returning to number 16?' Markham asked, sounding frustrated.

'No one, boss,' Burton replied in tones of equal exasperation.

'So nothing to say she didn't call on Mrs Craven via Derwent Lane . . . If she knocked at the conservatory window, Sheila would have thought nothing of letting her in the back way.'

'Carruthers says Sheila was easy-going about neighbours coming round the back,' Burton told him. 'It's only a low wall, so not like they had to clamber over a fence.'

'But nobody saw anything,' Markham repeated glumly. 'And in suburbia of all places . . . land of the proverbial twitching curtains.'

'Holiday time, guv. Plus the hot weather . . . everyone trying to keep cool and minding their own business.'

Perfect timing.

They had no better luck at St Michael the Archangel rectory in Cabot Road. The vicar Norman Collins was a courteous, whippet-thin middle-aged man with a slight stoop who Markham guessed must have been decidedly handsome in his youth. A cultured voice, aquiline features, fine dark eyes and a head of silver hair lent him an air of distinction which was entirely lacking in the owlish, balding deacon Graham Thorpe with whom he was deep in a discussion of parish affairs when the detectives broke into their meeting.

However inconvenient the interruption, Thorpe promptly produced tea and then effaced himself while the vicar expressed their sadness at the death of Sheila Craven in a few well-chosen phrases.

After they had left the handsome Victorian terraced house, Burton didn't mince her words.

'No Mrs Collins, so I bet that guy's got a brigade of ladies hovering in the wings,' she commented acidly.

'You weren't impressed, Kate?'

'Oh don't mind me, guv. It's just, he struck me as one of those clerical smoothies who always knows what to say.'

'Sincere?'

'Yes,' she conceded. 'Though all that about Sheila leading an exemplary Christian life sounded, well, a bit *glib* if you know what I mean . . . almost like he was dialling it in.'

'I suppose it's an occupational hazard that priests sometimes sound as if they're talking by rote,' Markham told her. 'There has to be an element of detachment.'

'Well he had almost film star looks . . . Not like that deacon. There's no danger of *him* having a *Thorn Birds* moment,' she laughed as they stood at the bottom of the rectory drive. 'He reminded me of the head librarian at the university . . . bald and boring.'

'Quite a sensitive face, though,' Markham countered. 'And no doubt used to fading into the background while the Reverend holds centre stage.'

'At any rate, there's two more who can't be ruled out,' she sighed. 'No one was around to confirm the Rev was working on his sermon . . . and unless a neighbour saw Thorpe deadheading those roses, he could easily have been round at the Copse finishing Sheila off.'

Crossly, she kicked a stray pebble from the gravel drive.

'It's all so *pat* . . . everything like one of those villages in an Agatha Christie novel.'

'Remember the Old Carton case, Kate,' Markham reminded her. 'We know what can fester beneath a community's cosy exterior.'

'*God yes*,' she said with feeling, looking back at the rectory. As she watched, there was a movement behind the downstairs bay window. Someone was waiting to see them depart.

'Back to base,' Markham said. 'Medway may be a sleepy backwater, but hopefully we're making ripples.'

And drawing a killer into the open.

CHAPTER 3

'So, no dice with the healing centre then?'

Doyle was clearly disappointed as they reviewed matters the next morning.

'Wednesday's half day closing,' Burton informed him. 'And anyway, the centre's usually only open in the afternoons. Henry Morland teaches on the European studies degree course, so he's at the university most mornings.' She paused, riffling through a manila folder before producing a head-and-shoulders black and white portrait. 'There he is, totally respectable . . . looks like an accountant or something.'

'Ditched the beard and weird getup then,' Doyle concluded. 'Must've decided it'd spoil his chances of career progression,' he added sourly.

The young detective was the proud possessor of a degree in Criminal Law. but he was clearly fascinated by Morland's colourful background, Noakes's mentorship having fostered an interest in all things esoteric and 'far out'.

'One of that lot from the Copse — Prof Windling at number 5, retired from the uni as head of modern history last year cos of health issues — said Morland's gone all Eastern Orthodox,' Doyle confided. 'Icons and incense and bells and all the rest of it.'

'Perfectly irreproachable,' Markham said calmly.

'Not entirely, guv,' Doyle asserted stoutly. 'More like a fad for dodgy mystics and *freakiness*.'

'How so?'

'Well, the prof didn't seem all that comfortable with Morland's approach . . . said he had this obsession with "rehabilitating" Rasputin. He insisted all the stuff about seducing women was just him testing his restraint and pitting himself against the Devil.'

Markham was interested to see where this led. 'Go on,' he said.

'The way Morland tells it, Rasputin was some sort of Christ-like outsider . . . totally misunderstood . . . next best thing to a saint.'

'Actually, I think the Orthodox Church *did* make Rasputin a saint,' Burton interjected earnestly.

Carruthers didn't like the sound of any of it. 'The bloke was downright sinister,' he muttered. 'Like some kind of religious Doctor Feelgood.'

Burton pursed her lips.

'Maybe Morland's colleagues are just jealous,' she mused. 'Let's face it, dons and lecturers are worse than prima donnas when it comes to that.'

An interesting remark in the context of her relationship with the head of Bromgrove University's criminal profiling unit, Markham thought.

Doyle looked deeply sceptical. 'I'm not sure about that, ma'am.' As Burton frowned, he added hastily, 'Or it could be Morland identified with Rasputin at some level? Banged on about him being misunderstood and slandered cos the same thing had happened to *him* when that woman ran to the *Gazette* about him being a perv.'

This struck Markham as an astute observation. 'An interesting hypothesis,' he said.

With a wary sidelong glance at Burton, Doyle ploughed on.

'Sounded to me like Morland's a creep. Mind you, the students lap up all his stories about Rasputin's enemies using him to topple the Romanovs . . . this power-behind-the throne stuff's all the rage on history courses nowadays.'

'I suppose Rasputin just ended up being the ideal scape-goat for everything that was wrong with Russia,' Burton said thoughtfully. 'On top of which, he was this peasant from Siberia messing around with aristocratic women, which went against the natural order.'

'So you're on Rasputin's side then, ma'am,' Doyle ventured, with a surreptitious wink at his Carruthers. 'Up the workers and all that.'

'Don't be facetious, Sergeant,' she rapped.

Carruthers clearly decided it was high time they turned aside from the byways of history.

'Look, in this case, it ain't the Rasputin lookalike who copped it,' he pointed out baldly, 'just some harmless old biddy who never hurt a soul.'

'Unless it turns out she had some kind of raunchy past,' Doyle speculated. 'Or she got mixed up in dodgy stuff at Morland's clinic.'

'*Oh for heaven's sake.*' Burton was evidently exasperated. 'How likely is that at her age!'

'I'm *serious*, ma'am,' the young sergeant sounded affronted. 'You hear about that kind of thing in the news . . . gaslighting the elderly.'

'Wouldn't the vicar be a more likely bet if it came to that?' Carruthers asked. 'If she was a churchgoer, *he'd* be more likely to influence her than some charlatan faith healer on the fringes . . . Plus, Morland was an ex-Catholic priest and it doesn't sound like she was the type to approve of that.'

'A good point, Carruthers,' Markham agreed. 'Norman Collins certainly had an impressive presence . . . easy to imagine him acquiring a certain following amongst his parishioners.' He turned to Burton. 'I recall you were struck by it, Kate.'

'Yes, the vicar definitely had an aura all right,' she confirmed. 'Tough on the nerdy deacon . . . put him well in the shade.' She thought for a moment. 'I can imagine Collins having a winning way with women. But he seemed quite worldly and shrewd — the type who'd see the elephant traps a long way off — so it's hard to imagine him winding up in some kind of pastoral mess.' She sighed. 'Neither Collins nor Graham Thorpe has a useful alibi, but they're not really contenders for prime suspect at this stage.'

'Unlike Morland,' said Doyle hopefully.

'The only problem there being, we don't know that Mrs Craven ever patronized Mr Morland's healing centre,' Markham pointed out. 'Which is why you and Carruthers need to clear that up this afternoon.'

Doyle was visibly delighted.

'You don't want to take Morland yourself, boss?'

'Kate and I are going to call at Medway High School,' the DI said evenly. 'It appears Mrs Craven knew the head-teacher Frances Langton, so hopefully we may glean more details to fill out our picture.'

The 'ginger ninja' looked as though he could hardly believe he and Carruthers were going to get first crack at the mysterious owner of the Healing Centre.

'I need hardly say, Sergeant, that I expect absolute profes-sionalism on your part,' Markham reminded the youngster. 'Whatever your interest in Rasputin and esoteric religious practices, you will confine yourself to the parameters of the current investigation, specifically any interaction between Mrs Craven and Mr Morland. We need to leave sensational-ism and prurient speculation out of the equation.'

After the two sergeants had left, Burton said resignedly, 'Doyle's full of it, sir, totally hung up on Rasputin and all this mystic mumbo jumbo.' She sighed. 'I suppose Noakes is egging him on. What do you make of it, sir?'

'What, Rasputin? A fantastic subject, sure, but the mythol-ogy is just that. I seem to remember watching some film about him once with Olivia . . . Pure schlock really, but compulsive viewing.'

There, he had said his ex's name easily enough, as though he was well over her and moving on with his life. Only, he had a suspicion that Burton was not deceived.

All she said, however, was, 'Morland's a colourful figure but it's a bit of a stretch to imagine him and Sheila Craven up to some kind of voodoo.'

'Natalie might be able to give us some more background,' he suggested. 'I'm seeing Noakes shortly.' He omitted any reference to dinner at Rossi's or Sunday lunch. 'I can pump him then.' He laughed. 'As for Doyle and Carruthers, I think the interview with Morland should dispel any overheated Gothic fantasies about Russian mystics.'

'Do you plan on *us* taking a look, guv?' She was loath to admit to her strong curiosity about the healing centre and its enigmatic proprietor.

'We can let the other two soften him up for us and then pay a visit tomorrow afternoon.'

'You don't reckon they'll end up alienating him?' she asked dubiously. 'After all, he *did* threaten to sue the *Gazette*. And if he gets on the blower to the DCI, there could be no end of complications.'

'You can give them a pep talk beforehand, Kate . . . reiterate the need for tact and diplomacy. Morland might actually be flattered by Doyle's interest—'

'Just so long as he doesn't make it too obvious he thinks Morland's been messing with OAPs,' she finished dourly.

'Oh I think he'll rein himself in, Kate. Doyle's an ambitious young detective who won't want Sidney fancying he's been infected by my "mystical streak".'

She grimaced. 'That *would* be career suicide all right.' Then, hesitantly, she continued, 'All this faith healing stuff's a bit unnerving, sir . . . We're meant to be living in the twenty-first century not the Dark Ages!'

'Morland can't be all that unorthodox, Kate. Medway's not exactly a hot spot for alternative culture. His clinic wouldn't have lasted this long if he were some totally dodgy guru preying on the vulnerable. You said something before about Rasputin being made a scapegoat for everything that went wrong in Russia. We need to be careful it doesn't happen in this investigation with Morland just because he's got some kind of Dionysian backstory.'

'Agreed, sir.' Burton looked at her watch. 'We're not due to see Frances Langton at the school till four . . . Think I'll go and give Doyle and Carruthers that "pep talk".' She smiled grimly. 'Then I'll do a briefing note for our meeting with the DCI tomorrow morning and sort out something for the press office.'

'You're a human dynamo,' Markham said admiringly, causing her to flush with pleasure.

'You're not so bad yourself, sir,' she rejoined gruffly.

'I run a strange sort of outfit here, though, don't I?' he laughed. 'I'm willing to bet DI Carstairs and his ilk don't have riveting debates about the likes of Rasputin.'

Her solemn expression softened.

'Nathan says you can't beat lateral thinking and free association, guv . . . *incubation* he calls it. Plus, you letting us bat ideas around is what gives our unit its distinctive flavour.'

'"Distinctive flavour" eh, Kate.' Markham smiled the rare, charming smile that transformed his ascetic features. 'I'm pretty sure Sidney and the high-ups have another name for it!' Seeing her poised to leave, he added casually, 'By the way, how's everything with you these days?'

'Me and Nathan had a bit of a bumpy spell, but we're working through things,' was the cautious reply. 'Mirroring exercises, role play and dialogue strategies,' she added defensively.

There was something poignant about the way she said this. Like a student desperate to get an A grade on her assignment. Conscientious in this as in everything, Burton was determined to do her homework, though it sounded about as romantic as watching paint dry. He could only imagine what Noakes would make of the role play element!

Schooling his expression to show nothing of what he felt, Markham merely said, 'Glad to hear it, Kate. Don't hesitate to ask if you need any time off.'

When hell freezes over, he thought as the door shut behind her.

* * *

Later that afternoon, as Burton drove them, with her customary punctilious observation of speed limits, to Medway High School. Markham said, 'We need to take in the Copse tomorrow, Kate, once we've recce'd the healing centre. I want to do a follow-up with Stella Fanshaw and Tricia Dent. Neither of them has a satisfactory alibi . . . according to Dent, she was hard at it rearranging her stock, while Fanshaw apparently checked up on flower arranging at Saint Michael the Archangel before coming home.'

'It all seems so improbable somehow, guv,' she sighed. 'I mean, the Copse set up is pure George Orwell, isn't it . . . shades of old maids cycling to Holy Communion through the morning mist and all that jazz.'

'As envisioned by John Major, aka "Captain Underpants",' he said with a rueful expression. 'Don't forget, Ms Dent apparently dated that DJ, George Parker, so she doesn't exactly fit the template of a sedate spinster.'

'You know what I mean, guv . . . It's the sheer *ordinariness* of it all that makes this case so *weird*.' She paused, scrupulously observing roundabout protocols. 'I was watching this drama on catch up the other night, *Manhunt*. It's all about the Night Stalker who did all those burglaries and rapes involving old people . . . Martin Clunes plays a blinder as the SIO.'

'Ah yes, I remember it, Kate. Colin Sutton, wasn't it? The one who put Levi Bellfield away . . . got justice for Amélie Delagrange, Marsha McDonnell and Milly Dowler?'

'That's right, sir. *Manhunt*'s really good . . . shows the perp unscrewing lightbulbs, forcing side doors, disabling telephones, slithering through ginnels and the rest of it . . . seriously spooky. But this case of ours, boss,' she raised her hands from the steering wheel and let them fall in a gesture of exasperation, 'we're talking mid-morning — broad daylight

38

— and a visitor smothering Sheila with one of her own cushions in the conservatory as if they'd dropped in for coffee and decided to finish her off by the by . . . almost as casual as brushing their teeth or part of their morning routine, like it was nothing at all.'

'I know what you mean, Kate. And I remember one of the senior detectives in *Manhunt* raging about the fact that if the victim only fell within the right age range — twenties to forties — it would've made the case sexy enough for the tabloids.'

'Exactly, boss. You can bet the *Gazette* will bury this one on page seventeen or right towards the back . . . because they can't show a pic of some pouting teenaged nympho.'

There was a note of bitterness in her voice that was unusual for Burton, but he carefully refrained from looking at her and she had herself in hand almost immediately.

'It's the whole setting, sir,' she went on more composedly. 'Suburbia, with the blasted dahlias bobbing away outside and nothing more exciting than the postman rocking up with a load of junk mail. Then someone holds a cushion over Sheila's face till she stops breathing . . . I mean, what would make anyone do that? Are we talking a gerontophilic,' even in her agitation, Burton did not omit technical precision, 'or someone who needed to shut her up for some reason?'

'Or a mixture of both.' Markham knew they had to be prepared to think the unthinkable.

'It was a gentle sort of killing,' she said almost pleadingly. 'As though they didn't want to hurt her.'

Just like Shipman, would have been Noakes's verdict. And look how that escalated.

All he said at this point, however, was, 'Agreed. The level of violence doesn't suggest a sadistic desire to linger over the process or protract it unnecessarily . . . which points to an impulse kill rather than premeditated murder.'

'But what could an inoffensive old lady have said or done that would make someone suddenly decide to kill her?'

'Your guess is as good as mine, Kate.'

He just hoped to God Sheila Craven's murder hadn't ignited a flame that wouldn't go out.

Now they were drawing up at Medway High, Burton parking in a space adjacent to the forecourt.

The school was built on the same model as Hope Academy's soulless sixties 'bunker' — a beige, Lego-brick, battery-hen edifice with all the charm of B&Q or a women's prison. Actually, on balance, Markham felt he preferred HMP Styal.

'Horrible, isn't it?' Burton breathed as they disembarked and contemplated the three-storey cement building with its modular cinder extensions.

Olivia was wont to say that Hope Academy's motto should have been 'Abandon hope all ye who enter here'. Looking at Medway High, Markham felt an even stronger note of despondency. 'Maybe inside it's all futuristic architecture and light-filled atriums.'

In the event, the school's interior was even more unprepossessing than its exterior, with the chlorotic off-white walls and submarine-like corridors clammily evocative of their experiences in the Ashley Dean investigation at Hope. Burton was resolutely tight-lipped, but Markham could tell from her taut expression that she didn't at all care to be reminded of that particular case. Light and air felt conspicuous by their absence, however, so it was difficult to avoid comparisons.

At least since it was holiday time, there were no marauding hordes whooping and hollering, which meant they were spared the customary hubbub of a juvenile exodus.

Frances Langton was decidedly attractive for a headteacher, Markham thought, having mentally prepared himself for something along the lines of Hope's bulldozing senior management. Slender, softly spoken and youthful, with long dark hair, a pale complexion and features of quattrocento delicacy, the headteacher couldn't have been further removed from the female 'juggernauts' whom the team had previously encountered at Hope Academy.

She had a reserve and fastidiousness that inflected her disclosures about Sheila Craven.

'Sheila was an exemplary Christian, Inspector,' she commented over refreshments brought by a smiling secretary.

This wasn't enough for Markham in the circumstances.

'Could you expand on that, Ms Langton,' he said courteously. 'Currently, we haven't got much sense of what Mrs Craven was like in terms of her personality.'

As in, Spare us the platitudes, Burton thought sardonically.

'Whatever you tell us is obviously in confidence,' Markham went on quietly. 'Unless of course it's directly germane to our enquiries.'

Frances Langton fingered the necklace of amber beads that set off her well-cut jade trouser suit.

'She was a good woman,' the headteacher repeated. 'But she enjoyed gossip and small talk . . . with the likes of Stella Fanshaw from the Copse and one or two others. Birds of a feather. It can make trouble in a community, you know . . .'

Markham rather thought he did, having learned from his ex how insidious and dangerous could be this gnawing of the inward worm in a certain type of woman. 'The Coven' was the nickname Olivia had bestowed on a similar clique at Hope.

'Did Sheila make some sort of trouble for you?' Burton asked bluntly.

'I think she . . . speculated about my friendship with Norman Collins.' A flush had burned into the pale cheek. 'Talked about it in such a way as to imply there was an unsuitable degree of intimacy, a familiarity between us that might prove detrimental to his ministry . . .'

'How do you know Sheila badmouthed you?' Burton pressed her.

'Eventually I worked it all out and found the proof of the pudding . . . plus people were willing to talk . . .' She tucked a stray strand of hair behind her ear with a careful deliberation that suggested she was thinking about how to package her dislike of Sheila Craven. 'Norman and I were friends and he was a school governor, but then he backed away . . . didn't want to engage with my strategic planning.

I'm pretty sure it had something to do with Sheila, though obviously I never confronted him about it.'

So the vicar had cooled on her, Burton thought, and it was most likely down to clacking tongues including Sheila Craven's.

Which added up to motive.

The head had no alibi. 'I came in early Monday morning to catch up on admin and paperwork.' A self-deprecating smile. 'The bane of my life.'

'No one else around?' Burton enquired.

'My PA came in about midday and a couple of the secretaries showed up after lunch. We're pretty flexible in holiday time. I think there were cleaners on the premises, but I kept my head down until the afternoon and nobody bothered me.'

It was only five minutes' walk from school to the Copse, Markham calculated. And he noticed that Frances Langton's office had a side door that led directly on to Warren Avenue, so she could easily have made it to Derwent Lane and back without a soul being any the wiser.

As though to emphasize that she had nothing to hide, after some inconsequential chat, the head let them out that way, her expression almost defying them to comment on the school's proximity to the Copse.

'So Sheila queered Langton's pitch with the padre,' Burton mused as they made their way round to her Fiesta. 'Then he went lukewarm on her school improvement plans . . . wouldn't back her up with the governors anymore.' Fastening her seatbelt, she mused. 'She wasn't all that keen on the Rossi crowd, though that story about Vincent Rossi claiming their little sister Giulia was being bullied didn't sound like a big deal . . . And it was obvious she didn't go a bundle on George Parker either.'

'I believe we've yet to meet Vincent,' Markham said, thinking that he would look out for this scion at dinner on Friday. 'Perhaps they let her down when it came to fundraising,' Markham said thoughtfully. 'Or it could be they're all too brash and ostentatious for her taste.' Frances Langton had struck him as possessing an innate pride and refinement, covered with a thin glaze of ice-cool reserve, that made her an intriguing proposition. Certainly he could easily imagine her as the target of jealous gossip.

'She wasn't giving anything away about Morland and the healing centre,' Burton continued. 'But having a couple of acupuncture sessions there doesn't add up to much.'

'Hmm, yes she was definitely cagey . . . Mind you, in her position she probably has to watch what she says.' As they approached the town centre, he asked, 'Have the FLOs located Desmond Pettifer yet?'

'Oh right, the nephew . . . He was off at some music festival in Wales . . . works as a promoter or something like that. They said he was pretty offhand when they broke the news, so he's obviously not that close to Sheila. He's due back in Bromgrove sometime tomorrow, sir.'

'Try and arrange a condolence visit for the afternoon please . . . Even if theirs was a long-distance relationship, I think it's important we get off on the right foot.' Not least if Pettifer entered the stakes as a potential suspect.

There were potential candidates for Sheila Craven's murder whichever way he looked, the DI thought uneasily. But the Golden Hour had been and gone, and a killer was gloating somewhere close at hand.

Time to step it up a gear.

CHAPTER 4

It was strange, Markham thought the following morning as he sat with Burton in the DCI's office, how his relationship with Sidney had become almost *affectionate* with the passage of time. The boss's dreadful nasal honk still affected his nerves like nails scraping down a chalkboard, and he disliked the woke-ridden management-speak as much as ever, but visits to the Holy of Holies were no longer such an ordeal as formerly.

Sidney himself, with his buzz cut, designer specs and sharp linen tailoring, looked like a hybrid of Prince William and an Italian football manager, though periodic outbreaks of eczema (notably in abeyance now that Noakes had retired) somewhat marred the impression of executive chic.

Olivia loathed Sidney who returned the compliment in spades, invariably referring to 'Markham's lady friend' with a knowing leer that suggested his doubts of their relationship lasting the course (actually, he had showed some prescience if it came to that). Calling him 'Judas Iscariot', a 'backstabbing snake' and various other choice epithets, she had early detected the king-size chip on Sidney's shoulder due to Markham's Oxbridge credentials, handsome looks (including thick black hair — a particular sore point for his follicle-challenged boss), courtly grace and total disdain for the sort of palm-greasing at which Sidney was so adept.

But Markham himself had come to realize that beneath the bombast and strident self-assertion, the DCI was in fact terminally insecure, not to mention 'pussy-whipped from here to eternity,' as Noakes said with reference to 'Brunhilde', his formidable spouse who ruled the roost at home. In fact, Sidney's allegiance to conventionality, class paranoia and deep-rooted horror of anything idiosyncratic or unusual (viz his DI's "feyness") reminded Markham of Muriel Noakes's anxious adherence to orthodoxy and the social norms, as though they represented protection against being perceived as an imposter who belonged outside the charmed circle of Bromgrove's middle-class elite. Interestingly, both the DCI and Mrs Noakes were rabid royalists, *his* particular favourite being the Countess of Wessex pictures of whom appeared with startling frequency in the Hall of Fame, as the photo-montage which took up the whole of one wall of the office and showed Sidney hobnobbing with assorted notables was irreverently known.

Yes, Markham thought to himself as he discreetly observed the DCI throning over acres of teak desk (he was a great champion of the "paperless office"), the flipside of what Olivia considered to be Sidney's mean-minded jealousy was undoubtedly some fear that had its roots deep in his upbringing — a dread of not being good enough. He could understand and pity this, as well as admiring Sidney's resilience in mustering strategies that allowed him to keep his sense of self intact. If that meant patronizing Markham for head-in-the-clouds dreaminess and 'making himself conspicuous', then so be it.

On this occasion, as it happened, and much to Markham's private amusement, Sidney was all affability as he discoursed on Rasputin and the Romanovs with Kate Burton, she having decided it might be as well — given the DCI's well-known nervousness around suspects with a litigious streak and his fear of sensationalism — to underline the team's respect for Henry Morland's academic and university credentials.

Burton and Sidney being psychology graduates with a keen interest in criminal profiling and proficient in all the politically correct jargon, they had found common ground in a way that he and Markham never quite managed. Burton's red brick educational antecedents and respectful earnestness (unmingled with servility) also stood her in good stead.

'A fascinating period of history, Inspector Burton,' the DCI brayed approvingly. 'I believe Prince Philip helped with the DNA testing when they located the Romanovs' bones in Ekaterinburg. Only natural that our royal family should want Nicholas and Alexandra properly honoured.'

Markham forbore from pointing out that guilt might have had something to do with it, seeing as George V shamefully vacillated about rescuing his cousins from the revolutionaries until it was too late.

It was obvious that Sidney was keener on the tsar and his family than the Mad Monk, but Burton was adroit. 'We've come a long way from all the *Hammer House of Horror* stuff,' she said earnestly. Her features a picture of innocent enthusiasm, she added, 'Doctor Morland's articles on the real extent of his political influence shed a whole new light on it all.' Markham had no doubt that Burton had mugged up on Morland's entire oeuvre with a view to making herself mistress of the subject in question.

Having artfully positioned herself as Henry Morland Ph.D.'s number one fan, Burton slipped in, 'Of course we'll need to speak with Doctor Morland, but really it's pretty much routine.' In the sense of ruling him out, was the clear implication.

Sidney visibly relaxed, reassured that the proprietor of the Healing Centre would be handled with kid gloves and there would be no scandalous rumours about Sheila Craven and the ex-priest.

The DCI's addiction to quick fixes — the 'Bushy Haired Stranger' or mentally deranged loner — was notorious in

CID, especially where there was any risk of the great and good or Bromgrove's reputation being tarnished by association with violent death. To his credit, however, Sidney had increasingly placed his trust in Markham's team to achieve results, even where they pursued lines of enquiry that threatened the established order. Now he said warily, 'Am I to take it that you're looking for someone with a local connection, Markham?'

'It seems very likely that Mrs Craven knew her killer, in view of how she died and the absence of defensive injuries,' he replied levelly, fully aware that a killer embedded in the community — quite probably a respectable citizen — was Sidney's worst nightmare.

'Nothing was taken from the property, sir,' Burton told him. 'There was money and jewellery in her bedroom upstairs, but it wasn't touched, and there was no sign the killer attempted to search any of the rooms.'

Sidney frowned. 'Could there be a link to her husband? Tom Craven was one of our own, so conceivably it's possible this might be someone with a grudge.'

Markham shook his head. 'Noakes thinks not, sir.'

The DCI passed a hand over his forehead, his expression suggesting he felt a migraine coming on.

'I presume you're proposing to involve George Noakes in some way then, Inspector,' he said heavily, as though inwardly cursing, *Just when I thought it was safe to come out!*

'As an occasional civilian consultant, sir,' Markham aimed for his best bedside manner, 'seeing as Noakes is familiar with Medway and the high street. Then there's Natalie . . . she has links to the university and local community. And obviously her work as a holistic practitioner,' or however she described herself these days, 'gives her the perfect calling card.'

'Access all areas,' Sidney said thinly.

'Something like that, sir.'

'Extraordinary the way that family somehow manages to enmesh itself in every CID investigation going.'

There was really no response to this observation, so Markham simply maintained a rictus smile till his jaw ached.

'Mrs Craven led a quiet life,' Burton said finally in an attempt to dispel the spectre of the Noakeses. 'So for now, we're looking at the neighbours, her church, shops on the high street, the local Italian.' Surreptitiously crossing her fingers behind her back, she continued brightly. 'The vicar at Saint Michael the Archangel and the headteacher from Medway High have been a great help. It's a question of getting a *feel* for the local networks, sir.'

'Just so long as you don't take too long about it,' was the faintly menacing response. 'I need hardly point out that the murder of an elderly woman in her own home is generating great concern *at the highest levels.*' Which, roughly translated, meant that the Chief Constable or some other head honcho was giving Sidney gyp.

Markham was swift to offer reassurance. 'We're throwing everything at this one, sir, including help from the criminal profiling unit.' Just as soon as he could pin down Nathan Finlayson . . .

In the meantime, Burton gave it the full Krafft-Ebing.

'Erotic age orientation . . . clinical targets . . . laboratory appraisal . . . *Kinsey* . . . DSM-IV . . . classifications systems . . . population-level occurrence . . . paraphilias . . . teleiophiles . . . etiology and psychosexual origins . . . *Journal of Forensic Psychiatry & Psychology* . . .'

With no apparent squeamishness, Sidney lapped it up, stroking the jutting chin formerly adorned by a wispy goatee ('cos he reckoned it makes him look like an egghead', was Noakes's withering verdict). After a discussion of psychological markers in the Night Stalker case, Burton concluded earnestly, 'It's possible the person we're looking for suffered some sort of abuse by an elderly person, sir, but the offender profile's still inchoate at this stage.'

Inchoate! Not for the first time, Markham thanked God for a second in command who had swallowed a thesaurus, to say nothing of the Diagnostic and Statistical Manual of Mental Disorders.

Well aware that Sidney would be secretly hoping their enquiries might point to a mental patient or some other social reject in preference to well-heeled suburbanites, the DI added suavely, 'Of course we'll be liaising closely with the Newman Hospital and Carradine Centre,' the latter being Bromgrove's homeless hub, 'keeping all options on the table, sir.'

Once safely back in Markham's office, Burton said, 'At the risk of sounding like Barry Lynch,' the station's slimy press officer, 'I'd say we got away with it, guv.'

He smiled. 'Thanks in no small part to your skill in disarming the DCI, Kate.'

'I guess he's not so bad if you can get on his wavelength,' she said diplomatically. 'He's quite the history buff . . . It was funny what he said about that tsar — Alexander the something — who was so strong he could bend iron pokers and silver cutlery with his bare hands . . . like some sort of Uri Geller . . . Noakes would have enjoyed that.' A giggle escaped her. 'Did you clock the way Sidney's PA kept looking around as though she was afraid sarge was going to jump out at her.'

'Not exactly kindred spirits her and Noakes,' he laughed. 'I think she took it the wrong way when he cracked that joke about PMTea . . . He was lucky she didn't set the diversity squad on him.'

'Knew it would be a lost cause, boss . . . all that inclusion training was water off a duck's back.'

'Well, at least now he's officially a civilian, I don't have to dread that officious woman from HR turning up here like the Wrath of God with complaints about the latest outrage to PC sensibilities.'

She chuckled before returning to the subject of Sheila Craven.

'We're not really looking for some random psycho here are we, guv?' she said, the mirth fading from her face. 'Rosemary Blake was positive that Sheila normally kept the conservatory's French doors locked unless she brought someone in round the back. The doors weren't forced, so she let them in—'

'Which means she had to have known them.'

'Exactly.' Burton's face was troubled. 'I know I trotted out all the behavioural psychology stuff for the DCI, guv, but Sheila's murder doesn't fit the template for sexual homicide. Dr Patel says she wasn't interfered with and it didn't present like an asphyxiation scenario or fetish activity.' She thought hard. 'Of course, it could be they just have got off on the act itself . . . having power over life and death . . . a bit like Shipman . . . all neat and tidy with the old folk looking like they'd just nodded off where they sat and him getting a kick from shooting them full of morphine . . .'

'You could well be right, Kate. Nothing to say we're not looking for someone with a psychosexual kink. Back there you mentioned the Night Stalker . . . Well, as I recall, there was quite a lot of theorizing about Delroy Grant's formative years and the fact that he was almost entirely brought up by his paternal grandmother in a rural community in Jamaica.'

'So his sexual tastes might've had something to do with her taking over the maternal role?'

'Correct . . . some kind of disordered response to disruption of the mother-child bond.'

'Or she could have abused him in some way?' Burton pressed.

Markham was suddenly very still, the well moulded lips set as though closed on a secret. For an instant, he was suddenly back with the sadistic stepfather who had stolen his own childhood. He was silent just long enough for Burton to wonder at it, before he replied in his usual tone, 'Some sort of trauma in infancy might well be a factor if it turns out we're dealing with a sexual attraction to the elderly.' The DI paused. 'But I'm not convinced that's what was going on here.'

Burton fiddled with her papers and briefcase while surreptitiously observing the guvnor. Small wonder that Sidney felt at such a disadvantage whenever he was in Markham's presence. The narrow, aristocratic face, high forehead, dark hair coming down in a peak, together with the look of fastidious reserve, could not have been in greater contrast to the rest of Bromgrove Station's high command. And then there were the fine dark eyes and penetrating gaze . . . unlike 'Blithering' Bretherton of whom Noakes was wont to say that his eyes were so near his nose they looked like they wanted to join themselves to it . . .

'Penny for them, Kate?'

'Just thinking that the DCI seemed to have mellowed, sir,' she lied, somewhat flustered.

'Well, he appeared reassured by your obvious respect for Dr Morland's pre-eminence as an expert on Rasputin and Tsarist Russia,' was the wry response. 'I was just waiting for you to get started on the tradition of holy fools . . . "God's foolishness is wiser than human wisdom and His weakness is stronger than human strength",' he intoned piously with a mischievous gleam.

She looked embarrassed. 'I probably overdid it a bit, guv.'

'It was most diverting. 'Just a pity Noakesy wasn't there to join in.' Sidney's reaction to his friend's theories about The Mad Monk didn't bear thinking about.

'The DCI took it quite well when you said that about him being a civilian consultant on this one.'

'Oh, there'll be some kind of quid pro quo exacted, never fear,' he observed cynically. 'But in the meantime, we've got the healing centre lined up for this afternoon?'

'That's right, boss. At four o'clock . . . Then we can take a look at the Copse and Sheila's neighbours.'

'What about Desmond Pettifer?'

'He's coming in to the station at six.'

'Good.' No one could say they were letting the grass grow, Markham thought. Aloud, he continued, 'Did we get anything useful from the SOCOs?'

'Nope, boss. The killer was forensically aware . . . literally did the deed and then wiped everything down. There's no useful DNA.'

'What about Doyle and Carruthers . . . Did they find the healing centre an Aladdin's cave of Rasputiniana?' There was a sardonic edge to Markham's query.

'I'll check in with them before we head off,' she said. 'Hopefully they didn't come across as giving the impression we think Morland's some amateur huckster into all kinds of mumbo jumbo.'

Markham laughed. 'I'm sure you'll be able to smooth over any awkwardness, Kate.' His gaze rested on her consideringly. 'I had the impression back there in Sidney's office that you're quite taken with the whole Rasputin legend.'

'Oh, I've always had a bit of a thing about Nicholas and Alexandra . . . awful to think of their children being butchered before they ever really lived.'

'I know what you mean, it's a compelling story. Olivia,' it was almost as though he was testing himself by bringing her into the conversation, 'found it intriguing too.'

After a faintly awkward pause, he continued, 'The DCI wouldn't like me impugning royalty, but arguably the empress's infatuation with Rasputin brought them all down.'

'Her son's haemophilia was the ticking time bomb,' she replied stoutly. 'Her being desperate for a cure is what gave Rasputin a hold over her. Really, it's no wonder she turned to religion.'

'So you're a "Rasputinist", then,' he teased.

She looked alarmed at this.

And even more alarmed when he added mischievously, 'There's a legend about Rasputin's genitalia ending up in some museum after the revolution . . . pickled in formaldehyde.'

Swiftly recovering her composure, his fellow DI shot back, 'Let's pray Noakes doesn't latch on to stories like that . . . might give them a coronary down at Rosemount.'

Markham chuckled. 'He's much safer sticking to General Gordon. Heaven only knows how I'm going to keep him from storming the healing centre.'

They smiled at each other in a moment of precious complicity.

With a gleam in the dark grey eyes, Markham then asked, 'What would the DCI say, if he heard us conversing like this, Kate? He'd be bound to disapprove.'

'Oh, I think he was pretty intrigued by it all, sir . . . The thing is, we don't seriously think Sheila Craven's part of some dodgy secret sect run by an ex-priest who fancies himself to be a reincarnation of Rasputin, do we? . . . I mean, that's just too far out for words.'

'Agreed. It seems highly improbable.' With a wry grin, he added, 'Though I'm sure the Gazette would love it.'

She pulled a face at that. 'There weren't a load of icons or religious knickknacks knocking around Sheila's house . . . nothing that stamped her as some sort of crank . . . She was just this perfectly respectable middle-of-the-road churchgoer—'

'Who made a dangerous enemy somewhere along the line.'

Burton shivered at that.

'While I'm fully alive to the danger of stereotyping Henry Morland,' Markham continued, 'he undoubtedly represents an exotic element in the mix . . . Do we know why he left the priesthood, by the way?'

'We're up against the usual *omertà* there, boss, but Bishop Buckley's chaplain *did* deign to tell me that "nothing unto-ward",' she air-quoted viciously, 'was in question.' Scowling, she added, 'He behaved like I was some kind of sleazy hack salivating over the prospect of exposing a pervy priest.'

'Given all the flak the Catholic church currently attracts, I suppose you can hardly blame him.'

'He implied there was some deep theological reason the likes of me are too thick to fathom. That or Morland was kicked out for being unsuitable.'

'You'll be able to ask him yourself shortly, Kate.'

This recalled her to their agenda for the afternoon. 'I'd better go and debrief the other two,' she sighed.

'What's the position on Morland's alibi?' Markham enquired.

'He wasn't at the university with it being the holidays . . . doing some gardening apparently . . . *another one* virtuously deadheading the roses.'

'And nobody saw him?'

'Sorry, guv, his neighbours are away, so no joy there.'

'What about whether Sheila ever had any treatment at the centre . . . do we know if she went there?'

'She had the occasional facial and pedicure . . . but Morland doesn't do those himself, and anyway she hadn't been in for several months.'

Another brick wall.

After Burton had left, Markham reflected on their successful meeting with the DCI. He had spied a picture of Sidney's eldest son Jake at his Sandhurst passing-out parade, so perhaps paternal pride had something to do with the new mellowness. Noakes generally didn't have much time for 'sprog Officer-Cadets', but he had quite warmed to Jake, a charming self-effacing young man, principally for the reason that he was 'nothing like his old man'. So perhaps there might be some safely neutral territory on which Sidney and Noakes could make small talk when they met.

Mind you, he'd be a fool to count on it.

* * *

The Healing Centre was an unpretentious unit next to the pub. From the outside it could have been a dentist's or newsagent's but for the discreet signage. Inside, however, it was a different story. Oriental rugs on parquet floors, watered silk lavender wallpaper and beautiful flower arrangements — white and purple lilacs, vases of roses and orchids and bowls of violets perfuming the air — gave the ground floor suite of five consulting rooms a feeling of intimate cosiness. A very *feminine* atmosphere, Markham reflected, but of course Morland's clientele would be preponderantly, if not exclusively, female.

The walls were covered with icons and what looked like vintage prints of palaces.

'*Tsarkoe Selo*, "the Tsar's village",' Morland told them, seeing their interest. 'Russia's equivalent of Marie Antoinette's

Petit Trianon. It was the Romanovs' enchanted paradise where they could be themselves and live a simple life.'

'With an army of servants in the wings,' Burton sniffed disapprovingly, peering at pictures of retainers in brightly coloured national costume. 'That's autocracy for you.'

'True,' their guide smiled. 'They were deplorably insulated from how the masses suffered.'

'The empress was a seriously beautiful woman,' Burton commented, examining a family group.

'Yes, you can't see it in these photographs, but Alexandra was very willowy with dark blue eyes and masses of reddish gold hair . . . very striking.'

Markham felt a sharp stab of pain at this, an image of Olivia rising up before him.

Morland mistook his wince for impatience.

'Let's adjourn upstairs,' he said smoothly. 'Otherwise I'm liable to get carried away discoursing on my favourite subject.'

His office on the first floor was functional and relatively utilitarian by comparison with the suite of rooms below, but it was nevertheless comfortable with plain leather chairs, desk and bookshelves in pine and more prints on vintage grey herringbone wallpaper.

There was no sign of any clients or staff, and Markham figured Morland had arranged it that way. Their interviewee offered coffee which the detectives courteously declined, engaging in some more desultory chat about the university and his research on Rasputin before cutting to the chase.

Asked about Sheila Craven's visits, he readily replied, 'I've checked my appointments book and she was here a few times last summer, only I didn't attend to her personally . . . I've a vague recollection of seeing her, but it was just a case of pleasantries and "how are you?", nothing more than that.'

Morland seemed perfectly calm and master of the situation, a musical speaking voice falling agreeably on their ears. He was personable and conservatively dressed in chinos and open-necked shirt, with close-cropped dark hair, long aquiline nose, mobile expressive mouth and alert hazel eyes behind clear-rimmed glasses. Aware of Burton's curious appraisal, he said, 'As you can see, I ditched the Summer of Love disguise a while ago.'

Embarrassed, Burton said, 'Sorry, it's just that it's quite a turnaround from the long-haired look.'

'Think nothing of it, Inspector,' was the easy reply. 'That belonged to my kabbalistic phase — identifying too strongly with Rasputin when I researched his connections to the *khlysty* . . . Russian apocalyptic sects, unhinged flagellants who sought God through all kinds of extreme practices like orgies and voluntary castration and cutting off women's breasts.' Just wait till Noakes found about *this*, Markham thought wryly.

'Did Rasputin belong to one of those groups?' Burton asked curiously.

'Well, they investigated him multiple times but couldn't nail him for it.' A dour smile. 'Shame the *Gazette* didn't cotton on to my research interests. Given their genius for getting the wrong end of the stick, they'd have had a field day.'

Markham found that he was warming to Henry Morland with his wry self-deprecation.

Burton was swift to take the opening.

'Is that what happened with the woman who went to the *Gazette*?' she asked. 'A misunderstanding?'

'Yes. She misinterpreted an applied kinesiology session.'

That was it. He offered no further details nor explanation. By tacit agreement, the detectives did not press him further.

It was the same with Morland's priestly career. He talked calmly about a 'period of spiritual debility' and 'being at odds with his superiors' (something with which Markham could sympathize), but they got nothing beyond that and were obliged to move on to a review of his qualifications (which were sound), the centre's various treatments and protocols. He was politely vague and noncommittal about the locals, giving the impression that he had taken no particular trouble to integrate himself into the life of the community.

Afterwards, mulling over the encounter as they sat round the corner in Markham's car, Burton said with unusual animation, 'That's an interesting bloke.' Wistfully, she added, 'The students are lucky . . . I bet his courses are packed out.' She grinned. 'And that was funny, what he said about Rasputin being so orthodox he could safely have gone on *Thought for the Day*.'

'We didn't learn much about Morland *personally*, though, apart from what he said about his interest in alternative medicine developing out of the research into Eastern mysticism.'

'True,' she conceded, 'but that about not knowing Sheila seemed genuine enough.'

'The place appears to be doing well financially,' Markham observed, 'and all the paperwork was in apple-pie order.'

'Probably all the female patients are titillated by him being an ex-priest.'

His lips twitched. 'Not very feminist of you, Kate, but doubtless accurate.'

'I was wondering . . .' She coloured and broke off. 'No, that's stupid.'

'Go on,' Markham urged .

'Well, he's obviously charismatic . . . a registered hypnotherapist and all the rest of it. There's lots of positive reviews online.' It was typical of her to have checked. 'What if someone fancied playing the "soul doctor" with Sheila, so they could get her to do what they wanted?'

'You mean like a *disciple* of Morland's?' Markham asked, intrigued.

Her blush deepened.

'Sounds a bit extreme . . . But when he was talking about autosuggestion and the way Rasputin cast a spell over Alexis and his mother, I wondered if some copycat had targeted Sheila like that, only for some reason they screwed up and ending by killing her.'

Markham looked thoughtful. 'Not extreme at all, Kate . . . As an elderly widow living on her own, she might well have been vulnerable to that kind of manipulation.'

Starting up the engine, he reflected that the interview with Morland had indeed been engrossing. He had no such expectations that the Copse would be half so interesting . . .

And so it proved.

Those of Sheila Craven's neighbours who were in the vicinity on Monday morning were all boringly unexceptionable and, as established by Doyle and Carruthers, alibied up to the hilt.

Stella Fanshaw fully lived up to Doyle's description of her as a 'bossy old trout'. Stocky, beady-eyed and belligerent, with a stiff blow-dried blue rinse that wouldn't have moved in a force nine gale, she was clearly irritated at having to account for her movements again while at the same time gratified at being interviewed by not one but *two* detective inspectors. She repeated the account that she had given their colleagues, waspishly pointing out that Rosemary Blake must have skimped on that morning's tasks, since strictly speaking she wasn't due to finish until half eleven 'on the dot' but had obviously packed up early and gone round to Sheila's since there was no sign of the cleaner when Stella arrived back from her detour to Saint Michael's. Markham guessed the hapless woman had already been apprised of her employer's displeasure as regarded bunking off early.

'Nobody saw Stella coming back into the Copse, though,' Burton said dispiritedly as they stood near the little central island, no doubt under observation from behind the net curtains at number 16. 'And we only have her word for it about dawdling at the church and getting back just before half eleven . . . for all we know, she might have been in and out of there in minutes then scooted off to Derwent Lane. The estate's a bit of a goldfish bowl, so she wouldn't have risked trying Sheila's front door.'

'Difficult to see Ms Fanshaw 'scooting' anywhere, but then again she's not particularly decrepit and she had the time,' Markham said thoughtfully. 'I suppose it's too much to hope we've got any sightings from Derwent Lane yet?'

'Zilch, guv. I've got Doyle and Carruthers on it but no one saw anything. A shady lane with flats and just a few semis set well back from the road . . . it was ideal really,' she said regretfully.

Looking back at number 16, Burton said, 'The shutters came down when we got on to the vicar and Frances Langton. You'd have thought an uncharitable word about those two never passed her or Sheila's lips . . . but I'm willing to bet there were regular gossip-fests.' Uneasily, she added, 'Morland talked about the Russian court being a strange closed world where everyone was plotting. Something about this case feels the same . . .'

As they walked over to Sheila Craven's doll's house, cordoned off with police tape, Burton's mobile rang. Watching her take the brief call, Markham saw her face change.

Bad news.

'Norman Collins is dead, sir,' she told him without preamble.

Markham was stunned. 'Foul play?' But he already knew the answer.

'Looks like it, guv.'

Suddenly the very air of the quiet little residential estate seemed to have changed.

Vibrations of evil.

CHAPTER 5: INTERLUDE

The rectangular high-walled rectory garden was immaculately tended, its trellises lined with climbing roses and late-flowering clematis, while trim little flowerbeds edged with boxwood sported carnations, dahlias, purple stocks and other blooms. Pleasant shady nooks were dotted about, and a gravelled path led to a large pond at the farthest end which adjoined the neighbouring graveyard of Saint Michael the Archangel Parish Church. The presence of SOCOs and uniformed officers swarming about seemed almost a sacrilege in such a tranquil Eden.

After suiting up, they joined Dr Patel who was waiting by the pond standing next to a tarpaulin shroud which covered the corpse of Norman Collins.

'He was bludgeoned while feeding his koi carp and then shoved into the pond to drown. I'd say the water's just over three feet deep but being injured disabled him.' Gesturing to an iron gate set in the wall at the rear of the garden, the medic added, 'That was open, so his attacker presumably came in the back way . . . There's no padlock, so it would have been easy to slip the latch. Alternatively, he let them in and went on feeding his fish without realizing the danger.'

Standing there with the drowsy hum of bees in the background and the heady scents of phlox and campanulas jostling for attention, Burton looked sick as she imagined the vicar's attacker watching him drown.

'Do we have a weapon, doctor?' Markham asked.

'Whoever did this must have brought it with them . . . Judging by the state of his skull, I'd say a paperweight or something like that.' The pathologist's face was sad. 'This is a lovely spot. At least he died surrounded by beauty.' Aware of Burton's tension, he added gently. 'No need for you to view the body. I'll send pictures over . . . He wouldn't have known anything after that initial blow to the head.'

The DI didn't look as though she found this to be much consolation. 'Time of death, doc?' she asked unsteadily.

'I'd say around eight o'clock yesterday evening,' was the quiet reply. Despite Markham's long-standing friendship with 'Dimples' Davidson, he found something refreshing in the lack of humming and hawing that attended this pronouncement, habituated as he was to their usual pathologist's stubborn reluctance to be drawn on specifics. 'Like getting blood out of a stone,' as Noakes used to say, though Doyle reckoned the reluctance was an affectation and Dimples secretly wanted to come across like gruff Dr Max DeBryn from *Inspector Morse*.

'Who found him?' Markham asked now.

The pathologist nodded to a little knot of uniforms surrounding a distraught-looking middle-aged woman.

'His cleaner Mrs Harrison . . . comes in most mornings. He's usually in his study when she arrives, so she knew something was off.'

Now it was time for Dr Patel and the paramedics to stretcher the remains out to the waiting ambulance in Cabot Road. Despite their best efforts, the canvas-covered bundle sagged and slithered clumsily as it was manoeuvred on to a gurney, Burton swallowing hard as she imagined its contents. The detectives, SOCOs and uniforms all stood to attention and bowed their heads as Norman Collins left his garden for the last time.

'I feel bad, guv,' Burton said as the little group disappeared. 'I'd almost made up my mind it had to be *him* who was up to something shady with Sheila Craven.'

'What kind of shady?'

'Mind games or hypnosis or suggestion, something like that . . . Being her vicar, he was the one best placed to exert emotional pressure. Sheila was devout, so she would have been easy pickings . . . And he had the magnetism. I could just picture him holding forth from the pulpit . . . dominating everyone like some wicked cardinal out of Shakespeare.'

Markham could see his colleague was badly shaken.

'You're not alone thinking along those lines, Kate, so don't be too hard on yourself. Mr Collins struck me as a formidable personality with hidden depths, a complex character . . . certainly out of the usual run of clergymen.'

There was a sudden commotion behind them at the other end of the garden which turned out to be Graham Thorpe remonstrating with one of the uniforms.

'It's all right,' Markham dismissed the constable with a nod. 'Mr Thorpe is the deceased's deacon.'

Thorpe, in shirtsleeves and perspiring heavily, removed his glasses and put them in his top pocket as though he didn't want to perceive his surroundings too clearly.

'What's happened? Was it an accident . . . did he collapse or something?'

Markham looked at the man's plain, earnest features, blotchy with agitation.

'When did you last see Mr Collins?' he parried.

'At evensong yesterday evening, Inspector,' the other replied promptly. The service finished at six. We chatted briefly in the sacristy before going our separate ways.'

'And there was nothing out of the ordinary about him?' the DI pressed. 'Mr Collins didn't step out of his usual routine or appear to have anything on his mind?'

'There was just one thing I thought was a bit odd . . . He inserted a litany to Saint Michael the Archangel right at the end of the sermon. . .'

Burton looked at him blankly. 'But isn't that normal? I mean, seeing as that's the name of the church . . . isn't Saint Michael the patron saint or something?'

'Well, it wasn't part of the liturgy for the *day*.' The deacon plucked at his shirt where it stuck to his underarms, as though suddenly conscious of the great soup plates of sweat that were spreading across the cheap nylon. Markham was struck by pity for the man who had drawn the short straw when looks were being handed out. Stamping his authority on a congregation would have been effortless for Norman Collins, but the deacon would have had to work much harder.

'It was a bit OTT really,' Thorpe said, 'the way he tacked on prayers for protection against evil spirits who prowl about the world.'

Markham felt a chill come over him and it seemed in that moment that the pleasant garden was full of shadows.

Had Norman Collins intuited the identity of Sheila Craven's killer? Or did he just sense the presence of a lurking threat without knowing who it was he had to fear?

Now was not the time, but the DI determined to enlist Noakes on the morrow for an inspection of St Michael's and its grounds. Meanwhile, the church would be cordoned off and uniforms posted to prevent an influx of rubberneckers.

'What happened, Inspector?'

His attention was recalled to Graham Thorpe.

'I'm not at liberty to give you details, Mr Thorpe. All I can say at this stage is that the vicar died in suspicious circumstances.'

The deacon automatically made the sign of the cross and wiped his forehead. He looked as though he was about to keel over, but Markham knew from long experience that appearances could be deceptive.

Burton was clearly thinking along similar lines. 'Where did you go after evensong?' she asked bluntly.

The man drew himself up. 'Straight home of course.'

'Anyone able to vouch for you?' she persisted.

'I live alone,' he said stiffly. 'I've known the vicar for fifteen years and he was faithful to all his parish duties.'

It was a curiously opaque response.

'Cold fish, isn't he?' Burton commented after he had left a short time later. 'Like cod on a fishmonger's slab . . . and that awful limp handshake.' She shook her head. 'Mind you, when all's said and done, I don't see him as the murdering type.'

As daylight began to forsake the rectory garden. Markham suddenly felt wiped out. Burton too looked exhausted.

'You should get off, Kate,' he said. 'Tomorrow's likely to be full-on, so I want you to snatch some rest before we're plunged into briefings and bulletins and the rest of the hoopla.' At least they did not have to worry about notifying Norman Collins's next-of-kin, his deacon having confirmed that the vicar had no living relatives.

A thought struck Burton.

'What about Desmond Pettifer?' she asked. 'We were supposed to see him at the station.'

Markham was too flattened for the bereavement courtesies. 'That'll keep. Just leave a message . . . explain the situation and rearrange if you can.'

'Wilco.'

And still she lingered. Almost as though there was nothing waiting for her at home.

Markham was strongly tempted to invite her to join him, Olivia and Noakes for supper at Rossi's. But the situation with his ex was delicate, and her jealous insecurity regarding Burton would be unconducive to a relaxing occasion. Then there was the fact that Noakes was hardly likely to approve of him inviting Burton, especially since he knew she had once carried a torch for Markham and more than likely guessed this had caused problems with Olivia. Besides which, Markham had a burning curiosity to know the state of play between Olivia and Mathew Sullivan but would feel constrained from putting out feelers with Burton at the table taking it all in.

As she squared her shoulders, perhaps shrugging off any disappointment that she wasn't included in his plans for the evening, Burton looked more vulnerable than usual. Suddenly, Markham had a poignant image of what she must have been like at about four or five years old, pretending that everything was all right even when it wasn't. However, her voice was resolutely cheery as she said goodnight, declining his offer to drop her off. He felt a wave of affection for his doughty little colleague as he watched her retreating back, feeling more sure than ever that things had gone badly awry between herself and Nathan Finlayson and making a mental resolution to touch base with the psychologist as soon as possible. He liked Finlayson (whom Noakes had nicknamed 'Shippers' on account of his startling resemblance to serial killer Dr Harold Shipman) and felt obscurely as though he had wronged the man by virtue of his own latent attraction to Burton — very much a slow-burn affair that had evolved over the course of their partnership and his increasing admiration for her.

In the meantime, supper with Noakes and Olivia at Rossi's beckoned.

Before he left, he said a silent prayer for Norman Collins, hoping that in some fourth dimension the dead man's soul was rejoicing in flowers whose beauty far exceeded any earthly specimens.

* * *

'I reckon the missus would like this place,' Noakes commented appreciatively as he wolfed down his starter of *fritto misto* while Olivia and Markham tackled their *bruschetta* at a more sedate pace. 'Dead cosy an' rustic . . . Mind you, all them crucifixes are a bit weird,' he said, casting furtive looks as the ornate wood and wrought iron crosses which, interspersed with antique gilt mirrors, hung on the exposed brick walls.

'The Rossis are bound to be devout Catholics,' Olivia said, 'so it's a nod to their religious heritage.' Mischievously, she added, 'There's something positively Gothic about it all, so your mate Rasputin would feel right at home here, George.' She was the only person other than Muriel to call Markham's wingman by his first name, which merely intensified the doggy devotion with which he habitually regarded her.

'You could do a project at Hope,' he said in a happy burst of inspiration. 'Seeing as they're all big lefties up there, you'd be onto a winner telling 'em about Rusky toffs copping it from the peasants.'

'On the basis that they were evil tyrants, eh, Noakesy?' Markham said deadpan.

'Oh aye, dead wicked an' cruel . . . Grand Duke something or other sliced his Borzoi down the middle after someone asked how good his sword were.'

This coinciding with the arrival of Olivia's lamb cutlets, she looked as though she could well have dispensed with such details.

Noakes was monetarily distracted by his spaghetti carbonara, but swiftly returned to the fray. 'Seriously luv, some *Down with the Aristos* stuff an' you'd probably be in line for deputy head.'

'You've forgotten, there isn't a vacancy right now, George,' she said quietly.

There was an awkward silence as Mathew Sullivan's name hung in the air.

'Oh yeah, I'd forgotten about Mat the Lad,' Noakes said with elaborate casualness. 'How's it going with him these days?'

Markham continued eating his sea bass with every appearance of equanimity, but in reality he was intensely anxious to hear the answer.

'Oh, you know, we're fellow sufferers, George,' she said airily. 'He's got grand plans for the new term, but it'll be an uphill battle getting them accepted.' Which implied their association was purely professional but didn't explain why

Sullivan had been spotted squiring Olivia here, there and everywhere, Markham thought savagely.

'Seeing anyone these days, is he?' Noakes asked slyly. 'He ducked a few five-a-side sessions, so I figured his love life must've picked up.'

'He's a slave to the job, George, so I'm not sure there's much time for anything else right now,' she replied with forced calm, closing the subject down.

His ex looked as striking as ever, Markham decided, a simple shift dress in mint green suiting her pale colouring, though it couldn't disguise the fact that she had lost weight. The thick red-gold hair was coiled in a chignon, strands curling loosely round her face and softening the finely-cut features which to his concerned eye looked more sharply etched than he remembered.

He wondered how things truly stood between her and Mat Sullivan whom he consciously avoided these days despite being personally fond of Hope's lanky, witty deputy head.

He had been pretty sure that Sullivan was ninety-nine and a half per cent homosexual, but since the Ashley Dean investigation the teacher had dated various women, so who knew what might happen if there was a spark. There had always been a certain chemistry between Sullivan and Olivia.

Of one thing Markham *was* sure, and that was that he didn't have the right to probe or cross-question Olivia. He felt there was still something between them, however . . . a frisson, an undercurrent. Or was it just wishful thinking?

Eventually came pudding — tiramisu and Bakewell tart for the men and lemon sorbet for Olivia — when they turned to the burning topic of Markham's current investigation.

Noakes listened with rapt attention as Markham expanded on the interview with Henry Morland.

'Sounds like a cool customer,' he said when Markham had concluded.

'Well, he certainly wasn't giving anything away.'

'You don' think he's up to owt iffy then?' It was obvious Noakes was disappointed that no revelations about defrocking or spiritualist dodginess were forthcoming.

'He was fascinating on the wonders of Imperial Russia — Kate was in the seventh heaven.' Markham was aware of Olivia stiffening and the fact that Noakes had registered it, but resolved he wasn't going to have Burton banished from the conversation. She didn't deserve that.

'Could hardly tear herself away,' he continued calmly. 'Inside is like a shrine to late nineteenth-century Russia . . . Quite surreal finding somewhere like that in Bromgrove.'

'Maybe I should pay a visit,' Olivia said.

It sounded almost like a challenge.

'I'd be very interested to hear what you think,' was all he said, however.

'So what next then?' Noakes demanded. 'This Bakewell's champion,' he added approvingly. 'Proper jammy instead of that nasty stringy stuff.'

'I thought you and I could scope out Saint Michael the Archangel tomorrow morning,' Markham replied.

'Check out the graveyard, you mean?' his friend said eagerly. 'See if there's any OAPs stashed there?'

'God, George, you're the life and death of the party tonight,' Olivia said with mock horror. But she looked wistful, and Markham could almost fancy she had been on the point of asking to join their little expedition. However, she didn't make the request and the moment passed. Perhaps it was for the best, he decided, given her scorched-earth policy when it came to the subject of her personal life.

Noakes looked as though he would like to have Olivia along, but with surprising tact followed Markham's lead and made no suggestion that they should make an outing of it. 'Don' forget you're both coming to ours for your dinner on Sunday,' he reminded them. 'Looking forward to it,' was Olivia's polite response, though Markham suspected she privately dreaded witnessing Muriel's ill-concealed glee that the two of them had split up.

'That lot over there are getting pretty rowdy,' Noakes observed as Francesco Rossi brought their coffees. 'The big mouth is George Parker,' he informed his companions. 'His phiz was plastered all over the *Gazette* last week for Bromgrove Music Week.'

The restaurateur was apologetic. 'It's always . . . lively when Mr Parker's in,' he told them. 'But Matteo and Marina'll keep them in order, and Vincent's quite friendly with that crowd, so he won't let things get out of hand.'

'That bloke's the image of Silvio Berlusconi,' Olivia observed as Francesco glided away. 'Is the gorgeous blonde girl behind the door his daughter?'

'Yes, she's the manager,' Markham replied.

'And the Italian Stallion next to her?'

'Matteo her fiancé.'

'What about the tall guy standing at the noisy table?' Olivia asked. 'He seems to be getting on well with them.'

'That's Vincent.' Ed Frayling was standing closer to their table than she had realized.

'Sorry,' she blushed. 'They're all so striking, I just had to get the rundown.'

The waiter grinned. 'Agreed,' he said. 'They're handsome all right . . . I try not to hate them for it.' He wasn't so bad in the looks department himself, Olivia thought appraisingly, but the Rossis had the edge when it came to height. 'My shift's nearly over,' he said courteously, 'so I'll say goodnight . . . I'm due at a gig in town.'

'You're a musician?' she asked.

'Guitar and vocals, though nothing big league . . . well not yet. I want to start my own music magazine too when my boat comes in or I can find someone to sponsor me. Right now, I'm just scrabbling around hoping to catch someone's eye.' He grinned. 'Preferably the big boys, though as yet they don't see me as the next One To Watch.'

With a cheery wave, he was off.

Markham's gaze followed him. Frayling was an engaging character, yet he sensed a certain despondency beneath the resolutely upbeat persona.

Could this up and coming musician possibly have hit on Sheila Craven or other patrons for money?

No, he decided. Ed Frayling's frankness and ready admission of career issues simply didn't fit the suspect profile. Waiting tables was the favoured option these days for many an artistic wannabe, and the young waiter was clearly philosophical about his chances of attracting the spotlight. No doubt his level-headed girlfriend helped to keep him grounded.

Serena Rossi suddenly appeared at their table, having sprung from nowhere. She looked very tired but her smile was warm.

Clearly gratified by Markham's compliments on the meal, she said diffidently, 'Inspector, there's a gentleman at that table over there who wondered if he could just have a word.'

Oh God. He had a particular horror of being buttonholed by members of the public who wanted to 'bend his ear' — in other words, bore for Britain — about the deficiencies in local policing.

'Nothing like that,' she said, swiftly registering his dismay. 'His name's Des Pettifer . . . He said you'd arranged to see him earlier.'

Full marks to Pettifer for discretion, since it didn't look as though he had said anything about his aunt's death, Markham thought as he followed Senora Rossi to the raucous table. On the other hand, wasn't there something callous in him being out on the town at such a time . . .

'Well, well, well, if it isn't CID's blue-eyed boy,' a thick-set fair-haired man slurred. Fleshy and with slightly blood-shot eyes, he had the kind of good looks that quickly went to seed. 'Come to arrest me for breach of the peace?'

'Easy, George.' Vincent Rossi placed a warning hand on the DJ's shoulder. 'You should always stay on the right side of the police.' He gave an old-fashioned bow to Markham. 'Especially one as distinguished as the Inspector.' The Italian accent was more marked than that of his parents, maybe as a sign of loyalty to the home country, and he had certainly inherited their easy charm.

A small dark-haired man pushed his chair back. 'Des Pettifer,' he said. 'Why don't we step outside for a minute, Inspector. I could do with some fresh air.' The careful enunciation signalled that he was tipsy. He turned to the others. 'Back in a mo.' Weaving his way unsteadily ahead of Markham, he led the way outside.

Despite an instinctive distaste for the man who was carousing without a care in the world so soon after his aunt's death, Markham offered his condolences. Pettifer made no pretence of exaggerated grief but responded perfectly correctly. As to alibi, he was apparently on the road to Wrexham at the time of Sheila Craven's murder.

'Nowt to say he couldn't have done for her an' then legged it,' Noakes grunted on Markham's return to their table, eyeing Pettifer balefully as he rejoined George Parker.

'True . . . We'll check for sightings of his car in the vicinity of the Copse that morning, but to be honest there seems no reason to doubt him at this stage.'

'What about the old woman's will . . . was her nevvy expecting to get his hands on the dibs?' Noakes persisted.

'Her solicitor promised to give me a few minutes tomorrow morning, so hopefully I'll find out then if anyone had expectations worth killing for,' Markham replied. 'Sidney emailed me earlier to say Sheila's funeral is half eleven on Monday—'

'So soon?' Olivia interjected. 'Isn't that a bit speedy in the circumstances?'

'Don' tell me . . . strings being pulled as per bleeding usual,' Noakes muttered. 'Is Pettifer some sort of VIP then?'

'Reading between the lines, I think it's more to do with Tom Craven having been one of our own,' Markham told him. 'Plus, she apparently stipulated for St Michael's and they'll be wanting a decent interval between her funeral and Norman Collins's service which is bound to be a big affair with visiting clergy and all the rest of it.'

'God yeah . . . To think of the padre being bumped off too!' Noakes exclaimed. At the surprised expression of a passing waitress, he added *sotto voce*, 'Summat's gotta be up with that church.'

'Well, we can suss the vibes tomorrow, Noakesy. The others can crack on with checking people's alibis for Mr Collins.'

'Maybe Sheila Craven was like one of those neurotic women Rasputin attracted,' Olivia mused, her thoughts turning once more to the original subject of their conversation. 'Maybe she confided her secrets to the vicar and somehow *that's* what led to their deaths.'

'What, you mean like who'd been cheating at bowls?' Noakes guffawed.

She punched his arm lightly. 'No, George. Something more weighty than that . . . *something worth killing for.*'

Her words rang in the DI's ears after they went their separate ways, Noakes offering to drive Olivia home and thus pre-empting any awkwardness of the do-you-want-to-come-up-for-a-coffee variety between herself and Markham. He was in fact grateful for the reprieve, since he felt wrung out and ill-equipped emotionally to hear any revelations about his ex and Mathew Sullivan.

Something worth killing for.

Perhaps Sheila Craven's parish church might help them find some answers.

CHAPTER 6: TAKING STOCK

Saint Michael the Archangel Parish Church was a Victorian building of slightly dingy, pale-yellow stone designed on severe Neo-Romanesque lines and set in a sprawling plot that appeared heavily overgrown in parts, with tangled rose bushes, unmown grass, trailing ivy and brambles almost obscuring the monuments in the oldest section at the far end adjacent to Molyneux Road. Of a piece with the old-fashioned rectory, thought Markham, as he recalled their meeting with Norman Collins in his study with its high back leather chairs, cherrywood table and armchairs covered in green velvet pile.

Observing the narrow-gabled structure, softened only by its rose window over the pediment, Noakes professed himself unimpressed as they walked towards the porch. 'Shame it's the same colour as the lavs in town,' he said, nodding amiably to the young constable who saluted at their approach.

Markham found that he quite liked the classical symmetry of the exterior. He was agreeably surprised by the interior too.

There was no transept, just a rib-vaulted nave with pine pews on either side ending in an arched, burnt-orange terracotta sanctuary that held a simple wooden altar beneath a gilt-framed devotional painting and carved mahogany tabernacle. Colonnaded arches along the side walls lent the interior a crypt-like atmosphere of ancient catacombs, with statues and candle-stands in each of the recesses, while to the left of the altar a white marble Christ presided magisterially over the whole with arms outstretched. On the right was a bronze figure of Archangel Michael, his wings extended to their uttermost span and sword raised aloft in acknowledgment of the Creator's sovereignty. Two crimson and white damask banners hung above the nave on either side, as though to emphasize the archangel's martial credentials, while the green and red marble pulpit next to the figure of Christ had a red velvet parament embroidered with gold-lettered text that read: *The greatest glory comes in displeasing the wicked.* Above the pulpit was a white satin canopy supported by two slender barley-sugar columns in walnut wood, lending it the appearance of a mysterious palanquin.

Noakes shuffled up the shallow pulpit steps to investigate a lectionary on the reading stand.

'*Our adversary the Devil as a roaring lion goeth about seeking whom he may devour,*' he intoned lugubriously. 'Ties in with what you said about the padre getting wound up over Old Nick being on the prowl.'

At this, Markham had a sudden sharp feeling of unease, as if he sensed a presence lying in ambush, lurking in a hiding place just out of sight . . . waiting to ensnare another victim. Impatiently, he shook his head to clear it and inhaled deeply, savouring the chill, hassocky odour which was something he loved about old churches.

Now Noakes was investigating the panelled and glazed doors which gave access to three antiquated confessional boxes towards the back of the church on the right-hand side. 'Mebbe Mrs C came and sat in one of these,' he said with a superstitious reluctance to investigate their interiors. 'Mebbe she told the Reverend about summat that were troubling her . . .'

'Well, the seal of the confessional would prohibit him from betraying her confidence,' Markham replied, briefly inspecting each one.

'Yeah, but the Rev might've let it slip that she told him a secret . . . Or the killer could've been spying on Mrs C an' saw her going into one of them boxes.'

Again, Markham experienced an insidious sensation of evil very near, so close that it was as if the Devil stroked his face.

To dispel the feeling that something malign was creeping up behind him, stalking him step by step, Markham walked across to the sanctuary with its striking artwork above the altar. Noakes duly followed, though with furtive sideways glances that suggested he was not entirely at ease with the High-Church ambience.

'It's a Tissot print,' Markham said slowly as he gazed up at the picture. '*The Soul of the Good Thief.*'

Now Noakes was interested.

'They made that lad a saint,' he said. 'Saint Dismas. Fair enough really, seeing as Jesus said he could go straight to Paradise no questions asked.' The pug-dog features frowned. 'Don' think much of them angels swinging the wotsits.'

'Censers for incense.'

'Right. Well, they look well grumpy, like they don' really think he's pukka . . . as in he shouldn't be hitching a ride with them.'

Markham chuckled, but Noakes wasn't finished.

'An' making him midget-size ain't fair. Like he's a toy or summat.'

'I think the idea is to show him being borne aloft by the Seraphim, Noakesy. And let's not forget, angels are meant to be awe-inspiring divine messengers hence the difference in size.'

'They've got too many wings . . . I mean, why do they need *six*? And what's with the white mushy stuff at the bottom?'

'That's meant to be earth with the continents and seas . . . so you've got the good thief rising up from the globe far below.'

'Oh aye . . . looks more like scrambled egg or an omelette to me.'

'You're a hard man to please, Noakes,' Markham sighed.

'I s'pose the starry sky ain't bad.'

A minor concession.

The man Noakes thought of as the guvnor stood lost in thought, as though contemplating some inward vision.

Same old, same old, he told himself. But the ex-sergeant never minded when Markham 'went off on one' or indulged his bent for what Sidney called 'airy fairy claptrap'. He knew it was the DI's safety-valve and, besides, he liked the *specialness* of it all ... the way the guvnor made you feel life wasn't just humdrum and plodding along and there were strange mysteries out there.

Markham finally emerged from his abstraction.

The last recess on their left as they walked slowly up the nave towards the porch contained a simple wooden statue of Saint Michael the Archangel (sans spear, with folded wings and a benignant expression) along with prie-dieu. Noakes, predictably, could not resist taking a peek inside the little kneeler-cupboard. '*Hey*, I bet this was where the Rev came to say his prayers,' he pronounced, fingering the ribbons of a heavy missal with delighted curiosity. Screwing up his face, he recited with lip-smacking relish: '*Arise, O sleeper. I did not create you to be held a prisoner in hell.*'

'I think that's an Easter prayer, Noakesy,' Markham said, a shiver running up his spine at the ancient exhortation.

'Happen he were worried about Mrs C getting into heaven,' his friend remarked solemnly. 'So he had to do a bit extra. Probl'y lit candles for her an' that kind of stuff.'

Markham was touched by the earnest simplicity of his friend's conviction. He felt as if there was only a veil between himself and the murdered dead, and the least effort would be enough to tear it down. But it took George Noakes to make that aching sadness real and tangible — to reanimate those who cried out from the other world for justice.

'This is a beautiful church,' he commented, vowing within himself to avenge the murder of its priest.

'Outside's a bit of a mess, though,' Noakes observed. 'They could do with clearing out all the weeds an' them fallen trees down the far end . . . Happen they need a decent gardener.'

Markham found something attractive in the air of romantic abandonment, but Noakes was right about the graveyard being a bit of a Gothic ruin. The barebone beauty of autumn would be perfectly suited to its overgrown, dishevelled dilapidation.

They wandered over to a bench.

'You didn't get any *vibes* back there then, guv?' Noakes enquired hopefully.

'Not a one, I'm afraid,' Markham replied before adding, 'and there were no surprises in Sheila's will. I checked with her solicitors Maxwell and Fellowes in town . . . She left bequests to Saint Michael's along with various charities, plus six thousand to Desmond Pettifer and gifts to a few friends — a couple of hundred to Stella Fanshaw and small sums to her favourite waiters at Rossi's . . . nothing worth killing for and no life insurance policy or anything like that.'

'What about her house?' Noakes asked. 'Surely that's got to be worth a fair bit?'

'Left in trust to the North West Police Benevolent Fund.'

Noakes looked glum at learning this wasn't a case of "follow the money".

'Did you get any goss about the Copse or the high street?' he demanded with the air of a man desperate for some useful nugget of information.

'If by "goss" you mean incriminating facts about our suspects, Mr Maxwell was quite tight-lipped,' Markham told him. 'However, I *did* learn that there was some sort of fall-ing-out between Tricia Dent and the vicar's clique over her plans to stock antiquarian erotica.'

Noakes was intrigued. 'You mean mucky books?'

'Well, I imagine it's not the straightforward Linda Lovelace variety, more probably Marquis de Sade collectibles . . . tasteful porn, if that's not an oxymoron.'

His friend looked askance at this, lest the sleepers in that peaceful cemetery should rise up out of their coffins in protest at such profane goings-on.

Markham laughed at his expression.

'*Relax*, Noakesy, I don't believe she's a sexual deviant, and anyway it sounded like a storm in a teacup. From what Maxwell said, I gather the vicar regularly had to referee local squabbles as well as deal with outbreaks of hero worship.'

Noakes frowned. 'Hero worship?'

'Middle-aged parishioners vying for his attention,' Markham replied with a sardonic twitch of his lips.

'Was the Dent woman after him then?'

'Reading between the lines, it sounds as though Tricia Dent and Frances Langton might both have hankered after a closer intimacy with Norman Collins than certain parishioners — including Sheila Craven and Stella Fanshaw — considered seemly.'

Noakes rolled his eyes. 'Lemme get this right . . . You mean the Rev dropped them two cos of some interfering old biddies who should've minded their own beeswax?'

'Pretty much, yes . . . but petty stuff like that happens all the time in small communities. I'm not sure it adds up to anything significant.' Thoughtfully, he added, 'More interesting is the fact that Tricia Dent was seen leaving Bookworm around twenty-five to eleven on Monday morning . . . a detail she omitted to mention when we interviewed her.'

'Who spotted her?'

'Vincent Rossi. He'd gone in to Rossi's early so he could have a coffee and read the papers before getting on with the deep clean . . . says he definitely saw her leaving the shop as though she was in a hurry.'

'What did she say when you tackled her about it?' Noakes asked eagerly.

'She told Burton that she was, unusually for her, getting a headache from the musty smell of old books, so she just popped out for a breath of fresh air . . . went round the block a few times to clear her head . . . was only gone for about twenty minutes, which is why she had forgotten all about it.'

'Anyone see her take this little stroll?' Noakes's tone was deeply mistrustful.

'No one,' Markham replied levelly. 'So there's no way of disproving her account . . . I can't say I particularly warmed to the woman. She dated George Parker for a time, but there was an acrimonious breakup which must've left her feeling very vulnerable and perhaps explains why she was drawn to the vicar—'

'Until his groupies put the mockers on it,' Noakes interjected dourly.

'Like I say, not the most congenial of interviewees, but as things stand there's nothing which puts her squarely in the frame.'

Other than the fact that it looked as though she had lied to them, he thought.

'We c'n mull it all over when you come for your dinner tomorrow,' Noakes said consolingly. 'Mind you, there'll be no turning up here for Sunday Service with it still being a crime scene.'

'The SOCOs will be finished up later today apparently, so I believe "smells and bells" are still on.'

'*Champion*,' Noakes beamed. He looked back towards the church. 'Thass quite an interesting place,' he said. 'I reckon it might be an OK service. So long as we don' get one of them sky pilots who shouts about voices coming from heaven, like he thinks he's God booming out of a cloud.'

'I would have thought you'd enjoy a spot of liturgical tub-thumping, Noakesy.'

'Oh aye, but some folk get carried away and forget there's the loudspeakers, so no call to bawl.'

They lingered companionably a while longer, Noakes simply happy to be with the guvnor while Markham, lost in his own thoughts, asked himself which was the lovelier — sunrise or sunset? On balance, he thought the latter. Better to sink below the horizon of this world, so as to rise again in God . . . Had Norman Collins been engaged in similar abstract metaphysical speculation, he wondered. Or had he worried about a *specific* human soul hurtling headlong down to Hell?

He became aware that Noakes was shuffling his feet, as though to get the blood pumping.

'Come on, you old curmudgeon,' he laughed affectionately. 'I'll give you a lift . . . And then I'd better see how the alibis for Norman Collins are shaping up.'

Noakes looked wistful at this, as though he wouldn't mind going through alibis at the station rather than attending to the list of jobs Muriel would no doubt have lined up for his Saturday afternoon. But the DI didn't wish to push his luck with Sidney by smuggling his friend into CID at the weekend.

'By the by,' he said casually as they buckled up, 'Have you seen anything of Nathan Finlayson lately?'

'Ole Shippers?' Noakes's piggy eyes were shrewd. Chris Carstairs told Doyle he saw him an' Burton in town going into the Relate offices next to Holland and Barrett. Must've decided they needed some navel-gazing counselling service to sort thesselves out, It's the seven year itch an' all that . . . though more like seven minutes with *them*.' He scratched his chin reflectively. 'Me an' Doyle took Shippers out to the pub last week, but he got all shirty when we asked how it were going.' A sidelong glance. 'He didn't look too happy when *your* name came up.'

Markham felt a pang. From the sound of it, Finlayson — like Olivia — suspected there was unfinished business between Kate Burton and himself. Despite being essentially a laid-back, easy-going character, her fiancé could hardly be expected to welcome such a state of affairs.

And it was true that he had feelings for Kate, though he hardly knew how to articulate the perturbing nature of the attraction . . .

'We just have to give them space,' he said, aware that it sounded lame. 'They're bound to work it out for themselves.'

With unwonted tact, Noakes refrained from further comment. 'The missus is really looking forward to seeing you an' Olivia for your dinner tomorrow,' he said like some portly Cupid bent on smoothing the path of true love.

Well aware that his ex was likely to find Muriel Noakes's hospitality about as welcome as a dose of venereal disease, Markham forced a smile. 'I'm sure Sunday service will give us quite an appetite,' he said politely, comforted by the fact that Olivia had texted to say she would join them at Saint Michael's. Fortunately, Muriel would be attending the early morning service at Saint Mary's Cathedral, so at least that was one less social hurdle to be surmounted.

'Roast beef with all the trimmings,' Noakes said happily, oblivious of Markham's internal soliloquy. '*That* should set you up.'

As though their romantic difficulties could be solved through the medium of Yorkshire pudding! But the DI just smiled affectionately at his passenger as they headed out of the church carpark.

'Perfect Sabbath fare,' he agreed as they left Saint Michael's behind.

* * *

The Sunday service was unremarkable, though with a reasonably sizeable congregation, attendance having no doubt been boosted by the notoriety attaching to Norman Collins's murder. A mild-looking shrivelled little clergyman delivered an interesting sermon on Saint Jean-Marie Vianney, the Curé d'Ars, whose feast day in the Catholic calendar had occurred on the Friday when the vicar's body was discovered. Without directly referring to the murder, he spoke of a pastor's responsibility to ensure that his flock could 'gauge the goodness of the Master by the behaviour of the servant' and implied that the parishioners of Saint Michael the Archangel had been blessed with an incumbent in that mould.

'Quite moving,' was Olivia's verdict afterwards. 'I seem to remember the Curé d'Ars was the one who ended up listening to confessions eighteen hours a day for thirty-five years?'

'*Seriously*?' Noakes was impressed. 'You'd end up with piles at that rate!'

'Straight up,' Olivia smiled. 'He was famous for knowing people's sins before they confessed them.'

'RC though,' Noakes said doubtfully, the "No Popery" strain in his Methodist upbringing rearing its head.

'Yes, but a pretty appropriate choice seeing as Saint Michael is so High-Church.' With a mischievous smile, she continued, 'The curé was no milk-and-water type . . . he tried to ban dancing in his parish because he said dances were attended by the Devil and an occasion of sin.'

Noakes, a regular on the ballroom dancing circuit, didn't like the sound of this one little bit. 'Out of order saying that, if you ask me,' he muttered.

Olivia replied deadpan, 'Oh, he was a man on a mission . . . looked out the hired musicians and offered them more than their usual fee so they would agree to down tools. It made him very unpopular.'

Her friend looked as though this was just the sort of Jesuitical wiliness he would have expected.

'How d'you know all this anyway?' he asked.

'There's nothing like a convent girl, George,' she laughed. 'Mum and Dad sent me to nuns for my first school . . . once they'd been assured no one would try to convert me or make me bow down before any nasty idols.'

Noakes looked somewhat embarrassed. 'No offence,' he mumbled.

'And none taken,' she replied, resting a hand lightly on his arm, which affectionate gesture caused him to blush to the roots of his hair.

'Sounds an interesting kind of guy,' he conceded once the corned beef colour had subsided. 'An' that were neat, what the sky pilot said about a good priest being like the fella in the Gospel who had lots of stuff in his treasure chest.' Noakes was distinctly more comfortable with biblical citation than stories about saintly curés, Markham thought suppressing a smile his friend's irrepressible tendency to refer to clergymen as 'sky pilots' had been another reason why the vicar of St Chad's had rapidly cooled towards the pair of them, he recalled with a rueful shrug.

He felt somewhat apprehensive as they headed to Noakes's car, aware that Olivia found encounters with Muriel, whom she was wont to call Hyacinth Bouquet and 'Mrs Fratefully Naice' under her breath, an ordeal at the best of times.

And these were not exactly the best of times, though Muriel had been careful to exude high-minded sympathy and concern in the wake of their split. 'So very *sad*, but not really *surprising*,' she had gushed to him. 'Being a police wife requires *special qualities*' (the implication being qualities that Muriel presumably possessed and Olivia did not).

However, though Muriel was initially somewhat stiff and stately towards Markham's ex — playing the "gracious lady" in an aggressively floral shirtwaister and pearls, with her blonde bouffant freshly lacquered in honour of the handsome DI — she gradually unbent over the course of the meal, becoming almost friendly when Olivia praised the melt-in-the-mouth Yorkshire pudding and asked for a second helping. Normally inclined to deprecate the 'scrawny anorexic look' and 'people who subsisted on Pot Noodles' (i.e. Olivia), she merely delivered a few complacent bromides about domestically-focused wifedom (i.e. her own) before the talk turned to Rasputin and the Romanovs. Natalie too — displaying a Cheddar gorge of cleavage and sultry eye make-up in Markham's honour — abandoned her usual surliness towards Olivia and listened with unusual attention as their guest talked about the doomed imperial family and their ill-fated obsession with the Mad Monk.

'There's actually a Rasputin vodka, you know,' she said.

Trust the voddy queen to know all about that, Olivia thought with an inner eye roll.

'The vicar who's just died was a *marvellous* priest by all accounts,' Muriel said, clearly happier with sanctity in the form of an Anglican clergyman than some grubby Slav renegade. 'As you know, *we* prefer Saint Mary's Cathedral,' this being where Noakes was towed on high days and holidays, 'but that's such a *delightful* little church. Of course,' with a knowing look, 'he was never able to please *everyone*. And being such a *striking* man,' here she simpered at Markham, 'there was the problem of him getting trapped by star-struck ladies who jostled for attention. So *sad* when women *take advantage*.'

Which is no doubt how Muriel viewed her own relationship with Markham, Olivia thought, grinding her teeth at the avalanche of meaningful italics . . . the subliminal message being that a sensitive, unworldly policeman had been snared by a siren bent on getting him into bed. Then she caught Markham's eye and the resentment receded. It was of a piece with his decency, she reflected resignedly, that he always regarded Muriel Noakes with generous compassion, preferring to ignore her anxious consolidation of class hierarchy and focus on the vulnerable woman beneath the fussy, irritating veneer. For *her* part, though, she felt she could happily have emptied the gravy boat (Royal Doulton obvs) over Muriel's lacquered bonce.

Finding her voice, she adopted a tone of bright interest, 'The vicar was apt to be pestered then?'

Gratified by Olivia's deferential attitude, Muriel unbent still further. 'Oh yes. The headteacher at Medway High and the woman who runs the bookshop were both after him . . . So *inappropriate* to carry on like that. Apparently the poor man had his work cut out fending them off.'

Somehow, Markham couldn't imagine Frances Langton forcing herself on anyone. Tricia Dent might be another matter, though. There had been something about her that made him think of a slightly dilapidated house to let, only there were no takers . . .

Natalie cut in impatiently, 'Women like that *always* have a crush on the priest if he's halfway decent looking.'

Olivia suppressed a grin at the way Natalie had been making stealthy inroads on the red wine decanter (Waterford) that Muriel now nudged out of her daughter's reach.

'What do *you* make of these murders, Natalie?' Markham asked with the old-world courtesy that never failed him on such occasions. 'With your clinical training, you must have formed an impression.'

Clinical training! *Oh, for God's sake, Gil, she's a two-bit beautician with delusions of grandeur*, Olivia wanted to scream.

But Markham regarded the daughter of the house as if there was no other person in the room, causing her to preen and flick the savagely peroxided mane in a manner that made Olivia want to slap her.

'I reckon it's gerry-bashing,' she said with an air of self-importance.

Markham didn't turn a hair. 'Gerontophilia?'

Vigorous nodding. 'Yeah . . . Like the Stockwell Strangler.'

Muriel abruptly left the table to fetch her Queen of Puddings. While being as heavily addicted as Noakes and her daughter to true crime documentaries, she felt there was something vaguely indecorous in being too up-front about it — as though it marked them out as emotional weirdos. It was why she was always ultra-careful to place her books about the Yorkshire Ripper and other criminal luminaries at the very bottom of her pile of library books, underneath Maeve Binchy and Barbara Taylor Bradford.

'*Hmm* . . . the Kenneth Erskine case. It's interesting that you should say that, Natalie,' Markham continued with his customary cast-iron charm. 'Kate Burton was thinking along similar lines.'

Natalie wasn't at all sure she cared to be bracketed with that plain woman who clearly had the hots for Markham, but she experienced a certain sly satisfaction as she clocked Olivia Mullen's frozen expression. Her dad went overboard for Olivia's fairy-tale number, but clearly something about Markham's frumpy colleague had got under her skin . . . Not that Burton was *so* frumpy these days, mind you. She'd seen her in town a fortnight ago looking almost, well, glamorous. Or as near to glamorous as that type was able to manage.

Suddenly aware of Markham's eyes fixed upon her, Natalie was jolted back to the present.

'Yeah . . . but Erskine was special needs . . . mental age of eleven,' she said, casting around for some sort of intelligent contribution. 'Whereas it sounds like this one knows what they're about.'

'Have you had any dealings with Henry Morland or the healing centre, Natalie?' Markham asked. 'I imagine your services are much in demand these days, so you may be too busy for a backwater like the high street.'

Pass me the sick bucket, Olivia thought sourly. *FFS, Gil, you're making her sound like Apothecary to the Queen!*

Markham never took his eyes off Natalie, who was visibly delighted that "DI Dreamboat" was regarding her with such earnestness. As Olivia observed Noakes's happy expression, she felt a twinge of compunction and inwardly chided herself for being uncharitable. Why couldn't she be less neurotic and more understanding about the foibles of others? 'I love your spikiness, Liv,' Markham had once told her, but she had always felt this moral deficit when around him. Whereas with Mat Sullivan . . .

Don't go there, Liv, don't go there, she told herself, registering Natalie's peepers trained on her face.

'I went to some of *Doctor* Morland's lectures on Russia . . . part of my course on political change.' There was a triumphant sidelong glance at Olivia as Natalie said this — *See, you're not the only intellectual in Bromgrove!* — but Olivia bore it very well, reaching for the decanter to tranquilize her irritation.

'I haven't been down the centre for a while,' Natalie continued. *You mean, never*, thought Olivia wrathfully. 'But he's *ever* so interesting about history stuff.'

History stuff! OMG. Olivia took a hefty swig of the Bordeaux.

Muriel reappeared with the Queen of Puddings, visibly relieved that the Stockwell Strangler appeared to have left the stage.

To Markham's polite enquiries regarding the healing centre, she returned a decided negative. 'Of course, I know the late

Queen was, and dear King Charles is, *devoted* to homeopathic remedies, but being blessed with *inner resources*, I never felt the *need* for a consultation.'

Not half! went Olivia's internal monologue, as she recalled Muriel's infatuation with Dr Yasir Nariman in the Beautiful Bodies investigation.

Markham caught her eye. *Easy, Liv, easy!*

Muriel clearly disapproved of Henry Morland for leaving the priesthood (albeit the left footers) but had equally clearly hoovered up every crumb of gossip about the charismatic proprietor of the clinic.

'So you don't think Morland's been modelling himself on Rasputin and getting up to all sorts with sweet old ladies?' Olivia demanded bluntly.

'We have to remember his calling as a man of the cloth,' was Muriel's chilly response.

'*Ex* man of the cloth,' Olivia shot back pointedly.

After they had left the Noakeses, coffee having never seemed so interminable and protracted, Olivia said crossly, 'Muriel's a sucker for charismatic dark and handsome types, Gil.' Then, with a burst of laughter, 'I can just imagine her capitulating to Rasputin hook, line and sinker.' Raising her voice an octave, she trilled, '*Oh Father Grigory, tell us how you cured the Tsarevich and saved Holy Mother Russia* . . . Yuck!'

'It's her romantic streak, Liv,' he replied gently. 'You know she's devoted to the idea of Monarchy.'

'*We must not let daylight in upon magic* . . . Walter Bagehot has a lot to answer for,' Olivia replied irritably. 'Lethal for the likes of Muriel.'

There was a silence between them, though not unfriendly.

'Drop me off, Gil,' she said finally. 'I wish I could come to Sheila Craven's funeral, moral support and all that, but I'm not sure I'll be able to get time off.'

'No worries, Liv. I appreciate the thought.'

Their glances locked in a long, wordless moment.

It was enough.

CHAPTER 7

Sheila Craven's funeral on Monday 8 August fell in a period of wonderfully mild weather typical of an Indian Summer, with a police guard of honour and strong parish turnout planned to give this faithful parishioner the send-off she deserved.

Markham, however, felt gritty-eyed and weary from a poor night's sleep. Always prone to uneasy slumbers during a murder investigation, he had dreamed the previous night of Grigory Rasputin who stood in Norman Collins's fragrant garden with arm upraised (in blessing or warning), his strange, irresistible eyes glowing like coals . . . *We are fools for Christ's sake.* Markham had awoken in the small hours, shuddering and slick with sweat, the words ringing in his ears.

Wandering into his study (as paperless as Sidney could desire, since the DI used it mainly for meditation), Markham spent a long time as dawn broke over Bromgrove contemplating the hillocky municipal graveyard whose proximity somehow kept his murdered dead close.

Thick as autumnal leaves that strew the brooks in shady Vallombrosa.

Murmuring a line of Olivia's favourite poetry, he surveyed the ranks of clustering headstones and monuments in the rimy early morning light.

Suddenly his gaze alighted on a statue of Archangel Michael guarding some nineteenth-century grandee's tomb with alabaster wings raised aloft. There was something about the angel's disdainful hauteur and tightly compressed lips that reminded him of his old Classics master, an elderly clergyman and confirmed misogynist who had little patience with 'overwrought females'.

Was unbalanced female fervour at the root of these murders? he wondered. Had Sheila Craven and Norman Collins died after becoming enmeshed in some peculiar imbroglio that hinged on relations between the vicar and his women parishioners? It seemed almost too much of a cliché to be credible.

The opaline glow of sunrise gilded the outdoors as Markham finally padded into the galley kitchen of his apartment to brew strong black coffee and mull over the various competing scenarios.

If it was not a question of pastoral shenanigans, then what?

Had Sheila Craven got herself involved with a younger man . . . a toyboy? Someone she had encountered at Rossi's perhaps? Or had she, God forbid, stumbled across some nefarious goings-on involving her nephew and the likes of George Parker? Somehow that seemed the height of improbability.

Was it possible her murder was connected with the Copse and a dispute between neighbours? The problem being, there was no evidence of any feud or falling-out . . .

And in any case, where the heck did Norman Collins fit in?

Then there was the high street to consider. Sheila didn't appear to have had much to do with the Carnforths, though apparently she and her husband had dropped in to the Medway Inn from time to time before Tom Craven fell ill. Nor had the team been able to establish a strong link between Sheila and the healing centre. There was no denying Henry Morland's enigmatic, vaguely sinister aura, but Markham struggled to see the former Catholic priest as a cold-blooded killer. As he sipped his coffee — scalding hot to wake him up — he recalled something Morland had said just before he and Burton left the centre after interviewing him. As they paused before a picture of the doomed tsar and his family, Morland observed quietly, 'Strange isn't it, how the Romanovs made the reverse journey that Rasputin did, ending up leaving their palace in Petrograd to be murdered in Siberia . . . When the girls were executed, they had amulets round their necks containing Rasputin's picture and a prayer. Terrible to think that on their way down to the cellar in Ekaterinburg they had to go past pornographic graffiti showing their mother and Rasputin making love, with Nicholas watching from the side. I find it unbearably sad that this was virtually the last thing they saw . . .' Morland's face and words spoke of a sensitive romanticist and aesthete, but not a hardened murderer. On the other hand, given his past, he was presumably well-schooled in hiding his true nature.

Half-heartedly, Markham made himself some toast, his mind still swarming with possibilities.

Could Burton be right about some unhinged acolyte of Morland's attempting to bring Sheila under their sway? And if so, to what purpose? *Financial gain . . . lust*? He baulked at the latter, but knew it couldn't be ruled out.

Suddenly he recalled the missal Noakes had found in the prie-dieu at the back of Saint Michael's with that text his friend was certain Norman Collins had perused before he died.

Arise, O sleeper. I did not create you to be held a prisoner in hell.

What if the vicar hadn't been contemplating Sheila Craven's eternal destiny but was concerned about someone else? Someone who had stirred latent, almost unthinkable, suspicions that refused to be suppressed . . . someone he feared was in thrall to hellish impulses . . . A prisoner of sin. Had he attempted the role of counsellor before realizing, too late, that he had placed himself in mortal danger?

Absently chewing his toast, Markham wandered back through to the study where he opened the window, inhaling deeply so as to banish the cobwebby fug that he seemed unable to shake off.

It promised to be a fine day, though he fancied that summer was on the turn and he could detect the deciduous tang of autumn.

Sadly, he reflected that the stark brooding beauty of September and October was Olivia's favourite time of year, his ex being wont to compare the cemetery's swirls and drifts of wind-dishevelled leaves to souls of the dead wandering abroad.

The austere features softened still further as he recalled her standing out there during one particular equinoctial gale, passionately declaiming Shakespeare to the graveyard's inscrutable stone cherubs: '*Blow winds, and crack your cheeks! Rage! Blow! You cataracts and hurricanoes, spout till you have drenched our steeples!*' The expression on the face of the cemetery superintendent as he came upon Olivia impersonating King Lear was priceless, the man giving both of them a wide berth after that particular encounter.

As memories suddenly flooded his mind, he found himself missing Olivia with a fierceness that took him unawares., Most of all he missed her caustic irreverence and the sense of mischief that meant he was never bored in her company. And then there was the sex. From that point of view, they were a perfect fit, so perhaps Muriel wasn't wrong in seeing Liv as a siren luring him onto the rocks . . . His attraction to Kate Burton, while undeniable, had none of the raw, visceral urgency that made him ache for Olivia at night . . .

He pulled himself up as the reverie threatened to become more erotic. These were fine thoughts to be entertaining on the morning of a funeral!

Rein yourself in, Markham. Rein yourself in.

He had arranged to meet Noakes and the others later at Saint Michael's. The DCI was due to attend, so it wouldn't do for him to turn up looking ravaged and hollow-eyed. With Sidney being no great fan of Olivia, the last thing he wanted was his line manager imagining he was somehow undone by longing. And his entire being revolted against having to endure what he knew would be Sidney's commiseration on his plight: 'So terribly *sad*, Markham, when these things happen, but the important thing is to *stay busy* and *focused* and *not look back*.'

When it came to schadenfreude and meaningful italics, the DCI left Muriel Noakes in the starting blocks. He could only be thankful that Sidney didn't as yet appear to have cottoned on to Olivia's relationship (if that's what it was) with Mathew Sullivan. Once alerted to *that* development by the sour grapevine, his boss would no doubt have a field day, implying that it confirmed his darkest misgivings about the moral laxity of teachers in the state sector (for all Sidney's parroting of leftie PC claptrap, he had chosen private education for his own precious offspring).

Markham firmly recalled his thoughts to Sheila Craven. Today was all about commemorating *her* life in the church where she had worshiped for so many years.

His gaze was drawn irresistibly to those stone angels beyond the window, their faces smooth and unwrinkled, glowing with simple pleasure in the wonder and goodness of creation, sin and suffering to them merely a distant dream, guessed at but never experienced. His own religious faith was uncertain and troubled, but he knew what he wanted for Sheila was a crucial moment of recognition: for her to be called by name and summoned into the Kingdom, like Dismas the Good Thief in that strange, mysterious painting above Saint Michael's altar . . . not just turned into an angel playing a harp on some fluffy cloud, but validated and absorbed into a new order. He had never known the pensioner living her quiet suburban life in the Copse, but it somehow mattered desperately to him now that the Moving Finger should single her out and call her from nothingness into the wonder of new life. Whatever had happened in Sheila Craven's past, he badly wanted her to be reaffirmed in all her individuality at the funeral, not simply cancelled out by a callous murderer.

He knew exactly how Sidney would respond to such flights of fancy. 'So *important* to retain *professional detachment* and not be distracted by *morbid introspection*, Inspector. Remember, the public doesn't want *spookiness* and *ghost stories* and *hauntings*, just good solid legwork.'

Noakes understood the *spookiness* that drove him on. None better. His former wingman knew too that he wanted resurrection for his murdered dead, in this life as well as the next. Not to show that death no longer had dominion over them, so much as to prove that human malice wasn't the end of everything and the dead didn't simply go down into the grave in silence; that those who met an untimely end weren't just extinguished, and the separation of death could be reversed . . .

It *wasn't* creepy hocus pocus, as Sidney might imply. More a balancing of the books. In the dark watches of the night, Markham entertained biblical musings: *How are the dead raised? With what kind of body do they come?* Ultimately, however, he knew that his own role was to guarantee a temporal 'happy ending' in the face of almost unbearable human suffering . . . He supposed that was really the point of all good detective novels: an unknotting of the uncertainties and confusions of the plot. If so, then *he*, Markham, was the man for the job; bent on finding an ending that made sense of all that had gone before. The difficulty being, that he couldn't as yet find a resolution to Sheila Craven's story, let alone that of Norman Collins . . . A satisfying plot had to respect the depths of the characters who acted it out, but he had never felt further away from understanding the motivations and impulses of the actors in this particular drama. There seemed to be no 'proper' ending in sight. No satisfactory *denouement*.

With an inward groan, and trying to drag his still wayward thoughts away from memories of those passionate nights entwined with Olivia, he adjourned to his bathroom to prepare for the day ahead.

* * *

In the event, it was a very beautiful funeral, with glorious splashes of colour in lavish bouquets placed on either side of the altar and next to the coffin on its trestles. The thickset, beetle-browed celebrant didn't appear to promise much, but the man delivered a surprisingly stirring address about darkness not swallowing up the light and death being transformed by Christ's help into something quite new, a kind of sleep from which the dead would waken to a new dawn, the 'waste sad time' transformed into an outpost of eternity.

Norman Collins was not forgotten, the officiating minister making no reference to the violent manner in which the vicar and his parishioner had met their end but simply coupling their names as faithful Christians who had lived exemplary lives. An impatient jerk of the head from Noakes suggested he didn't regard the bit about exemplary behaviour as being a foregone conclusion, but Markham had no doubt the general tenor of the service met with his friend's approval, rousing oratory having been a feature of the Yorkshireman's Methodist upbringing and afternoons at Sunday School. At least, since this particular priest didn't mumble or boom like the Recording Angel, it was what Noakes would reckon 'a decent send-off'.

As the preacher concluded with a prayer that the Saviour's resurrection should rescue all souls in prison and those 'caught in the toils of sin', Markham's eyes wandered over the congregation.

The contingent from Rossi's occupied a pew near the front, Francesco and Serena and their handsome family making a striking picture, with Vincent and Matteo — son and son-in-law — broad-shouldered and solicitous as they shepherded the women into a bench. On spotting some of the older Rossi females wearing traditional mantillas, there was some muttering from Doyle and Carruthers about 'black crows', but they quickly subsided at a look from his fellow DI. Ed Frayling and Barbara Price, the latter stumpy in comparison with her boyfriend but kind-featured and visibly concerned for him, were in the row behind, along with sundry other personnel from the restaurant. Watching the Italian 'tribe', Markham fleetingly envied their cohesion — the sense that they were a tightly compacted unit ready to take on all comers, whether it be the police or anyone else.

Frances Langton, chic in a black midi flared skirt suit, her dark hair caught up in a velvet snood, looked stiff and strained as she stood in a bench behind Stella Fanshaw. Hardly surprising that the headteacher shouldn't choose to stand next to Fanshaw, he thought, given what she had let fall about a poisonous clique exiling her to the fringes of parish life.

Stella Fanshaw looked uncompromisingly squat and plain, wearing a hat like a squashed mushroom, in contrast with Frances Langton's effortless elegance. Watching closely, however, Markham thought Sheila Craven's neighbour seemed ill at ease, jiggling awkwardly in her Sunday Best footwear as though it pinched. Perhaps it was the prick of conscience, Markham thought grimly, as he observed the woman's edginess. Perhaps she felt compunction about the manner in which she had drawn Sheila Craven into her vendetta against Frances Langton and Tricia Dent.

Dent's rakishly tilted peekaboo veiled hat struck a flamboyant note above her bell-bottom trouser suit topped with a cashmere poncho. Like Frances Langton, she presumably wouldn't be shedding bitter tears for the late lamented — certainly not if Sheila Craven had put paid to her friendship with the vicar. Observing her pallor and the fixity of her expression, Markham assumed that her grief must have something to do with Norman Collins, and that the occasion was more about paying her respects to the murdered incumbent of Saint Michael's than mourning the demise of a woman whose loss she could scarcely have regretted.

Graham Thorpe stood halfway down the church, mixed in with the general congregation. Markham was surprised that he wasn't a concelebrant but, judging from the man's red-rimmed eyes, fidgetiness and patchy complexion, surmised that the deacon hadn't felt up to the rigours of a full-on funeral rite.

Emma and James Carnforth stood with Henry Morland towards the back of the church. They seemed to get on quite well, going by the obvious cordiality between the three of them and the way Morland put out a steadying hand as the pub landlady appeared to stumble going into the bench. Markham couldn't deny there was something chivalrous and caring about the former priest — something that had struck him when Morland spoke about Tsar Nicholas's doomed daughters and the poignant circumstances of their last hours. After visiting the healing centre and listening to the cultured academic, he had instinctively felt Morland to be a class act and knew Kate Burton experienced a similar response. But he also knew the infinite convolutions of the human psyche — its capacity to confound and surprise. Better than any-one, he knew not to judge by appearances. It was ironic, he reflected, that Morland with his well-cut clearly bespoke dark suit conveyed an infinitely more "clerical" impression than Graham Thorpe whose shiny black number and dingy collar appeared distinctly down-at-heel by comparison. Markham knew that Thorpe was unmarried but was intrigued to see the furtive looks he cast towards Frances Langton. The object of the deacon's attention appeared entirely oblivious, but the admiration in his eyes raised all sorts of interesting possibil-ities. Could it be, the DI wondered, that Thorpe had some kind of fixation with the elegant headteacher such that he imagined himself riding to her rescue on his shining white horse . . . avenging her honour by dispatching those who had made her unhappy. He saw that Noakes's attention had likewise been excited by this little bit of byplay, his friend giving a meaningful nod towards the deacon.

Desmond Pettifer, pale but composed, processed into the church with his aunt's coffin — nothing unusual in that — but it was somewhat of a surprise to see George Parker join the congregation, slinking in at the back just after the organist had struck up the processional. Of course, he and Pettifer were drinking buddies, but it seemed unusual even so. The dark glasses Parker sported seemed positively designed to draw attention to his "anonymity". If the neck craning and peering of his fellow-worshipers, were anything to go by — Emma Carnforth, in particular, unashamedly gawking till her husband nudged her — then the DJ had achieved optimum "impact". In Markham's experience of funerals, mourners always kept one eye on what was going on at the back of the church (while doing their best not to be obvious about it). So no doubt Parker had counted on his Greta Garbo moment producing its intended effect.

With Christian obsequies, optimism will always *insist* on breaking through. Despite the absence of helpful "vibes" from the congregation, Markham had the strange sense of finally belonging to a well-constructed plot in which there was the chance for him and the team to ensure that everything turned out well in the end.

He didn't know how they were going to accomplish it. But he suddenly felt a surge of hope that they could somehow make sense of a seemingly arbitrary and cruel pattern that had wrought the deaths of two innocents.

'*I have called you by your name, you are Mine.*'

As the congregation joined in the responses to the celebrant's exhortation that Sheila Craven and Norman Collins should know their Maker 'with unveiled faces', Markham silently vowed again to ensure the enigma was resolved and theirs would not be the dark side of the moon. Glancing at the set faces of his colleagues, he knew they shared his determination.

His attention was distracted from the celebrant's moving commendation by the DCI honking violently into a handkerchief (at least Sidney's hay fever meant he was distracted from observing Noakes, resplendent in the Politburo suit he reserved especially for such occasions). Clearly Sidney had been apprised that the deceased's nephew had celebrity connections (or what passed as such in Bromgrove) and therefore decided to grace the occasion with his presence. Superintendent Bretherton — bald, dome-headed and beaky-nosed — wore his usual stodgy aspect, eyeing

Markham's team with a vinegary expression as though to suggest he anticipated no particular pleasure from the notion of them being coadjutors in the fight against what Noakes called 'Evilution'.

Noakes himself was very well pleased at the high Anglican traditionalism of the service, joining in all the hymns with such fervour as to imply he regarded the injunction 'Raise Ye a Joyful Noise Unto the Lord' in the light of a personal imperative. Watching as Bromgrove CID collectively winced and cringed through his friend's enthusiastic rendition of 'He Who Would Valiant Be', Markham felt once more an aching sense of loss, knowing how Olivia would have relished the entire scenario.

'What's happening about the eats?' His wingman got straight down to brass tacks as soon as Sheila Craven's coffin had departed to the crematorium (family and close friends only, thank heaven).

'The parish centre, Noakesy,' Doyle replied.

'Didn't know there was one.'

'Straight up, sarge,' Carruthers piped up. 'Round the back of the graveyard on Molyneux Road . . . the verger bloke or whoever he is said they're laying on a buffet and what have you.'

'It ain't on the order of service thingy,' Noakes said suspiciously.

'Yeah, that's cos they didn't want everybody and their dog rocking up,' Doyle explained. 'They wanted to keep it, well, *select* . . . just the favoured few.'

'Right you are. That means *us*, then.' Noakes was happy to have that cleared up.

'Let's get round there,' Markham said resignedly, giving way with good grace. Sidney and Bretherton had disappeared, so with luck Noakes's dogged demolition of the funeral baked eats wouldn't bring down the wrath of his superiors upon his head. '*So unbecoming for CID to behave as if they don't know the meaning of a square meal.*' Not that, Markham reminded himself, Noakes could technically be classed as CID anymore.

Markham was vaguely uneasy as they filed out. There was the feeling of having missed something important — something crucial that was lost amidst the flowers and incense and hymns . . . something overlooked that would not be recalled. Despite that surge of hope during the service, a doubt gnawed at the edges of his consciousness, making him curiously reluctant to leave.

'Let's be on our way,' he repeated mechanically, casting a surreptitious back towards the church. The building looked serene, its pale-yellow brickwork bathed in gentle sunlight. But he still felt that it called out to him not to leave yet . . . that there was something he needed to know.

His colleagues were exchanging looks of the *OMG-he's-away with-the-fairies* variety. Even Burton looked politely longsuffering, as though it was to be expected that the guvnor should fall into a trance at the merest whiff of incense.

'After you, Kate,' he said trenchantly, giving himself a mental shake. Whatever secrets the church harboured, nothing could be gained by lingering in its overgrown graveyard. Perhaps something would be gleaned through mingling with mourners at the wake. He had the sense of the souls of the dead being but a little way above his head waiting for the next move.

* * *

The parish centre looked more like a bingo hall, Noakes observed with a sniff as they arrived at the tired little white-washed single-storey building for Sheila Craven's wake.

'What about the cross over the door, sarge?' Doyle laughed. 'That's a bit of a giveaway.'

'You wouldn't think it were anything special,' the other replied, unmoved. 'Bit of a let-down after the church.'

But inside was welcoming enough, with a buffet laid out at the far end and a team of parishioners cheerfully bringing out more food and drink from the kitchen at the side of the room.

'I trust the refreshments meet your exacting standards, Noakesy,' Markham murmured as he surveyed the tables spread with platters of appetizing finger food along with mini tarts, cupcakes, trifles and gateaux. 'It doesn't look like Sidney and Bretherton are around, but for goodness' sake, try not to look as though you're auditioning for an episode of *Man v Food*.'

Noakes grinned unrepentantly.

'Sidney'll be busy greasing up to George Parker an' that reporter from the *Gazette* who showed up,' he replied. 'I'm surprised Gavin Conors didn't try to muscle in . . . probl'y couldn't face the church an' didn't reckon on anyone famous being there.'

There was a long-standing antipathy between Noakes and Conors — the *Gazette*'s reptile-in-chief — that had on one notorious occasion flared up into fisticuffs, and it was clear the former DS was delighted at the thought of 'getting one over' on his old adversary.

'Well even so,' Markham warned, 'the idea is that we're here to pay our respects as opposed to—'

'Filling our boots,' Carruthers concluded.

'Exactly, Sergeant,' Markham said with a hint of asperity. 'You took the words right out of my mouth.' The DI cast a quick look round the room which was starting to fill up. 'Obviously we should also be on the alert,' he added quietly.

But on the alert for what? he wondered as his colleagues joined the queue for food.

On such occasions, there was always the hope that people's emotional make-up would be laid bare and the team might see them without their defences — might see a face full of anger, or fear . . . or *guilt*.

As the initially subdued hum gradually became more cheerful, however, with voices rising in appreciation of the generous hospitality, Markham didn't feel particularly sanguine about the likelihood of a break in the case.

Ed Frayling and Barbara Price materialized in front of him. It occurred to Markham that some might say Barbara was punching above her weight in dating the slim, auburn-haired young waiter, but she had a sweet smile and something almost maternal in her manner.

'Can we get you something, Inspector?' Ed asked courteously. 'Times like this, I automatically go into "waiter mode" — don't feel comfortable tucking in while there's folk who haven't been served.'

'I'm fine, thanks,' Markham smiled. 'Surely it's a bit of a busman's holiday if you're expected to roll your sleeves up, Mr Frayling.'

'Oh that's nothing,' the other laughed. 'Look at Francesco and Serena, they're already getting stuck in.'

It was quite true, the older couple having joined the kitchen team behind the serving hatch, Francesco dispensing jovial bonhomie while Serena scuttled about. Marina and Matteo, meanwhile, weaved deftly between the tables where older mourners were sitting, checking that everyone was comfortable.

'They wanted to sort the catering,' Barbara explained. 'But the Parish Council insisted on doing it.'

'A tug of love, you might say.' Ed grinned but his voice was sad as he added, 'Saint Michael's felt it was the last thing they could do for Sheila and the vicar. There's quite a few here from the choir here today . . . Sheila was such a stalwart.'

His girlfriend laid a hand on his arm. 'Come on, let's leave Mr Markham in peace . . . We can always offer to do the washing up if you're that desperate to help.'

'You're on, Barb.' He winked at her, and the plain Jane face lit up in a manner that was quite touching to see.

Kate Burton joined the DI.

'I suppose it's too much to hope that anyone has let their guard down,' he said wearily.

'Well actually, I did see what looked like the tail end of a row between Frances Langton and Stella Fanshaw.'

'Indeed?'

'Yes, I slipped out round the back to see what's out there — nothing special, just this little paved courtyard and shrubbery — and they seemed to be having words. Fanshaw had this really angry turkey-cock face and Langton said something like, "Haven't you done enough damage?" Fanshaw stalked off when she saw me listening, don't know where she got to . . . And Langton came in here and sat down with Graham Thorpe. I reckon he's keener than she is.'

'Well done, Kate, that's very interesting. Any other discoveries?'

'Folk are giving Tricia Dent a wide berth . . . definitely looks like she's Number One on the Unpopular People list. And Emma Carnforth seems very cosy with the ex-priest — hanging on his every word — though you'd think they'd be poles apart.'

'What about the lot from Rossi's?'

'Well, they seem fine — just your typical big-hearted Italian family and everyone seems to like them.' She paused. 'There's something a bit off with Vincent, though.'

'The son?'

'Yeah. He got quite snappish when Ed and Barbara were playing with the little girl, Giulia. Overdoing the macho big brother bit, if you ask me.'

'Maybe he felt the family was on parade and didn't want her getting overexcited.'

'Something was definitely up with him, his eyes were everywhere . . . But I suppose he was looking out for Desmond Pettifer and the DJ chum. Looks as though Pettifer's done a bunk actually. One of the old dears back there was having a moan about how the younger generation don't have any manners.'

Markham chuckled. 'Well, I'd say all is not lost, given the way Marina and Matteo are pulling their weight . . . quite a charm offensive.'

'They're a nice couple,' Burton agreed. 'She's got a smile and a cheery word for everyone, and he just gets on with it. Great work ethic. If they ever retire, Francesco and Serena can be sure the restaurant will be in safe hands.'

'Talking of work ethic, Kate, I think it's time to extricate our colleagues from this gathering and get back to base.'

'Sarge has serious designs on that pavlova they're bringing out, guv. But,' with an eye roll, 'I'll get Marina to sort him a goody bag so he won't feel deprived.' She hesitated. 'Is he coming back to the station with us?'

'Yes, though let's be discreet about it. No point in annoying the DCI unnecessarily.'

Faint hope! But he needed Noakes there while they shared their impressions and thrashed out next steps. Almost as though the ex-DS was his talisman. Sheila Craven and Norman Collins would not be truly at rest until he followed the clues, wherever they led.

As in the church, he then had a sudden sense that something significant had happened but could not identify the source of his conviction.

CHAPTER 8

There was no sign of DCI Sidney back at the station, and no one raised so much as an eyebrow on seeing Noakes accompany his former colleagues to Markham's office. As far as the former DS was concerned, there was nothing unusual about him coming on board and no shortage of precedents. He and Doyle were devotees of the police procedural drama *Ridley* which featured a former DI brought back as a consultant eighteen months into his retirement. Such was their mutual addiction, that Burton had acidly suggested they might like to offer themselves as script advisers on the next series. It was a mystery to Markham's fellow DI how Noakes had got Rosemount to agree to this 'freelance policing', but she supposed there were aspects of his life she was far better off not knowing. As things stood, he was on the books as CID's 'outside contractor' (with squatter's rights, as Carruthers put it).

As they mulled over their impressions of the funeral and wake, it emerged that Noakes too had picked up on the simmering tension between Frances Langton and Stella Fanshaw, having shamelessly earwigged the headteacher's conversation with Graham Thorpe.

'That weedy deacon's dead gone on Miss Jean Brodie,' he observed cannily, 'but she ain't having any of it . . . only sees him as good for having a whinge.'

'What sort of whinge?' Carruthers asked eagerly.

'About that one from the Copse, the Fanshaw woman . . . the way she stirred things an' made trouble so the Rev ended up giving Langton the cold shoulder . . . how it spoiled their beautiful friendship blah de blah.'

Doyle sniggered. 'God, that's hardly tactful if Thorpe's got a thing for her.'

'Well, he were up for the whole shoulder to cry on number. Didn't sound like he were a big fan of Fanshaw . . . said summat about clacking tongues an' folk should stay out of other people's affairs.'

'Where did Ms Fanshaw get to?' Markham asked. 'I don't recall seeing her in the parish hall.'

'Stormed off in a huff after the barney outside.' Noakes had clearly been eavesdropping to some purpose. 'According to Langton, she said something about not staying to be insulted an' it were all a charade an' she couldn't stand hypocrites.' Regretfully, he added, 'Thorpe clocked me standing next to their table an' changed the subject pronto.'

'So perhaps she went home then,' Markham said thoughtfully. 'I wonder what she meant about "hypocrites".'

'Could've been talking about the Eyeties.' Noakes saw Burton stiffen. 'I mean that lot from the restaurant, the Romanos.'

'You mean the *Rossi family*,' Carruthers grinned, thinking that sarge made them sound like some kind of trapeze act.

'Same difference . . . Anyway, the lad who's engaged to their daughter—'

'Matteo,' Burton interjected, being a stickler for accuracy.

'Yeah, the Italian Stallion. I heard him telling the daughter it were a bit rich the way her mum an' dad expected them all to pitch in after the snotty way Sheila Craven behaved every time she came in the restaurant —sending food back an' picking on any half decent looking waitresses . . . plus saying they flirted with ole Tom when he were alive.'

Burton frowned. 'But everyone seemed fond of Sheila at Rossi's.'

'Oh, *pur-lease* . . . They weren't going to badmouth some sweet old lady,' Noakes pointed out. 'Specially not one who turned up murdered,' he added cynically.

'People can become cranky as they get older,' Doyle said, thinking of some of his nan's friends. 'Aches and pains, that sort of thing,' he added charitably. 'And there's different values too.' He remembered his nan had taken a dim view of his ex-girlfriend's amorous approach to the opposite sex once she'd had a few drinks.

'Tom thought his missus walked on water,' Noakes put in. 'But she could be tricky all right. What happened with him — the cancer an' all that — must've hit her hard. Not surprising if she went a bit bitter an' twisted.'

'Did you make any other discoveries, Noakesy?' Markham asked as his friend opened the goody bag disclosing a somewhat squished pavlova (not that the aesthetics were likely to prove any obstacle to hearty enjoyment).

'The woman who runs the pub has got the hots for the ex-padre,' he said through a mouthful of cream.

Burton winced at the vulgarity.

'Sounded like he were giving her a mini-lecture on Russian history . . . banging on about how Tsar Nicholas an' Rasputin an' Alexandra were in some eternal triangle thingy but it were sweet an' innocent an' no hanky panky. He said it were terrible how they were slandered an' then came out with some story about the Mad Monk being attacked by a woman with no nose on account of having syphilis.' Noakes scooped up the last of the meringue. 'Enough to put anyone off their vol-au-vents, but Mrs Mop couldn't get enough . . . all starry-eyed an' goggling at him like he's God Almighty.'

'I heard someone say *Mrs Carnforth* runs a local history group,' Carruthers remarked, not without a certain sly pleasure in puncturing Noakes's more carnal scenario. 'Probably wanted him to do a talk or something like that.'

'Well, *Mr C* didn't get much of a look-in,' the older man grunted. 'Mind you, he were busy stuffing his face.'

'Pot Kettle Black, Noakesy,' Markham observed wryly.

'Did anyone spot what was up with Vincent Rossi? Apart from having to be nice about Sheila,' Burton asked. 'He looked out of sorts, kind of glowering on the sidelines.'

'I reckon he was miffed at George Parker's no show,' Doyle ventured.

'Not to mention Pettifer,' Carruthers murmured. 'A case of Hamlet without the Prince.'

'They probably met up together once Parker finished gladhanding Sidney an' Bretherton,' Noakes suggested. 'You jus' wait, Sidney'll have made sure the bloke from the *Gazette* snapped 'em together . . . another sleb for the Hall of Fame.'

It was more than likely, Markham reflected grimly.

'Anything else catch your attention?' he asked the team.

'People were giving Tricia Dent the evils,' Doyle said. 'I couldn't see why she put herself through it. Henry Morland an' that waiter's drippy girlfriend were the only ones who bothered to talk to her . . . and it didn't look like they got much change out of her.'

'You'd have thought Frances Langton might be on Dent's side,' Burton mused. 'Seeing as the two of them got on the wrong side of the parish gossips and ended up as pariahs.'

'Yeah, but if both of 'em fancied their chances with the Rev, they were most likely *rivals*,' Carruthers said bluntly. 'Anyway, it didn't look like they were mates.'

Markham suddenly felt unaccountably weary as the talk went round in circles, the earlier surge of optimism he had experienced back in the church evaporating.

He got up and walked across to the window, his gaze wandering over the carpark leylandii to the roofs of the town centre. Livelier than Medway, even on a Monday afternoon there would be plenty of activity and bustle, with sixth formers 'bunking off' from Hope Academy and other local schools for a spot of illicit retail therapy. He wondered what Olivia was doing at that moment. No doubt she was getting up close and personal with Mat Sullivan, he conjectured miserably.

The funeral and wake had left him feeling flat and drained.

'Isn't the air close today?' he heard Burton murmur behind him.

'Yeah, an' the rain's not far away neither,' came Noakes's retort to groans from the youngsters.

Despite himself, Markham smiled at the desperate witticism. Knowing him so well, his former wingman had picked up on his despondency and was trying to lighten the atmosphere. As was often the case with Noakes, his words were mysteriously empowered to mean more than they might initially seem to, and the daft wordplay paradoxically gave his boss a shot in the arm. He owed it to the team to press on. If Olivia was here, she would undoubtedly exhort him to channel George Bernard Shaw: 'Every day I perform two acts of heroic virtue. I get up and I go to bed.'

Noakes's piggy eyes were intent on him when he turned around. Forcing some energy into his voice, the DI said, 'Let's take a quick break and then meet back here to evaluate our suspects' movements for last Thursday evening when Mr Collins was killed.'

For all the use *that* was likely to be!

Burton bustled off with Doyle and Carruthers in tow, Markham grateful for her sensitivity in making a swift exit so as to leave him alone with Noakes.

'Chris Carstairs told me he saw Mat Sullivan in the Grapes the other day with Guy Raynor,' his friend remarked with elaborate casualness. 'Said they looked well cosy . . . no eyes for anybody else. Guess thass why we ain't seen Sullivan at five-a-side.'

Markham's heart leaped at this piece of intelligence. Raynor was the wonderfully handsome Gay Federation rep whose beautifully planed and chiselled face and haughty pub-lic-school manner (he was in fact an alumnus of Hope Academy) provoked admiration and resentment in equal measure.

'I allus thought ole Mat might be the type who swings both ways,' Noakes said, carefully not looking at Markham. 'Bisexual.' He scrunched up the paper bag, having scrutinized it thoroughly in case he had missed any meringue. 'An' the lads down at football said he'd had girlfriends. But if him an' Raynor are an item, then he must've had second thoughts . . . cos Raynor's got no time for closet queens, it's strictly *man-to-man* with him . . . always banging on about the *fraternity* an' *loyalty*. He won't stand for anyone else muscling in neither . . . specially not a woman.'

Markham was simultaneously relieved that Kate Burton wasn't around to hear Noakes's decidedly un-PC pronouncements and touched by his friend's clumsy attempt to reassure him that there was no prospect of a sexual relationship between Mat Sullivan and Olivia.

After Noakes had sidled out of the office leaving him to chew over this latest revelation, Markham pondered what it might mean for his future.

If Mat Sullivan had decided that he was not, in the final analysis, available to women but Olivia was infatuated with her colleague and imagined that she could 'change' him, then she was storing up significant unhappiness for herself. Markham had flattered himself that her altered looks might have had something to do with missing *him*, but it could just as well be connected with unrequited love for Sullivan.

Even if Olivia and Sullivan *weren't* having a physical relationship, Markham wasn't sure he cared for the idea of some sort of trade-off whereby they shared a platonically intense complicity that steered clear of sexual consummation.

He could see how the clever deputy head, with his sardonic wit and ironic detachment, would find Olivia's elegance and caustic humour imaginatively, if not physically, stirring — enough so that they had become close allies, both professionally and personally.

On the other hand, he suspected that Noakes was right about Guy Raynor not tolerating a rival, and certainly not a woman. There would be no "eternal triangle" involving

Olivia, Mat Sullivan and Guy Raynor, of that he was reasonably sure.

It was a strange situation, and while he hated to think of Olivia being unhappy, he was selfish enough to draw comfort from the fact that it sounded as though she faced defeat in the battle for Mat Sullivan's romantic affections. However powerful the emotional dynamic that bound them, and whatever Sullivan's private ambivalence about his sexuality, it was unlikely to survive the advent of Guy Raynor who was more likely to regard Olivia as some kind of predator than treat her as a friend.

The sound of the town hall clock chiming the hour brought him up short with a guilty start. Forcing thoughts of Olivia from him, he reached for a manila folder and was soon wrestling with the imponderables of his investigation. There *had* to be something they had missed . . . something that would crack the case wide open . . .

Two hours later, however, with Noakes having been obliged to return to Rosemount and the others visibly flagging, Markham was forced to admit that they were no further forward, though there seemed to be general agreement that the nexus between Frances Langton, Stella Fanshaw and Tricia Dent should be probed further.

'Let's get Graham Thorpe in tomorrow and apply some pressure,' he decided. 'A formal interview here should help to focus his mind,' he added grimly. 'If there are parish secrets, then he's our best bet for finding out about skeletons in the cupboard.' Catching Burton's eye, he grimaced. 'Unfortunate choice of words,' he said wearily.

It sounded almost like a prophecy.

* * *

Tuesday morning found his team (minus Noakes) assembled again in Markham's office.

The DI had passed an easier night thanks to Noakes's revelation about Olivia and Mat Sullivan and was keen to refocus the enquiry by drilling down into parish business at Saint Michael's.

They were hammering out the interview strategy for Graham Thorpe when a call came through for Markham. One look at his face during the lengthy conversation told Kate Burton this was not good news.

Pale but composed, he told them, 'Stella Fanshaw's been found dead in the church.'

'As in *suicide*,' Doyle blurted out, 'cos it was *her* that killed Sheila and the vicar?'

'Apparently she was strangled,' Markham replied. 'Dr Patel's over there now waiting to brief us.'

'Who found her?' Carruthers asked.

'Graham Thorpe when he came to set up for Matins just before nine.'

Doyle was aghast. '*Jesus.*'

'I trust that's a prayer, Sergeant.'

The young DS swallowed, remembering his boss's intense dislike of profanity.

'Sorry, guv,' he mumbled, flushing.

Carruthers shot him a sympathetic look. 'Interesting that Thorpe was the one to find her,' he said.

'Hardly,' Burton snapped, 'seeing as he's the deacon and that's his usual routine.'

Now it was Doyle's turn to sympathize. *Her Royal Arsiness*, his eyes telegraphed Carruthers as eloquently as if he had said the words out loud.

Markham paused and drew a deep breath.

'We also have a missing person on our hands,' he continued levelly. 'George Parker failed to turn up last night for the *Best North West DJ Awards* in Manchester.'

Doyle was nonplussed. 'Maybe he just felt bushed after Sheila Craven's funeral,' he suggested. 'Or he could've gone on the lash with Desmond Pettifer, probl'y felt he deserved some fun after buttering up Sidney . . . and then he was too wrecked to make it over there.'

The DI shook his head. 'Mr Parker was in the running for an award himself, so this was quite a big deal . . . his agent says no way would he have missed it. And anyway, Desmond Pettifer apparently parted with him just after three yesterday afternoon at his flat in Medway Gardens. A car was coming to pick him up at seven, so he definitely planned to go to Manchester.'

'Well maybe *Parker's* our man then,' Carruthers suggested. 'It would make sense for him to do a bunk and lie doggo if *he* killed Sheila and Norman Collins and then lost it with Stella because she was on to him.'

'Motive?' Burton rapped.

'Dunno, ma'am,' came Carruthers's reluctant reply.

'A neighbour spotted Mr Parker heading out again around four,' Markham informed them. 'But he never returned and hasn't been seen since. Given the circumstances, I'm concerned for his safety.'

'D'you reckon him and Stella were *both* on to the killer, boss?' Doyle asked in bewilderment. 'So then he had to get rid of the two of them?'

'Or maybe this is some kind of spree killer . . . some sick whackjob in it for kicks,' Carruthers put in quietly.

Suddenly, in his mind's eye, like a mysterious prompting of his subconscious, Markham saw the overgrown cemetery of Saint Michael's with its mouldering turf and neglected monuments. Turning to his fellow DI, he instructed urgently, 'Once we're finished with Dr Patel, I want uniforms to conduct a thorough search of that graveyard, Kate.'

Startled, she said, 'What are you expecting to find, guv?'

'Another body,' was the steady reply.

* * *

Stella Fanshaw had been strangled with her own scarf and her body propped in a sitting position in a pew halfway down the church. She had the same awful mottled complexion as

Sheila Craven, but other than that, her posture and expression were suggestive of a worshiper lost in prayer.

'They came up behind her . . . she wouldnt've have seen them.' The pathologist's eyes were compassionate as he gently tilted their victim's head from left to right, handling it with the tenderness of a lover. 'Off to her eternal reward with no prolonged pain or suffering.'

A surprise attack, wondered Markham, or the follow-up to some earlier confrontation . . .

'Time of death, doc?' he asked.

Dr Patel, refreshingly, showed no signs of playing hard to get.

'Judging by rectal temperature,' at which Doyle flinched perceptibly, 'and other signs, I would say around four or five o'clock yesterday afternoon.' Observing Doyle's wan looks, the medic said kindly to Carruthers, 'Why don't you two take a turn around outside while I fill your boss in.' Roger the Dodger, as Noakes called him, was admirably quick on the uptake, steering his colleague outside before Doyle upchucked up all over the pathologist's immaculate brogues.

'Your young friend appears to be taking this hard, Inspector,' Patel observed mildly as the two sergeants disappeared through the porch.

'Very devoted to his grandmother,' was the succinct reply.

'Ah, I see. Admirable.'

The pathologist, with minimum fuss, oversaw the removal of the body by paramedics. Markham and his fellow DI bowing their heads in reverence as he murmured, *'Truth is greater than the sun; some day or other all will come to light. Remember, the way to Truth is paved with skeletons over which we dare to walk. Our way may lie in complete darkness, but our hope burns as bright as ever.'* Catching Burton's questioning eye, he added kindly, 'Mahatma Gandhi, Inspector.' Nothing was so much to Burton's taste as an ecumenical reference, Markham thought, noting with amusement how his colleague watched the retreating procession with decided approval.

After this removal of the body, stillness enveloped them once more. *The Silence of Ages*, Markham thought as he savoured the moment of recollection. The chill, musty air of the church was such an agreeable antidote to the stale frowsiness of CID, he felt as though he could have remained there for ever.

Pabulum mortis, he reflected, momentarily lost in thought. Or if it came to dealing with Sidney and Bretherton, the more likely translation would be *Kicking Up a Stink*.

He needed to get on the front foot pronto before news of what he felt increasingly sure in his bones was a double murder seeped into the public domain.

Burton was ready. 'I'll get on with coordinating the sweep of the graveyard, sir,' she murmured. Then, softly, 'You think he's there, right guv?'

'Yes, Kate.' Markham spoke with infinite sadness. 'I think George Parker is somewhere hereabouts.' He shivered, as though the church's dim interior had laid cold fingers on him. 'I think this place is the killer's motherlode . . . they won't move far from its orbit.'

Watching from the porch as his colleague marshalled a search party, he thought of all the graveyards he had visited during his CID career. Despite the sombreness of the scene before him, he grinned as he recalled Noakes's irreverent comments on the theme of Death, his friend having relished the time when gravediggers and crematorium workers in Bromgrove went on strike and the *Gazette* promptly predicted that there would be a spate of 'panic dying'. Sidney had been decidedly unimpressed when Noakes pinned to the CID bulletin board the picture editor's Photograph of the Week, this being a chalked message that had mysteriously appeared on the gatepost leading into the municipal cemetery with the sublime message: *Sunday Eleven O'clock. Hearse Boot-Sale*.

He had no doubt Noakes would want to get in on the action at Saint Michael's and was willing to bet that Doyle had already tipped his mentor the wink that 'something big was going down'. The DCI wouldn't like it, but Markham felt he could do with just about anyone rather than his "outside contractor". Somehow he would wangle it so that his friend stayed close. If people thought it was weakness or a character flaw, then too bad. A double homicide on top of the other two deaths meant he needed all the support he could get.

But *was* this a double homicide? Was George Parker really out there somewhere in the cemetery's wilderness? Or was his hunch really a misstep?

Pacing up and down the porch, Markham's gaze fell on the stone bas-relief of a flying eagle. Fourth of the four animals at the Throne described in the Book of Revelation; taken to represent the fourth evangelist . . . but to his mind, there was something cruel and predatory in the meat-hook beak and talons. More hunter than symbol of holiness . . .

Burton rejoined him, flushed with excitement.

'The oldest section backs onto Molyneux Road, guv,' she said. 'One of the walk-in mausoleums seems like it's been interfered with—'

'In what way?' he caught her tone.

'Well, it's pretty dilapidated and practically falling down . . . The council or church authority must've been worried about kids or vandals getting in and put up a sort of retractable grille affair across the front. Mind you,' she added grimly, 'it's the usual bodge job, because it looks like someone jemmied it open and then re-padlocked it . . . It was the shiny new padlock that looked out of place.'

'Excellent work, Kate.'

'It was one of the uniforms who spotted it, sir.'

That was Kate Burton all over, unwilling to take the credit for someone else's discovery. He could tell from her face that there was more.

'It's pretty dark and grimy, but we shone a flashlight inside . . . there's something wrapped in refuse sacks towards the back, underneath a little stained-glass window.' She paused before adding quietly, 'About the right size for a body.'

'Lead the way,' Markham instructed, his features rigid as if turned to stone.

Despite the heavy police presence in and around Saint Michael's, silence hung over the graveyard's tangled wilderness like a pall. The grounds were at once picturesque and eerie, with cypresses and ivy-clad trees shading thickets of columns, crosses, obelisks, urns, caskets and chests. Nature seemed to have run amok, and an odour of decay and damp mustiness clogged their nostrils.

Eventually, they arrived in front of a narrow crumbling structure in grey stone which looked like a Gothic Hansel and Gretel hideaway, with intricately ornamented corbels supporting a gabled roof of slate. Markham started as he looked up and recognized the animals from Revelation: the lion, the ox, the eagle and one with human lineaments . . . a sly narrow face that seemed to sneer. *Too late, too late!* Doyle and Carruthers were already there, contemplating the mausoleum with a mixture of fascination and repulsion.

Handed a torch, he looked inside and saw the long-shrouded shape stretched out sideways under the stained-glass window which depicted an amethyst-robed bearded figure holding lilies and a carpenter's square. Saint Joseph, patron of the happy death, Markham thought with hysterical laughter rising in his throat. *The happy death. Oh dear God.*

Paper-suited SOCOs were hovering waiting for his direction.

'Anyone got bolt cutters?' he asked.

An officer stepped forward and cut the padlock.

Curtly, he gestured with the torch. 'Right, in you go.'

A forensics officer ducked into the shadowy vestibule and crouched over the black garbage bags, like some modern-day necromancer re-enacting the raising of Lazarus.

Only there was to be no Lazarus moment — no second chance for the man whose corpse, laid on its side, had been dumped in the crumbling monument.

George Parker looked back at Markham, lips drawn back from his expensive orthodontics in a ghastly snarl, the gaping neck wound a defiant rebuke to venerable Saint Joseph with his sheaf of chaste white blooms. The DJ's expensively barbered silver fox hair was discoloured with dried blood, while his fabled piercing blue eyes were glazed and unseeing.

The other members of the team duly took their turn with the torch, Doyle handing it back to Markham with hands that shook slightly.

Burton cleared her throat.

'The killer must be decompensating, sir,' she said. 'This one's not like the others. It's disorganized . . . *messy*.'

'That or it's more *personal* for some reason,' he mused.

Still the terrible hush all around them.

Doyle's voice, cracking with apprehension, broke into the silence.

'So they murdered Fanshaw and Parker *in the same afternoon*,' he said incredulously. 'Must be a maniac.'

'There will be a pattern, an underlying rationale, Sergeant,' Markham observed calmly, but inside his thoughts were in turmoil. It was barely twenty-four hours since Sheila Craven's funeral, so how could this have happened? Events were moving faster than in any other investigation he had headed. *Too fast for him.*

Aloud, he said, 'We need to get Dr Patel back here asap. I also want Desmond Pettifer located and full details of the victims' next-of-kin.'

'On it, boss,' Burton said crisply.

With a sinking heart, he knew that a press conference was now unavoidable and they were headed down the whole *Serial Killer on the Rampage* route.

He shone the torch over George Parker's ravaged features one last time.

The old proverb had it that "the eyes are windows to the soul", but Parker's unseeing, filmy stare offered merely an infinity of pain. Heedless of SOCOs, uniforms and assorted personnel waiting to get started, the DI contemplated the tableau 'as though he was memorizing it,' Doyle commented afterwards to Carruthers.

Indeed he was.

Memoriam Moratorium.

And then on with the pursuit.

CHAPTER 9

The press conference on the morning of Wednesday 10 August was every bit as fraught as Markham had feared, the ladies and gentlemen of the tabloids being in no mood to cut Bromgrove CID any slack.

Kicking proceedings off himself, since he thought it unfair to have Kate Burton soak up all the venom (despite her undoubted skill in parrying Gavin Conors's sly innuendo), Markham could not recall a more edgy PR encounter. Oleaginous Barry Lynch from the press office (he of the wandering hands) was unlikely to pronounce this time, as per his usual formula, that they had 'got away with it', the DI reflected grimly as he engaged in the time-honoured fencing.

'Isn't it true that the police took their eye off the ball?' Conors demanded belligerently, looking like a cross between a bookie's runner and minor mafioso in his tobacco-coloured suit and garish psychedelic tie, thinning hair slicked back and porcine jowls fairly quivering with confected indignation. 'After all, you didn't tell the public there was a serial killer at large who was targeting,' a pregnant pause before the coup de grace, 'God-fearing parishioners at a local church.' Hands thrown in the air with practised outrage, he added, 'You didn't issue any warning that there could be a religious fanatic out there bent on,' his voice cracked as though from emotion, '*slaughtering the innocent.*'

Bloody hell, Doyle observed, exchanging glances with Carruthers, Conors is giving it the full RADA. Must have taken lessons. Sidney was clearly fit to be tied, eczema flaring up so it looked as if he had psoriasis and his eyes shooting daggers at Markham. The DI, meanwhile, sat there cool as a cucumber, like he'd just stepped out of an ice bath, though the briefing room was uncomfortably stuffy. You had to hand it to the guvnor, the way he never let anyone get under his guard (except for Noakesy), Doyle thought.

'There are no indications that these murders were perpetrated by a religious fanatic,' Markham said with steely control. 'It's unhelpful to engage in speculation at this stage and,' he felt a twinge of self-disgust at descending to the standard ploy, 'insensitive to the feelings of the bereaved.'

That shut Conors up momentarily, but his sidekick, a hard-faced peroxide blonde, took aim.

'How will *the bereaved* feel about CID dragging their feet over dodgy goings-on involving the local vicar? It looks like a cover-up from where *we're* sitting.'

Markham's voice dripped with disdain. 'I won't dignify that allegation with a response.'

Atta boy, Lord Snooty! Doyle thought delightedly, relishing his guvnor's patrician contempt towards the assorted reptiles.

Gavin Conors was never squelched for long.

'So what can you tell us about the progress of your investigation, Inspector? *Is* there a maniac on the loose? Or,' he dropped his voice an octave for maximum melodramatic effect, 'are these murders something to do with *church corruption* and,' a sorrowful shake of the head, '*scandal* in high places.'

God help us, Carruthers thought disgustedly, Conors can't decide whether this is *Midsomer Murders* or *The Da Vinci Code*.

Markham bestowed a frigid smile on his questioner, the haughty aquiline features positively guaranteed to irritate the hell out of Conors, Burton reflected with pleasure.

By contrast with her Daniel Day Lewis lookalike boss, the journalist had never looked more sweatily out of his depth as he tried to insinuate that there might be some kind of nefariousness centring on Saint Michael's.

'We are following up a *number* of lines of enquiry,' the DI said calmly. 'I should point out that we have found *nothing* to indicate impropriety on the part of *any* church personnel. And Mr George Parker had no connection to the parish.' Or at least none that they had discovered.

'What about Father — oops *sorry*,' the peroxide blonde feigned embarrassment, 'I meant *Mister* Morland from the Healing Centre . . . will you be speaking to him in light of his, er,' another burst of simulated discomfiture, '*controversial* background.'

'Obviously, we'll be speaking to *all* locals who crossed paths with the victims,' Markham replied pleasantly. 'Naturally this will include high street businesses including *Doctor* Morland's. I'm sure the press will wish to avoid irresponsible reporting that might compromise the police investigation or,' his voice hardened, 'that could be construed as *defamatory.*'

Game, Set and Match, Carruthers thought admiringly. The *Gazette* wouldn't want to tangle with Morland again, not after the way he went on the offensive the last time it attempted to make mischief.

Having seen Kate Burton earlier with her nose buried in the *Diagnostic and Statistical Manual of Mental Disorders*, Markham gracefully passed the baton.

'Inspector Burton is the lead on our offender profiling together with Professor Nathan Finlayson from Bromgrove University,' he said before Conors and his sidekick could get their second wind and renew the assault. In his experience, there was nothing like a spot of *Cracker* and pop psychology to deflect the media from contentious interrogation.

Burton duly obliged, blinding them with science.

DCI Sidney visibly relaxed as Markham's fellow DI launched into an analysis of sexual sadism disorder and associated paraphilic fetishes.

Blimey, thought Doyle as she chuntered on about phallometric testing and psychiatric comorbidities to an enraptured audience, just talk dirty and they're happy as pigs in muck, the slimy gits. He grinned involuntarily recalling Noakes's story about the BBC announcer who introduced a news bulletin with the immortal words, 'This is the British Broadcorping Castration.' Catching a swivel-eyed glower from Sidney, he hastily adjusted his features as Burton flogged away gamely.

Afterwards, when they were safely back in Markham's office, he asked with incredulity, 'Are we really treating these as *sex murders*, guv?'

The DI sighed heavily and didn't return a direct answer.

'Depressing, isn't it,' he said to the room at large with withering irony, 'to think that the first books to be printed in English were the Bible and Chaucer's *Canterbury Tales* . . . but lo and behold, in only half a millennium we've reached Gavin Conors's *Sex Files* on page three of the *Gazette* . . . *There's progress for you.*'

'That lot are suckers for sound bites.' Burton sounded almost as deflated. 'And at least the sex stuff makes it sound like it could be some random nutter as opposed to one of the neighbours.'

Markham wasn't at all sure that he preferred the random nutter scenario to that of neighbour homicide but forced a smile. 'You did well, Kate. The DCI practically expired with relief when you got Conor and his chum to shut up about religious sleaze.'

'Yeah, what the heck was *that* all about?' Doyle interjected. 'It seemed like they didn't care whether they fingered Collins or Morland just so long as they got a "Pervy Priest" headline out of it.'

'As Kate says, the hacks think in sound bites,' Markham said with another heartfelt sigh, thinking that it was no wonder if Noakes spoke of 'Evilution'. Then, rousing himself, he continued, 'The preliminary report from forensics suggests that George Parker was struck down in the graveyard and dragged into the mausoleum.'

'So he wasn't killed because he walked in on chummy throttling Stella Fanshaw?' Doyle asked.

'No. It looks like Parker met our killer in the graveyard by appointment, either before or after the attack on Stella Fanshaw . . . Dr Patel reckons the murders were closely proximate, possibly within an hour of each other.'

Carruthers turned to Kate Burton. 'Christ, p'raps what you said about blood lust back there is where it's at, ma'am, and this is some total psycho who gets off watching people suffer.' Abruptly, he registered Markham's narrowed eyes. 'Sorry, sir, I know you don't like, er—'

'Taking the Lord's name in vain,' Doyle finished primly, secretly pleased that he wasn't the only one to have blotted his copybook in this respect.

'Quite, Sergeant, so let's try and remember that, shall we.' Markham let the rebuke sink in before resuming. 'All our suspects need reinterviewing. I want an account of *everyone's* movements for yesterday afternoon and evening. Make Desmond Pettifer a priority, seeing as he and Mr Parker "absconded" from the wake.'

'What about Graham Thorpe?' Doyle asked eagerly. 'He's *gotta* be in the running, what with him being the one to find Fanshaw.'

'Yes,' Markham said thoughtfully. 'It might yield dividends if he gets the idea that we're interested in Frances Langton . . . *that* might loosen his tongue.'

After dispatching Doyle and Carruthers to their respective assignments, the DI turned to Kate Burton. 'I'd better have a word with the DCI, Kate.' A wry grimace. 'And seeing as you generally have a mollifying influence on him, I'd like you there with me.'

'No worries, sir,' she said loyally. Then, with the puckishness she occasionally displayed, 'He probably just wants us to "show our workings" before putting us in detention for poor homework.'

Markham chuckled. 'He'll be getting it in the neck from high command, the poor sod.'

Burton blinked in surprise at the rare vulgarism, noting that the boss was looking somewhat ravaged.

'How did it go with the next-of-kin, guv?' Typically, he had insisted on doing the dreaded bereavement visits himself.

'Stella Fanshaw's sister lives in sheltered housing out by Old Carton. She's in poor health, but a niece lives locally and came over straight away. Decent people . . . I don't think they really took it in.'

'The shock won't register till later,' Burton said sagely.

'George Parker was a Barnado's boy. There doesn't appear to be any family to speak of.' Markham's face took on a marble rigidity that his colleague knew all too well. 'He dragged himself up by his bootstraps, so maybe the loud and obnoxious persona was a defence mechanism. The poor soul had everything to live for . . .'

'He dated Tricia Dent.'

'*Of course* . . . I'd forgotten that, Kate. Once we've got Sidney out of the way, can you check in with her as a matter of priority, get her unvarnished reaction so to speak.'

Unless she's the one we're looking for and has no reason to be surprised.

The thought in both their minds remained unspoken.

'Will do, guv . . . There's bound to be other, er, liaisons that'll need following up, not to mention competitors and rivals and that kind of thing.'

'Well, the music industry and showbiz are notorious for jealousy and "temperament", so we have to cover that angle.'

Burton caught the note of scepticism. 'But you don't think it's a case of microphones at dawn?' she queried pithily.

Markham smiled grimly. 'Neatly put. You're right, though. I *don't* feel the answer lies in disc jockey land . . . Too much of a coincidence that he and Stella Fanshaw died like that, so close on the heels of the other two murders. It feels like it *has* to lead back to Medway and the high street.'

'Don't worry, boss, we're on it.' Burton, endearingly, tried to project total conviction that they would crack the case, though in truth her confidence was at rock bottom.

'Why don't you have some, er, time out after seeing the DCI. I can handle everything this end.'

He grinned. 'You mean a trip to Doggie Dickerson's.'

'Well, you know a good workout always helps after—'

'Going ten rounds with Sidney.'

She grinned back. 'Something like that.'

'Good idea, Kate.' He knew she would understand his other addiction. 'And I'd like you to bring Noakesy up to speed. Then the pair of you can come round to my place later and we can thrash out a strategy.'

He was touched at the way her woebegone expression lightened. 'I'll bring takeaway,' she said happily.

'Nothing too healthy or salad-based . . . otherwise the old devil will only turn his nose up.' *And above all, nothing vegan.*

'Righto, sir. *The Lotus Garden* round the corner from me and Nathan is pretty good. Does great veggie dishes . . . as well as chow mein and spring rolls and the rest of it.'

'Sounds a winner.'

Olivia adored Chinese takeaway, he thought with a sudden lancing pang, before smiling at his subordinate lest she see the pain in his eyes.

Burton wasn't fooled, however. The DI missed the answering flash of anguish on her own face, before she said brightly, 'Right, it's a date.' Realizing what she had said, her pale cheeks took a deeper shade, as if her heart had sent its blood pumping at full gallop. 'I mean—'

'Nothing like a chowfest for recharging the batteries,' he said easily. Then, imitating Sidney's adenoidal blare, '"Though I don't know why it is that you and your team are *obsessed* with your stomachs, Inspector . . . always knee-deep in *cartons* and *fast-food paraphernalia* whenever I set eyes on you."'

The tension evaporated. She grinned.

'Nathan says it's like the salivating of Pavlov's dogs . . . we're programmed so that crime makes us hungry,' she said shyly.

'I seem to recall a seminar where Nathan asked CID what they had learned from those salivating dogs, whereupon Noakesy piped up that *he'd* learned not to back them till he'd seen them race three or four times.'

She giggled. 'The DCI was *furious.*'

'Well, Sidney is spared his nemesis today, so we can but hope that works to our advantage.' With old-fashioned courtliness, he rose and gestured towards the door. 'After you.'

* * *

The Bromgrove Police Boxing Club in Marsh Lane was the absolute antithesis of the town's gyms for the upwardly mobile, being a dingy, insalubrious outfit where CID's finest and the local criminal fraternity knocked seven bells out of each other in the ring before taking the party back onto the streets in their more usual roles as hunters and hunted.

DCI Sidney and the top brass strongly objected to such blurring of the boundaries and, in particular, baulked at the club's major-domo in the person of its villainous-looking proprietor who was heavily impregnated with *eau de Johnnie Walker* and looked like a cross between a punk poet (think Alice Cooper or Noel Fielding) and Fagin, with overtones of Gandalf and Black Sabbath. Alternating funereal frockcoats with mobster suits, his wardrobe was even more dire than Noakes's, while the effect of an extraordinary horsehair wig, yellow tombstone teeth and eyepatch was less swashbuckling gallant and more Long John Silver. In fact, DI Carstairs had done a whip-round the previous Christmas to present Doggie (in addition to the customary offerings of whisky and cigars) with a stuffed parrot, going to some lengths to ensure that the toy duly squawked 'Pieces of Eight' when squeezed. The old reprobate had been much gratified by what he saw as a becoming tribute to his distinctive dress sense.

Doggie (best not to interrogate the origins of his moniker) highly approved of Noakes, who shared his un-PC world view and 'had no airs about him' (an understatement if ever there was one). But Markham was always especially welcome, as Doggie's 'fav'rite 'spector' and an empathetic, studiously courteous audience who reacted with grave sympathy to the whole history of his being dumped by Marlene (of bingo hall fame) before finding romantic bliss with Evelyn to whom he was now respectably (more or less) engaged. The DI was always happy to give advice on the best way to outwit the environmental health busybodies and listened attentively when he talked about crime (something with which he had more than a passing acquaintance, and not just as a spectator), weighing his observations with the same deliberation that Doggie gave them.

Now, head on one side, as they stood in the newly renovated (after a fashion) 'premium locker room', with its temperamental showers and dodgy sauna, Doggie surveyed his faithful patron with rheumy-eyed concern.

'You're looking tired, Mr Markham.'

'Getting old, Dogs.'

This elicited an alarming wheezy cackle and a punch on the arm.

'Get out of it! You're in your prime . . . Remember the pasting you gave Mr Carstairs just the other week.' With a knowing leer, 'The latest dolly-bird's making him all soft an' flabby.'

Perhaps detecting something in Markham's expression which suggested that there was no danger of romance distracting him any time soon, Doggie continued hastily, ''Course, I know you've got your hands full with the gerry murders . . . an' now the pop star fella who copped it in the graveyard.'

Glumly, Markham supposed the appellation 'gerry murders', though typically un-PC, was more or less accurate given the ages of Sheila Craven, Norman Collins and Stella Fanshaw. At his meeting with Sidney, the DCI was almost indecently keen that George Parker's murder should be treated as an unrelated homicide, but in his bones Markham felt it had to be linked to the other three . . .

'Talking of rock icons, you're looking uncommonly Goth today, Dogs,' he said, taking in the other's 'alternative' outfit of black cargo trousers teamed with a dark t-shirt and outsize black jacket (mercifully no leggings).

'Thass down to Evie's nephew,' the other replied, looking simultaneously proud and embarrassed. 'He does gigs an' all that.' A nervous shuffle. 'Hasn't got me into eyeliner and piercings. I ain't ready for The Full Monty just yet.'

Nor were the gym's customers, Markham thought with an inward shudder at the prospect of Doggie in eyeliner. Nothing more calculated to make Noakes conclude that his fellow un-PC ideologue had defected to the dark side!

'Um, very . . . edgy,' he murmured.

Doggie appeared satisfied with this.

Markham ploughed on, 'What sort of gigs does your, er, nephew-in-law,' was there even such a thing, 'do?'

'Heavy metal.'

Markham was none the wiser but made various non-committal noises.

'He c'n be a sulky little git,' Doggie confided. 'Between you an' me, he's got an ego the size of St Mary's Cathedral an' reckons the promoters are tossers for not seeing that he's the Next Big Thing.'

As Doggie looked expectant, Markham ventured, 'Well, it's a cut-throat world.' He broke off before he could say anything crass about it being dog eat dog. Doggie enjoyed a pun as much as the next man, but this was perhaps too close to home. 'I imagine it's more about who you know than how good you are really . . . luck of the draw kind of thing.'

'Xactly what Evie says,' Doggie proclaimed complacently, delighted at Markham's endorsement of his fiancée's wisdom. 'It's all about contacts an' they're thin on the ground right now . . . Evie says he should cut his losses, find a proper job an' settle down. There's a nice steady girlfriend panting to get him down the aisle. But thass the younger generation for you . . . never know when they're on to a good thing.' Philosophically, he added, 'Allus think the grass is greener on the other side.'

Now Doggie tapped his bulbous, veiny nose. 'I know you can't talk about how it's all going with your case, Mr Markham. But happen the music man got on the wrong side of someone in the business an' it was someone else that did for the gerries . . . which means you've got two sickoes out there.'

'My boss is pretty much of the same opinion, Dogs.'

Now the frowsy proprietor positively glowed. 'You reckon?' he exclaimed delightedly. 'Looks like me being round you an' the other gents from CID has started to rub off.'

God, that's all he needed. Doggie Dickerson joining Noakes as another honorary civilian contractor. Mind you, he'd give a lot to see Sidney's face if he suggested putting Doggie on the payroll!

'More than likely, Dogs,' was all he said, however.

Doggie prided himself on not crowding patrons and knowing when it was time to give them space.

With a phlegmy cough, he concluded, 'Good luck checking out the music scene, Mr Markham.' Cordially, he suggested, 'Benny Squint's around if you fancy a bout . . . An' Mr Carstairs is knocking around somewhere too.' There was a wistful note in his voice as he added, 'I ain't seen Mr Noakes lately, though.'

'Well, the new job's keeping him busy, Dogs. Not to mention the lady wife.'

Doggie guffawed. 'Oh yeah, Mrs "An' Another Thing" . . . she allus has to have the last word, that one.'

God help Noakes if Muriel ever got wind of such indiscretions. Luckily, she and Doggie Dickerson were unlikely to end up cheek by jowl in any of Mrs Noakes's customary haunts.

'Right, Dogs, think I might treat myself to a sauna.' Though such an appellation surely breached the Trade Descriptions Act. Markham did his best to look inscrutable. 'With a case like this one, a shot of mindfulness is called for.'

Doggie looked enraptured at the notion of his premises boasting such holistic credentials.

'Nothing like steam for freeing your mind up, Mr Markham.'

'Quite so, Dogs.'

'Tell Mr Noakes I asked after him.'

'Will do.'

The proprietor seemed loath to depart.

'Last time he was in, he told me about this wake he was at one time . . .'

'Occupational hazard in our line of business, Dogs.'

Noises reminiscent of a carburettor came from the other.

'This woman came up to him an' said, "The corpse's brother wants to know if you'd like a cup of tea".'

If that wasn't true, then it ought to be, Markham reflected with a chuckle as Doggie Dickerson lurched unsteadily away.

Right, time to sample Doggie Dickerson's version of a Nordic sauna. And if that didn't banish the spectre of DCI Sidney, he would see who was available for a cathartic pummelling. *Benny Squint, look to your laurels*!

* * *

The mood was more serious later that day when Burton and Noakes joined the DI in his apartment at the Sweepstakes.

The food was a great success, however, with Noakes pronouncing his chicken chow mein, sweet and sour pork, dim sum and jumbo meat spring rolls 'champion' (his highest accolade), while Markham and Burton tucked into crispy aromatic duck with chop suey.

By mutual consent, the trio chatted about inconsequential matters while eating, but once settled with strong coffee, they got down to business.

Briskly, Burton launched into the alibis.

'Graham Thorpe dropped Frances Langton off after the wake then went home—'

Noakes winked. 'She didn't invite him in for a coffee then?'

'No she didn't,' Burton said severely. 'She was "wrung out" after the funeral and didn't feel up to company . . . The same with the Carnforths, Ed Frayling and Barbara Price. Francesco and Serena Rossi went back to the restaurant to get ready for the evening shift . . . Marina and Matteo went for a walk on Bromgrove Rise . . .'

'Cosy coupledom all round,' Noakes grunted. 'What about Mister Rasputin?' he asked suspiciously. 'Where'd he slope off to?'

'Dr Morland went over to Old Carton Woods apparently. He wanted to clear his head.'

'Oh aye, another fresh air fiend . . . very convenient.' Noakes crunched his prawn crackers balefully. 'What about the DJ's ex?' he demanded. 'The one everyone treated like she'd got leprosy.'

'Ed and Barbara dropped Tricia Dent off on their way home. Barbara said they were a bit worried about her, but she just wanted to be alone.' Burton frowned. 'She seemed quite spacey when we told her what had happened. She didn't seem to take it in about Mr Parker . . . no reaction at all. She's registered at Medway Health Centre, so I've asked them to arrange a house call.'

'Was it genuine, Kate,' Markham asked, 'or could she have been faking?'

'It looked genuine enough to me, boss. I wondered if maybe she'd taken something and it was a bad reaction.'

'Talking of stoners, what happened with Pettifer?' Noakes wanted to know.

'He eventually answered his door,' Burton replied. 'But it was obvious he'd been on a massive bender—'

'Bet he sobered up fast enough when he heard the news about Fanshaw an' Parker.'

'Seemed pretty shocked to me, sarge . . . If he's an actor, then he deserves an Oscar,' she said slowly.

'If I had a pound for every time I heard that, I'd be a bleeding millionaire,' Noakes groused. Then, 'What about Big Vinny? The rest of them Romanos are like the Von Trapps . . . all cy carey-sharey an' cheesy grins, but he's a right mardy arse.'

Burton grinned despite herself. 'I think the Von Trapps were Austrian, sarge,' she said.

'Same difference,' retorted the Unquenchable One. 'So go on then, where did ole misery guts end up?'

'Sorry to disappoint you, sarge, but Vincent took the little girl Giulia home after the wake. He was on babysitting duty apparently.' She smiled at his incredulous expression. 'Italians are big on family responsibility . . . very child-centred.'

'Them alibis add up to a big fat zero!' Noakes burst out. 'All of 'em had opportunity.'

'What about motive, though?' Burton sighed with exasperation. 'I was coming round to the idea of some kind of parish imbroglio . . . er, entanglement,' she translated, knowing Noakes's dislike of 'Big Words' (especially the continental variety). 'Something involving the vicar and female parishioners at Saint Michael's but George Parker being murdered bollixes the whole thing up.'

Noakes clasped pugilist's hands across his ample paunch (not flattered by a vermillion pullover) and took stock. 'If the doc's right about Parker copping it in the graveyard, then mebbe there's a whole other ball game going on . . . someone from the music scene,' Noakes said the words with the air of one holding his nose, 'who had a grudge . . . summat to do with turf wars. Y'know, Sex, Drugs an' Rock 'n' Roll,' he added, warming to his theme.

'Or professional rivalries,' Markham put in, thinking of his earlier conversation with Doggie.

'Any chance Parker got chased into the graveyard after he blundered in on top of Fanshaw?' Noakes wondered.

'It's possible,' Markham conceded, 'but Dr Patel thinks the attack would have been far more frenzied in that case, whereas the throat-cutting was done with clinical precision and there was no sign of defensive injuries . . . plus, forensics haven't found anything pointing to a pursuit.' He turned to Burton. 'Did you try leaning on Mr Thorpe, Kate . . . as in, give him the idea that we might be interested in Frances Langton?'

She frowned. 'Think he saw through it, boss . . . just clammed up and kept repeating that zombie mantra about the vicar being above reproach blah blah.'

Suddenly, the flat's buzzer rang.

Markham went into the hallway and picked up the intercom.

'Olivia,' he said, a muscle leaping in his jaw and his internal pressure gauge shooting off the scale. 'Come on up.'

CHAPTER 10

Crikey, was Kate Burton's first thought as Olivia joined them, *it looks like she's dropped a lot of weight (and couldn't really afford to in the first place)*. Although Markham's ex was elegant in a floaty print number and nude wedges, the abundant red hair secured with a statement barrette, her complexion was flour white, there were purple shadows under her grey-green eyes, and her high cheekbones seemed unnaturally prominent, almost poking through the skin.

Noakes was dismayed too. The missus had always been of the opinion that Olivia was anorexic, bulimic, or quite possibly both, while he insisted that the guvnor's naturally willowy partner thoroughly enjoyed her grub and ate like a horse. But looking at Olivia now, with her shoulder blades poking through that dress, the notion of an eating disorder didn't seem quite so far-fetched.

Markham installed Olivia in his own armchair by the living room window, and went to fetch a glass of her favourite Pinot Grigio. Meanwhile, Noakes padded through to the kitchen, returning with a hastily assembled plate of takeaway in the shape of prawn crackers, char siu buns and gyozas. He had planned to stake a claim to the leftovers, but there were times when you just had to think of the greater good.

Burton felt supremely awkward and uncomfortable, as Olivia acknowledged her stiffly before swiftly turning towards Noakes and smiling with genuine warmth.

'Blimey, George,' she laughed, 'this is enough for an army.' Then seeing concern writ large in her friend's battered features, she tried a couple of the dumplings. 'They're excellent,' she murmured appreciatively.

'Burton got 'em in from The Lotus Garden,' the other told her happily, oblivious of the way Olivia's smile faded at this information.

'It's Nathan's latest foodie "find",' Burton said heartily, increasingly certain that Olivia resented her closeness to the guvnor and hoping this reference to her fiancé would reassure the other woman she had no designs on Markham. But Olivia merely looked down and toyed with a prawn cracker.

Markham came back with Olivia's wine, placing a large glass clinking with ice on a side table next to the comfortable tartan check wingback. Noting with alarm how much weight she had lost, it seemed to him that she was almost swallowed up in the chair's depths.

But with the arrival of her drink, some of the tension seemed to dissolve. Grinning at Noakes, she said. 'Don't let on to Muriel about my plebeian tastes, George . . . she's *way* too classy to put ice in her wine.'

Markham chuckled.

'I set a bad example, drinking Châteauneuf-du-Pape with just about everything,' he said. 'Alongside Muriel, I'm afraid we're total philistines.'

Noakes was very pleased at the implied compliment to his wife, mentally storing it up for later.

'So, how's it going with the investigation?' Olivia asked, turning serious.

Manspreading on the Chesterfield, while Burton perched on the edge of the sofa (she never sprawled but always sat like a secretary waiting to take dictation), Noakes took Olivia through the latest developments in his own inimitable fashion, eliciting laughter with his monikers for suspects and un-PC analysis of the parochial setup. Olivia, Muriel and Doggie Dickerson were the only three people outside CID with whom sensitive information was ever shared (though Mrs Noakes would doubtless be less than enchanted to find herself classed with such an unholy trinity). As Doggie always said, *What's Said Here, Stays Here*. Markham knew that they would never betray his confidence.

'How strange,' Olivia said at the conclusion of Noakes's account. With typical impishness, she continued, 'Until this latest murder, I'd have put my money on some kind of seraglio involving the vicar and his parishioners.'

'What's one of them then?' Noakes asked curiously.

'A harem, George,' she replied with dancing eyes. 'Like they had in the Ottoman empire.'

Oh well, he wouldn't put anything past *foreigners*.

'But hey up, they're all crumblies,' he demurred, ignoring Burton's frown. 'Well past that sort of thing.'

Olivia felt a secret satisfaction in observing the PC Queen's discomfiture at the turn the conversation was taking.

With a saucy wink in Markham's direction, she intoned:

'Sexual intercourse began
In nineteen sixty-three.
Between the end of the Chatterley ban
And the Beatles' first LP.

'So you see, George, at least *some* older folk make the cut.'

Noakes knew exactly where he stood on Lady Chatterley and pervy types. 'Oh aye,' he grunted laconically.

Markham chuckled.

'I seem to recall Philip Larkin said something about nineteen sixty-three being too late for him, Liv.'

'I'm exercising poetic licence to make my point, Gil,' came the cheekily flirtatious retort. In that instant, she looked almost like the Olivia of old, her eyes alight with pleasure and excitement. Observing Markham's answering glow, Kate Burton felt as though the air had been sucked out of her lungs.

There's still something there, she thought wretchedly watching Olivia come to life under Markham's attentive regard.

Despite having won her way into the DI's inner circle, as she watched Markham, Olivia and Noakes together, Burton suddenly felt banished to the margins, excluded from the others' easy complicity. 'The Three Musketeers,' was how Olivia had once described them. And it was true. There was some mysterious affinity between the trio that Burton knew she didn't share . . . had never really shared. Oh it was true, she had drawn closer to Markham during the Sherwin College investigation in Oxford, telling him stuff about her upbringing and the private insecurities she kept from everyone else (including Nathan). And there were moments when she almost fancied the DI saw their relationship as somehow special . . . almost fancied there was something between them ready to flare up and ignite . . .

But seeing Olivia and Markham together, was an abrupt snuffing out of those nebulous yearnings to which she could hardly even put a name. Like the words of that hymn she remembered from church, about everyone's hopes flying forgotten as a dream dies at the opening day, the same way her stupid fantasies about Markham were destined to bite the dust. She knew Nathan felt short-changed as a result of her devotion to the boss and inwardly vowed to change the dynamic.

Stop pining for the moon!

For a moment, she was terrified that she had spoken the words aloud. Noakes was looking at her in that leery way of his, as though he was privy to her innermost feelings.

Well stuff that!

'I better get off, boss,' she said awkwardly. 'Nathan'll be wanting his tea.'

God, even as she said the words, she was cursing herself for sounding hopelessly bourgeois and unsophisticated. However, there was nothing for it but to appear blithe and unconcerned. 'D'you want me to drop you off, sarge?' she said, Noakes having cadged a lift to Markham's for their takeaway supper.

'Ta very much.'

Noakes's cordial tone took her by surprise, but then it occurred to her he would probably be glad to see her gone from the Sweepstakes, leaving the field clear for Olivia.

Markham's ex visibly perked up at the prospect of her departure.

Can't you see I'm all out of options, Burton thought bitterly. *Like I could ever seriously have imagined being in the running . . .*

Markham regarded her with grave kindness. 'I've monopolized you quite enough for one day, Kate,' he said.

Oh, if only.

'Let's set up a meeting with Nathan first thing tomorrow,' he continued. 'Think about the psychological angles some more . . . So far, this seems to be a case of two halves, but I want to probe potential links between George Parker, Saint Michael's and Medway High Street. There has to be a connection . . . something we're missing. Hopefully, looking at it from a profiler's perspective will bring things into focus.'

Burton was privately dubious but murmured politely, 'First thing in the morning, boss.'

Olivia caught Noakes's last lingering look at the gyozas.

'Hey Gil,' she said lightly, 'put these in some foil for George will you. They're scrumptious, but a bit too heavy for me.'

Markham smilingly complied and his friends duly took their leave, after a promise from the DI to check in with his former wingman the following day. 'Now a sleb's been killed, you can count on Sidney an' the rest of 'em driving you round the twist,' Noakes opined cheerfully in parting, Burton's glum expression an endorsement of this verdict.

After their departure, Markham and Olivia chatted easily, the former experiencing an exquisite relief in going over the case with the person who, after Noakes, understood him like no one else.

'But how are *you*, Liv?' he said finally. 'I trust they're not working you too hard at Hopeless,' he added gently, using her school's infamous nickname.

It was as near as he dared go to touching on Olivia's personal life.

'Oh, same old, same old. I could swing for "Call Me Tony", Gil, I really could,' she groaned, referring to Tony Brighouse the head. 'Right now, he's hell bent on shoehorning transgenderism into every corner of the curriculum.' She giggled. 'God only knows what's going to happen with the end-of-year play . . . Macbeth, but not as we know it. Mat's tearing his hair out.'

Taking courage, seeing as she had been the first to mention Sullivan's name, Markham replied with an attempt at insouciance, 'So how's it going with you and Mat?'

He noticed that her hand shook slightly as she took a hefty swig of her white wine. Without being asked, he hastened to top her up.

'I wanted to convince myself Mat wasn't homosexual, Gil . . .' she said unsteadily. 'And with you and me growing apart . . .'

With an effort, he refrained from contradicting her.

'Mat and I were always good friends,' she continued. 'We'd flirt and laugh together . . . get silly and plot against "Call Me Tony". Deep down, though, I knew he wasn't in love with me or anything like that.'

'Was that what you wanted?' Markham forced the words out with difficulty.

'I was flattered by the attention.' There was a pleading note in her voice as she said this.

Abruptly, Markham got up and went through to the kitchen. He hadn't been joking when he told the others that Châteauneuf-du-Pape went with everything . . . including his former partner's revelations about her attraction to Mat Sullivan! With surprising steadiness, he knocked back a glass before pouring himself a refill and returning to the living room.

Olivia looked somewhat flustered.

'I'm sorry, Gil,' she told him. 'We weren't getting on . . . and somehow Mat was there right at the moment when I needed comfort and diversion.'

Markham nodded, his throat tight. He was dying to ask Olivia if she and Sullivan had consummated their relationship but couldn't frame the question.

But she sensed his enquiry hanging in the air.

'We never exactly . . . got to fourth base,' she said, flushing to her hairline.

It was so unlike Olivia to shelter behind euphemisms, that Markham found the denial less than convincing. He said nothing, however.

Olivia shot him an uneasy glance, disconcerted by his silence. 'I'm not sure I ever really believed he liked me.'

'And then Guy Raynor hove into view.' For the life of him, Markham could not keep the edge out of his tone. *So now you're thrown back on me*, he reflected bitterly.

Something of what he felt must have shown in his face, because she said hastily, 'I never took you for granted, Gil. But I got caught up in a complicated situation.'

You can say that again, he thought sardonically. *What a sexual merry-go-round.*

'So Mat and Raynor became close,' he prompted.

She wondered how much he knew, concluding that he was too proud to ask.

'We were a sort of threesome,' she said awkwardly, 'but I came to feel I was outside with my nose pressed up against the glass . . . never really a part of it.'

It suddenly crossed her mind that perhaps this was how Kate Burton had felt round herself, Markham and Noakes, and for the first time she felt a spasm of pity for the woman she had come to see as her rival.

She tried to explain a thoroughly novel, not to say weird, situation. 'I guess I must have an element of sado-masochism in my make-up to have put up with it,' was the best she could manage.

'You were at a low ebb and infatuated,' Markham said levelly. 'It happens.'

Something in his clipped delivery made her colour up once more, the flush receding almost immediately to leave her deathly pale.

'Guy's ruthless,' she told him, confirming what Markham already knew from Noakes. 'I could see he thought I might try to corner Mat into marriage or some kind of commitment.'

'Is that what you were after . . . a commitment?'

'No.' Her voice was so low, he had to lean forward to catch her reply. Biting her lip, she added, 'I'm not sure what I wanted . . . it was a sort of dependence on Mat that I couldn't break, even without our being able to . . . follow through . . .'

'So Raynor was hostile towards you?'

'It was a kind of seesawing power struggle between us, but I couldn't compete with him where it really mattered.'

Markham could only be thankful that Noakes wasn't around to hear these confessional outpourings. His friend would have said the whole setup was like 'one of them godaw-ful navel-gazing foreign films with subtitles' that Olivia used to make him watch. After *The Unbearable Lightness of Being*, Noakes had indignantly called time on such cultural for-ays before returning happily to Clint Eastwood and endless reruns of *The Outlaw Josey Wales*. Even in the midst of his current woes, the memory made Markham smile.

Olivia took heart from the lightening of his expression.

'I know, I know, Gil,' she said. 'It's like *Jules et Jim* or a Terence Rattigan drama.' That particular playwright being another of Noakes's *bêtes noires*. 'A real emotional mess. When I saw a band on Guy's wedding-ring finger, it was like a dec-laration of intent.'

Markham was startled. 'You think Mat gave it to him?'

'I never liked to ask,' she said miserably. 'But Guy used to flaunt it . . . if we went for coffee, he always sat with his left hand hovering against his lips, like he was trying to tell me they were symbolically married or something.'

Markham chose his words carefully. 'If Mat's sexual per-suasion isn't certain, if he's tied-up-in-knots and "learning" or bisexual . . . he might be very susceptible to a forceful personality like Raynor.'

'I don't really understand these games, Gil. Haven't got a clue . . . But if Guy *is* courting Mat, then looks like it's working.'

'Are you going to give Mat an ultimatum . . . As in, "You've got to choose. Me or him"?'

Sadly, she replied, 'I can't help feeling I went to him with my heart on my sleeve, and he stamped on it . . . started pushing me away when he and Guy became emotionally involved.' Rather desperately, she glugged down some more Pinot Grigio. 'I guess what's important now, is to keep our friendship intact . . . Sex is sex. In the final analysis, it's not the important thing.'

It was pretty damn important for us, Markham thought ruefully, sex between himself and Olivia having always been dynamite, even in the worst of times.

'The intellectual side matters as well,' she went on with a hint of defiance in her manner. 'It's not all about novelty and sexual discovery.'

They'd had that too, Markham's inner monologue continued relentlessly, before misunderstandings and mistrust poisoned their relationship.

'If I'm honest, me and Guy had a violent reaction to each other,' Olivia admitted. 'He doesn't like me any more than I like him. And with him being such a tough, possessive character, the writing's on the wall . . . Guy wants *all* of Mat,' she added wryly, 'so there's just not enough of him to go round.' A pause and then, 'A proper love affair with Mat would have destroyed our friendship sooner or later, and I don't really want to jeopardize that.'

This was something Markham *could* appreciate, having always greatly enjoyed Sullivan's charming, self-deprecating company and reserved humour.

Seeing as Olivia was in the mood to confide, he said cautiously, 'I believe Mat's had the occasional heterosexual romance.'

'That's right, Gil. But whatever happened with *me*, it was just a flash in the pan . . . nothing that lasted . . . and, well, these days . . .' Her voice trailed off.

Mat Sullivan must have exerted quite a hold over her, Markham thought, for her to be so upset about this. Maybe she had imagined she would be "The One", so she waited and hoped, with the inevitable result that she suffered.

Mind you, when it came to love, half of it was suffering and half was happiness, he told himself cynically, so probably Olivia had decided that it was a bargain well worth striking.

Rapture had a realm beyond the bedroom, he mused, with Olivia and Mat Sullivan being good friends long before there was a question of anything sexual developing between them. He was generous enough to hope that the two teachers' personal closeness managed to survive the advent of Guy Rayner. He had the sense that there was almost an element of courtly love about Sullivan's feelings for Olivia . . . that she represented the elegant embodiment of beauty, wit and grace — all qualities that moved him — but, being a woman, was an unobtainable lady, a muse he could worship without the burden of physical expectations.

Oddly enough, something similar might be said of the potent romantic appeal Olivia held for Noakes with his troubadour-like devotion to her interests and habit of regarding her as more than a mere mortal . . .

Markham became aware that Olivia's eyes were fastened on his face and recalled himself to the present. For all the fleeting schadenfreude attendant on her disclosures (after all, he had suffered terribly from their estrangement), he was stirred by compassion for his ex who now faced defeat on the level that most mattered between a man and woman and doubtless feared that even her friendship with Sullivan might be going down the swanny. You only had to look at her weight loss to measure the pain.

'I've banged on long enough, Gil,' she said. 'And it looks like I drove Kate and George away into the bargain.'

'Not at all, Liv.' He hesitated. 'By the way, there's no need to use the buzzer when you come round here . . . Just use your keys.'

'It wouldn't feel right . . . not after everything,' she mumbled.

'Don't be daft. You know you're always welcome.'

Olivia looked as though she wished she could believe it.

'How's Judas Iscariot these days?' she asked with a faint gleam of her earlier mischievousness. 'Panting to pin these murders on his old friend the Bushy Haired Stranger?'

He grinned. 'Well, you know Sidney.'

She grimaced. 'All too well.'

'He'd be relieved if we could at least square away George Parker as a celebrity murder — a deranged fan or something of the sort,' Markham told her.

She shivered, even though the living room was bathed in late-evening sun.

'That still leaves you with a serial out there.'

'Yes . . . But I'm sure these killings are somehow connected, Liv, though it's difficult to envisage George Parker and the vicar as participants in some kind of vice ring.'

She laughed. 'Did they even know each other?'

'Parker did the odd bit for charity, including Saint Michael's choir appeal fund, so their paths crossed from time to time. But there's no evidence of him being majorly involved with Norman Collins or any of the parishioners.'

'What about the high street lot?'

'Well, he was a regular at Rossi's and friendly with Vincent Rossi . . . he also visited the pub occasionally, but smart wine bars in Bromgrove town centre were more his style . . . There's no evidence that he ever patronized the healing centre.'

Olivia snorted. 'Can't see him being into rock crystals or Rasputin.'

'Quite.' Markham reckoned Parker's tastes ran to quite a different type of 'rock'.

Thinking about her own complicated personal history, she asked. 'What about ex-girlfriends or boyfriends, embittered lovers, spurned groupies . . . that kind of thing?'

'Well, I believe he gave the local headteacher the brush-off when she wanted to book him for a couple of school functions.'

'Not glitzy enough,' she opined sagely.

'More than likely. And apparently he dated Tricia Dent, but it ended badly.'

'The one who sells,' she slipped into Noakes's Yorkshire vowels, '"mucky books"?'

'That's her . . . But Parker was thick as thieves with Sheila Craven's nephew Desmond Pettifer, so who knows what was going on there. Markham sounded very weary. 'God knows, I don't.'

'There's nowt so queer as folk,' Olivia said, continuing her impersonation of Noakes. Suddenly the humorous manner dropped away from her. 'Hang in there, Gil,' she said gently, 'You've cracked tougher cases than this.'

He smiled at her. 'Somehow it doesn't feel like that right now,' he replied. 'The vultures are circling,' he added, thinking of Gavin Conors, 'and the chief super wants to see me tomorrow . . . Somehow I don't think I'm in line for a commendation or anything like that.'

'Maybe the profiling brainstorm tomorrow will throw up something and Nathan will come up with a psychotic *ménage à trois* that will be the key to it all.'

He burst out laughing. 'I'd settle for something a lot more prosaic than that, Liv . . . a simple link between Parker and Saint Michael's for starters.'

She joined in the laughter but then her smile died away. 'I really had better be on my way. Tomorrow's one of those awful Enrichment Days and the kids will be high as kites. I'll need all my stamina to get through it . . . and hold back from telling "Call Me Tony" to stuff his rotten job.'

Markham chuckled.

'What's the theme for tomorrow then?'

'Dunno yet, but it's bound to be teeth-grindingly woke . . . the need to renounce binary models of sexuality or some such bollocks. Actually, I find the kids are basically non-judgmental and accepting of other people without all of this being constantly rammed down their throats. And I don't care if they want to identify as *goats* just so long as I get them through their GCSEs.'

'Tut-tut, Liv,' he adopted a tone of mock reproach. 'I'm afraid that's a very blinkered attitude. I seem to recall you were similarly unenthusiastic about that INSET on Unpacking White Privilege.'

She groaned theatrically. 'Don't remind me.' Self-consciously, she added, 'I won't even be able to moan to Mat cos he's doing a swap with Medway High.'

It struck Markham that she was trying to make Sullivan sound like just another colleague, but it was clear that she was by no means over the deputy head.

After Olivia had left, Markham finished off the red wine, sitting in the armchair she had vacated as darkness gradually stole over the room.

He had wanted to ask her to stay the night, but somehow the words just wouldn't come.

If he had asked, would she have said yes?

He wanted her back, while at the same time he wanted an end to the emotional pain of their relationship.

Olivia had turned down a proposal of marriage but maybe now, after being scourged by her experience with Sullivan, she saw him in a new light . . . On the other hand, something in him revolted at the notion of being her 'backup plan'. And there was the question of trust . . . It almost seemed that she saw him more as a *brother* than a lover now. In which case, he thought with a bitter twist of his lips, perhaps the best he could hope for were occasional acts of incest . . .

He debated opening another bottle, but the prospect of handling Chief Superintendent Ebury-Clarke with a massive hangover was enough to convince him this would not be a good idea.

His thoughts turned to the criminal profiling session and Olivia's talk of a psychotic *ménage à trois*. Was it possible something like that could be at the root of these murders?

Well, there was no obvious psychopath out there for his money.

He had no doubt that Nathan Finlayson would do his best (whatever his resentment about Kate Burton's divided affections), but it was unlikely to satisfy Sidney or Ebury-Clarke. The best he could hope for was to buy the team some time.

At least the heart to heart with Olivia made him feel somewhat less despondent about the future, since it was clear she didn't give much for her chances against Guy Raynor.

But did it mean she wanted *them* to try again though? Or had that boat well and truly sailed?

Oh for God's sake, he chided himself, stop going round in circles.

They had a killer to catch.

And unless they boxed clever, the predator they sought would most likely strike again.

CHAPTER 11

'OK, so this is zero hour, right?'

Doyle and Carruthers exchanged ironic glances at Professor Nathan Finlayson's opening pronouncement. *FFS, what does he think this is . . . Celebrity SAS?*

Markham had caught the look.

'Indeed, Nathan,' he said in a tone designed to squelch his two subordinates, who looked duly chastened.

The DI was pleased to note that both Finlayson and Burton appeared brighter and more at ease with each other than they had previously, despite the unsociable hour. For his own part, he was glad he had held off opening another bottle of Châteauneuf-du-Pape, since this six-a.m. meeting followed by battle with the chief super would require his utmost powers of concentration. At least the coffee Burton had provided was excellent. He really didn't think he could bear to start the day with 'gnat's piss', as Noakes described it, from the CID vending machine. There were croissants too and, contrary to his usual practice, he tucked in. Essential to soak up last night's alcohol.

'Tell us what you think, Nathan,' he said warmly.

'I believe your killer is male and local,' the psychologist said calmly.

They waited expectantly.

'It's not just that female serial killers are less common,' he continued. 'Of course, we all know women can be deadlier than men.'

Not half, Doyle thought.

'I'm not going to bore you rigid with the sociology and statistics.'

Doyle visibly sagged with relief on hearing this, though Finlayson was generally infinitely preferable to Burton with her everlasting DSM bible.

'What I *will* say, is that the manner, almost the audacity and *showiness*, of these crimes, in terms of the killer's confident *modus operandi* — attacking victims in various locations with disregard for the risk of discovery — along with the close proximity of the last two murders, militates in favour of the perpetrator being male.'

'Doc Patel didn't rule out it being a woman, though,' Carruthers countered. 'And aren't female serial killers more likely to target people they *know* — which looks like what's going on here — and draw them in . . . gain their confidence so they drop their guard?' It was obvious that at least this particular DS had paid close attention during Finlayson's recent seminar on gender differentials.

'But if there's some kind of sexual kink, *that* means it's more likely to be a bloke,' Doyle cut in, anxious to demonstrate that he too had been a receptive auditor.

'The vics weren't interfered with,' Carruthers objected.

'Shut up the pair of you,' Burton ordered, 'and let Nathan speak.'

'Sorry, ma'am,' came the abashed response.

Finlayson wasn't in the least put out, however.

'All your points are well taken, gents,' he said equably. 'Key for me is that these murders don't fit the covert profile most commonly found with female killers. Also, the method of dispatch — strangulation and bludgeoning — exhibits a brutalism that I would argue is *atypical* of women offenders.'

He paused to let them digest this.

'Not only that,' he resumed. 'Assuming that the same person is responsible for all the homicides in your series, then the lack of any significant decompression or cooling off period between the last two murders makes it more likely the killer is male and there is a sexual component involved, albeit quite possibly latent in that the suspect lacks insight into that aspect of his motivation.'

Doyle shot Carruthers a triumphant look. 'So you reckon they're a sex killer, Nate?'

Burton didn't look as though she liked this abbreviation of her partner's name, but the professor seemed perfectly relaxed. At least it was better than 'Shippers', Markham thought, suppressing a smile.

'There are elements of George Parker's murder that I believe point to some kind of sublimated sexual impulse,' the psychologist replied. 'Having examined the crime scene photographs, there appears to have been some disarrangement of the clothing and hair pointing to possible anthropophagic appropriation . . . removal of trophies,' he added benignly, as though this was the most natural thing in the world. 'Throat-cutting — mutilation of the vocal chords — also suggests a desire to possess the victim by rendering him powerless.'

'So you're saying the killer's maybe homosexual?' Carruthers sounded baffled. 'Cos they secretly fancied Parker?'

'I would say there's some kind of homosexual wish-fulfilment at work, but it's deeply internalized so the killer isn't explicitly accessing those repressed desires.'

Doyle's brow was furrowed. 'Lemme get this straight,' he said, glaring at Carruthers as the other smirked at the unfortunate phraseology. 'D'you mean that what happened in the cemetery doesn't have anything to do with Sheila Craven and the vicar and Stella Fanshaw . . . that laughing boy arranged to meet Parker so he could kill him?'

'I think it's quite possible that the excitement of the previous murders set off some kind of unstoppable reaction—'

'You mean, he *got off on killing*?' Doyle burst out incredulously.

'Something like that, yes . . .' he nodded slowly. 'In terms of causation, we don't know what triggered Sheila Craven's murder. With regard to the vicar and Stella Fanshaw, it may well have come down to expediency, in the sense of needing to silence them or remove a threat . . . But in the case of George Parker, well,' the psychologist's expression was unusually sombre, 'I'd say this particular offender was deriving enjoyment from the infliction of violence — had maybe discovered a *taste* for it . . .'

Burton cleared her throat.

'Dr Patel thinks they most likely inserted a knife into the throat wound several times post-mortem,' she said.

There was silence in Markham's office as the detectives visualized that shadowy figure probing the gaping orifice — lingering over his handiwork the better to relive the scene in later fantasies.

'Just a knife, d'you reckon?' Doyle asked faintly. 'Or . . . anything else?'

'There was no evidence of penile penetration, ejaculation or insertion of foreign objects,' Finlayson said matter-of-factly.

Doyle and Carruthers looked at each other as though, in light of what the psychologist was telling them, this was small comfort.

'As regards gender archetypes, there's all the evolutionary psychology and biological coefficients,' Finlayson went on, 'but I have a feeling you could do without chapter and verse right now.'

Too right. The sergeants' faces were eloquent in their plea to be spared the neurological specifics.

'This is all really useful, Nathan,' Markham said courteously. 'Do you have any pointers as to the perpetrator's age and occupation?'

The other shook his head. 'The most I would venture is to say they may have strong feelings about organized religion, based on the sacrilegious use of that mausoleum as the disposal site.'

'Wouldn't that just be a case of needs must though?' Carruthers challenged. 'After all, it was an ideal place to hide the body.'

'I think there was some deep-seated *need* to violate a tomb,' Finlayson said slowly.

'You mean cos he's a *necrophile*?' Doyle liked things to be clear-cut.

'That may well have been a factor,' the psychologist agreed. 'But it appears he arranged to meet Mr Parker at that specific location and went to considerable trouble to break into the sepulchre . . . shrouding the body and positioning it under a stained-glass window like some kind of biblical tableau.'

Markham suddenly recalled his feeling that it was almost a re-enactment of the Lazarus story.

'There were other less risky locations he could have chosen,' Finlayson continued, 'but he was focused on the cemetery at Saint Michael's and that particular vault.' After a moment's hesitation, he continued. 'Dedicated to Saint Joseph, wasn't it? Perhaps there's a clue there.'

Doyle looked blank. 'Saint Joseph as in married to the Virgin Mary . . . Jesus's adoptive dad or foster father?'

Joseph Most Chaste, Protector of Virgins. Markham was startled by the way the words seemed to come to him from nowhere, like a distant murmur from his past, the echo of a long-forgotten novena perhaps.

'There's a website for Saint Michael's with a history of the church and graveyard, including details of mausoleums,' Burton said. 'Easy enough for someone to find out which vaults were dedicated to particular saints.'

Carruthers pursed his lips. 'So we're looking for some freaky gay incel with a thing for Saint Joseph who knew all about the graveyard.'

'What's an incel?' his fellow sergeant asked.

'An "involuntary celibate" . . . As in someone who never gets any.'

'That gunman who went on the rampage in Plymouth was heavily influenced by incel culture,' Burton recalled. 'And incels have been linked to shootings in the States.'

'OK, so which of our suspects fits the description of a gay bloke with religious hang-ups and a complex about not getting their leg over?' Doyle demanded in a martyred tone.

Burton looked pained at such coarseness, but Markham considered the question with grave deliberation.

'Ed Frayling, Francesco Rossi, James Carnforth and Marina's fiancé Matteo are all in stable relationships,' he said.

'Which leaves Graham Thorpe and Henry Morland,' Carruthers put in. With growing excitement, he added, 'Both of them come from a religious background — deacon and ex-Catholic priest — and there's no sign of girlfriends or anything like that.'

'Yeah, but Morland got into trouble for potentially assaulting some woman,' Doyle shot back, 'so it doesn't look like he's homosexual.'

'That was according to the *Gazette*,' Carruthers said scornfully. 'And anyway, he could be closeted. What's to say all that about him being some kind of sex bomb and Rasputin lookalike ain't camouflage for being secretly gay with a hidden life?'

Doyle snorted rudely, but Finlayson smiled at Carruthers as at a particularly promising pupil who had demonstrated willingness to think outside the box.

'Graham Thorpe's a better bet if it comes to that,' Burton hypothesized. 'If Frances Langton's keeping him dangling and he hasn't tried to move things forward, he might be heavily conflicted about his sexuality.'

'But if he's after Langton, Thorpe's gotta be hetero, right?' Doyle demanded.

'Not necessarily,' Finlayson said. 'She might represent some idealized, unattainable woman he considers it *safe* to pursue, with the conventionality a cover for urges he has difficulty acknowledging even to himself.'

At these words, Markham thought of Mathew Sullivan and his affinity with Olivia which was based on a non-carnal romantic sensibility. Perhaps that's how it had started out with Graham Thorpe and Frances Langton, but then the relationship curdled leading Thorpe to lash out when he could no longer sublimate his repressed sexuality.

'Christ, it's beyond me,' Doyle burst out. Then, aware of Markham's cool regard, 'Sorry, boss, but you've got to admit, all that's pretty *deep*.'

'There's Vincent Rossi and Desmond Pettifer too,' Carruthers said cheerfully, rather enjoying his colleague's bemusement. 'Both male and single . . . Plus, the Rossis are bound to be religious, seeing as they're your typical Italian Catholic family.'

Markham remembered the ornate crosses that adorned the walls of Rossi's and Noakes's discomfiture at the baroque theatricality of it all.

Seeing that the guvnor appeared struck by his observations, Carruthers pressed home his advantage. 'Vincent and Desmond were both friends of Parker's,' he said. 'And Pettifer was the last person to see him alive.'

'Too big a stretch,' Doyle muttered. 'They're just two wheeler dealers giving it large . . . not choirboy types screwed up about Saint Joseph and purity or whatever.'

'Those suspects who are to all intents and purposes established in settled relationships can't be ruled out,' Finlayson pointed out in a tone of mild reproof. 'You need to remember, it's not unusual for those who are ambivalent about their sexuality to want the security of a more conventional lifestyle.'

Doyle's disgruntled expression said, *Oh God, back to square one then.*

But Carruthers was thoughtful.

'Yeah, like Jan Morris,' he said.

'*Eh*?' Doyle looked at him like he had lost his marbles.

'The famous travel writer who underwent sex reassignment surgery,' his colleague explained. 'The one who dialled in the news about Edmund Hillary conquering Everest . . . After transitioning from James to Jan, she went back to the woman she'd married before she transitioned and they lived together like a normal family . . . the four kids just had to accept it.'

'Oh yes,' Burton chimed in. 'She wrote *Conundrum*. I remember that bit where she talks about the surgeon in Casablanca saying "Au revoir, Monsieur" before she had the op and then "Bonjour, Mademoiselle" afterwards. I thought it was all pretty moving.'

You bloody would. Doyle contented himself with the muttered verdict, 'Sounds like a selfish piece of work.'

'It was an incredibly complex scenario,' Finlayson observed diplomatically. 'But many would agree with you about the selfishness, Sergeant . . . Germaine Greer for one.'

Yikes. Doyle wasn't at all sure he cared to be classed with a radical feminist, even if he did seem to agree with some of her views.

Finlayson smothered a smile. 'In her former life, Morris was a chorister at Christ Church Cathedral,' he said deadpan.

'Please tell me this isn't all about transgenderism,' Doyle groaned, recalling all too vividly one of their most controversial investigations in which Kate Burton had been lucky to escape with her life.

Finlayson laughed. 'No, I don't think so, Sergeant. But Jan Morris is worth remembering . . . if only as an example of the incredible fluidity and ambiguity in human relationships.'

Ta for the lesson.

But all Doyle said somewhat sulkily was, 'None of this gets us any further, though, does it? I mean, if you're right, potentially *all* the blokes are in the frame.'

Markham heard the note of negativity.

'I'm grateful that you've narrowed things down, Nathan,' he said crisply. 'It gives me something to offer Chief Superintendent Ebury-Clarke.' The chief super was nowhere near as star-struck as Sidney when it came to criminal profilers (his university degree was — of all things — Geology, whereas the DCI felt his degree in Psychology put him up there with the luminaries of *Cracker* and *Mindhunter* and any number of sexy TV profilers). But Markham at least felt marginally more confident now about his chances of ensuring Ebury-Clarke didn't reallocate the investigation or bring in Scotland Yard.

Finlayson's gaze was sympathetic.

'Here,' he pushed a manila folder across Markham's desk. 'There's some data, statistics and whatnot to keep you going.'

Markham locked eyes with 'Shippers'.

He knew the psychologist was a decent man who could make Kate Burton happy. He knew also that his umbilical connection with Olivia – as if he had a string knotted under his ribs tightly and inextricably knotted to a similar string beneath hers – meant it would be the height of selfishness to come between his colleague and a settled relationship.

Silently and, he hoped, selflessly, the DI wished the unassuming bearded Shipman lookalike all possible success in rebuilding his relationship with Kate Burton.

She's not for me, mate. Go for it and good luck!

The psychologist smiled as if to say, *Message received and understood.*

Forty minutes later, Markham confronted Chief Superintendent Ebury-Clarke across acres of polished mahogany in the latter's spacious domain on the top floor.

The chief super was a squat, somewhat toad-like man with a comb-over, rubicund complexion and thick-rimmed spectacles which made it difficult to read his expression. He and Noakes were sworn enemies, ever since the time when Markham's wingman, well refreshed at the Christmas Jewish Police Association dinner dance, shared a joke about the liberal Jewish father who told his kids that Judas Maccabeus would come down the chimney and ask them, 'Who wants to buy a present?'

Sidney would doubtless have told the Chief Super all about Noakes's 'freelance' activities, so the DI was careful to stick to the criminal profile agenda, sprinkling his summary with liberal references to 'our expert Professor Finlayson from the university'.

Ebury-Clarke regarded him suspiciously.

'Are you saying there's a viable suspect then?' he barked, looking distinctly unhappy with the notion of Graham Thorpe and Henry Morland as contenders for the top spot. Like Sidney, he clearly preferred the idea of a random psychopath to any suggestion that these murders might be the work of a prominent local figure.

'In terms of next steps, I want to bring in Thorpe, Morland, Pettifer and Vincent Rossi,' Markham said levelly. 'Based on Professor Finlayson's conclusions, they would seem to constitute our most promising suspect pool.'

The conversation was interrupted by the chief super's office telephone.

Ebury-Clarke looked distinctly shaken at the conclusion of the call, his jowly features turning pale.

'Your suspect pool is down one man,' he told Markham tersely. 'Vincent Rossi was found dead this morning.'

The DI's stomach lurched. 'How did he die, sir?'

'Fell downstairs and broke his neck. It *looks* like an accident, but in the circumstances . . .'

. . . *coming on top of four homicides, it was unlikely to be a natural death*, Markham thought grimly.

'Dr Patel's on the scene, so you'd better get round there sharpish. The address is 6 Cinder Lane. And Inspector,' the froglike eyes held a baleful expression, 'we stick with accidental death for the time being, otherwise we'll have a panic on our hands.'

'The family won't buy it, sir. Too much of a coincidence.'

Ebury-Clarke's eyes narrowed to slits.

'I'm counting on you to bring the family onside, Inspector,' he snapped. 'No unseemly outbursts or anyone going off-message.'

Onside. Off-message. God, he made it sound like a corporate manoeuvre.

But Markham held on to his temper despite his revulsion at Ebury-Clarke's cold-blooded way of talking. No point antagonizing a superior officer . . . not if he wanted to keep this case. And right now, he wanted it more than anything else in the world.

'Of course, sir,' he said pacifically.

Once safely clear of the chief super's office, he texted Noakes:

Meet me and the team at our favourite Italian as soon as you can get off. VR sleeping with the fishes.

Cryptic (and a touch melodramatic), but he couldn't risk being more direct. His friend would realize what had gone down but should anyone else come upon the message, it would look like banter between mates.

On his way to round up Kate and the others, Markham said a prayer for this latest victim. He hadn't really registered Vincent Rossi otherwise than as a darkly good-looking, somewhat louring presence in the Rossi family circle. But there had been an impression of quiet strength and dependability, notwithstanding a certain grouchiness at Sheila Craven's wake when responsibility for the whole affair seemed to devolve upon the Rossi clan. The parents, along with his sisters Marina and little Giulia, would be devastated. He could only hope their faith would see them through.

In the meantime, time to step up a gear.

That meant putting Morland, Thorpe and Pettifer under surveillance. If Nathan Finlayson was right about the suspect profile, those three had to be his priority.

It would take very little for Ebury-Clarke to pass the investigation over to the big boys at AMIT, so he was living on borrowed time.

Somehow he had to make the killer break cover.

* * *

Cinder Lane was a quiet leafy street a little way outside Bromgrove town centre. With its mixture of modernistic dormer bungalows and chalet-style properties in Cotswold stone, it exuded quiet middle-class affluence. The police cars, crime scene tape and ambulance parked outside number 6 told a more sinister story, however.

Once kitted up in paper suits, Dr Patel met them at the foot of an impressive floating glass staircase which led from the open plan ground floor to the bedrooms. Markham had an impression of whitewashed walls, minimalist black leather furniture and gleaming onyx floor tiles along with lots of glass, chrome and stainless steel before his attention was riveted by the body which lay splayed at the bottom of the stairs, lying at an unnatural angle that showed the neck was broken. A strand of dried blood at the corner of one eye, along with the sagging jaw and glazed wide-open eyes, gave the young restaurateur the incongruous look of a drunk who had come off worse in a street brawl.

Suddenly Markham thought of Serena Rossi. Vincent would not want his mother to see him like this.

'Who found him?' he asked a hovering sergeant.

'The cleaner, sir.'

'Has the family been informed?

'Not yet, sir,' came the reply. 'Apparently they're getting ready for the lunchtime service.'

'Good, let's keep it like that until I can get over there. Kate, I want you to put a call through to the duty manager or whoever's in charge. Then post a couple of plain clothes outside. Tell them, no one allowed in or out of the restaurant without my say so . . . oh, except for George Noakes. He can hold the fort and keep the family on an even keel until we get there. Everything low-key . . . like we're just stopping them being pestered about George Parker. He met her gaze squarely. 'Give the impression Noakesy's an FLO or something.'

I might have known! But Kate Burton's mild exasperation was tinged with relief. Her old sparring partner had a definite knack when it came to dealing with the bereaved, so he could be trusted with this. And the situation was unusually sensitive in that the Rossis themselves couldn't be ruled out as suspects.

Markham turned to the pathologist. 'What would you say we're looking at, Dr Patel?'

'The poor man's condition is consistent with an accident last night, only . . .'

'What's bothering you?' Markham prompted.

'There's bruising on his forearms . . . fairly recent I would say, as though from someone gripping him tightly.'

'Any chance it could be sports injuries?'

'Possibly.' But the medic was clearly uneasy. 'There's a bottle of what looks like ketamine in the kitchen too . . . One of the side effects is blurred vision, so if the deceased was abusing drugs he could well have become disorientated.'

'Any sign of him being force fed the stuff?'

'Not that I could see . . . But if a visitor called around with a couple of cans, easy enough for them to slip the ketamine into a beer or whatever and then just leave it ready for you to find—'

'Making it look like Mr Rossi was into recreational drugs,' Markham finished grimly. It made him angry that, not content with killing Vincent, the killer had tried to take his good name away too.

'The landing's laid out as a snug, so if they went up there for a chinwag it would have been ideal in terms of manhandling him towards the stairs,' Patel continued.

'Is that what you think happened, doc?' It was rare that Markham made such a blunt appeal, but he badly needed to know. Of course the killer would have worn gloves, but a nod from Patel would help make the case for Vincent Rossi being victim number five.

The pathologist's gentle gaze was typically direct. 'I think this is a homicide, Inspector,' he said quietly. 'As things stand, the post-mortem is unlikely to prove it conclusively, but speaking personally I would say you're looking at another one.'

'Thank you.'

'You're welcome, Inspector.' The other's eyes held a wealth of compassion. 'If you'll permit, I will just say a brief prayer.'

Patel said, 'Sogyal Rinpoche, the Tibetan master tells us, "What is born will die. What has been gathered will be dispersed" . . . We pray that our brother now beholds in death's mirror the true meaning of life reflected.'

Markham found himself almost unbearably moved.

We see through a glass darkly; but then face to face.

'Much appreciated, doctor.'

Dr Patel gestured to the waiting paramedics, somehow investing the little cortege with ineffable dignity. The detectives bowed their heads as Vincent Rossi left his home for the final time.

'*Sir*,' Doyle said urgently as they fanned through the property looking for clues, 'Vincent was down to look after the kid sister this afternoon with it being the summer holidays . . . there's a reminder pinned on the fridge, one of those magnetic diary planners. No way would he have been necking ketamine, *no way*.'

Markham knew that Doyle came from a closeknit Lancashire clan (Nan the matriarch and everyone else duly subservient), not unlike the Rossis with their emphasis on traditional values above all else. So he gave due credence to the young sergeant's viewpoint.

'He just wouldn't get off his face, guv,' Doyle insisted. 'His mum would *crucify* him.'

The DI was inclined to believe it. Vincent Rossi had struck him as a family man first and foremost. And he knew that Italian men were apt to adore their mothers and female relatives. Somehow it just didn't *fit* that protective Vincent would have abdicated his responsibilities and indulged in a casual ketamine orgy.

No, Markham was certain that their killer felt compelled to eliminate Vincent because the young Italian was on to him.

But would they be able to uncover what it was that Vincent had found out?

'Well done, Sergeant,' he said to Doyle, aware how much this investigation had unsettled the youngster. 'I think we should get over to Rossi's now and see what the family can tell us.'

* * *

Noakes was already at the restaurant when the team arrived, sitting at a table with proprietors. 'The waiters haven't come on shift yet,' he told the DI. 'It's just kitchen staff out back.' Speaking out of the corner of his mouth, he added, 'I haven't said owt, jus' told them you needed to have a word.' Serena Rossi's strained expression, however, suggested that she already suspected this was bad news.

At a nod from Markham, Kate Burton gently suggested to the parents that they should go somewhere private. Upon which, Serena set up a bloodcurdling wail that brought Marina and Matteo rushing from the kitchen.

'Oh no, oh my God no. He's dead, isn't he? My Vincent's dead!'

His face full of compassion, Markham gave a nod of confirmation.

As the anguished mother rocked to and fro, Noakes knelt down beside her.

'Come on, lass. You gotta be strong for the rest of 'em now. Your boy's counting on you to hold it together, you can't let him down now.'

Serena Rossi looked at the big awkward Yorkshireman, his pug-like features full of sympathy and concern. Very carefully, he took one of her slim hands into his own huge one and squeezed it, almost trying to contract his stocky frame so as not to overwhelm the woman with his massiveness. The woman looked at the paw into which her own small hand had disappeared as though mesmerized.

'Whatever happened, you're his mum an' you'll always be his mum. Nobody can ever take that away from you,' Noakes said in a voice so soft that Doyle and Carruthers could hardly believe this was the former terror — the legendary bogeyman — of CID whose countenance was usually all thunder and lightning.

'Vincent was all for family, right. So that means you gotta keep things going, like he'd expect you to.' Somehow his voice had a hypnotic effect, while the rest of them might as well not have been in the room. 'Never fear, you'll see your lad again,' Noakes continued, striking a free, confident tone that took it for granted. And then this avowed anti-Papist, said something extraordinary in the rough, veiled voice that Doyle and Carruthers barely recognized. 'Go an' say Hail Marys an' a Rosary an' whatever for him. But then we want you right back here to help us find out what happened.'

With her gaze riveted on Noakes's face, somehow deriving comfort from those curranty eyes fixed on hers, Serena Rossi managed to take a proper breath instead of little shallow gasps and allowed herself to be guided by Burton and Doyle out of the dining room.

The subsequent interview with Francesco Rossi was one of the hardest of Markham's career, the proud head of the clan literally crumpling before him, punctured like some pitiful paper bag.

But then Serena Rossi came back into the dining room, with a new light in her eyes, leading little Giulia by the hand.

Noakes squatted down on his haunches.

'How do,' he said politely. 'Are you going to help us then?'

Little Giulia looked up at the big, clumsy, tomato-faced ex detective, her coal-black eyes a-glitter. Whatever she saw in Noakes's countenance seemed to reassure her.

'I remember Vinnie got really cross one time when Auntie Barbara called,' she said.

'How come, sweetheart?' Again, such was his gentleness, that no one from CID would have recognized their resident philistine (or the Grinch, as younger officers called him).

'She came round one night and they were yelling at each other . . . something about Uncle Ed and Vinnie being angry with him. I shouldn't have been listening, but I was thirsty and came out of my room to get a drink . . .'

'Go on, luv.' The grumpy Saint Bernard's features were as relaxed as possible to reassure the child. 'Can you remember anything else?'

'Vinnie said Uncle Ed should grow something and Barbara mustn't be cross about him not wanting to get married.' Giulia screwed up her face with the effort of remembering and cracked her knuckles with the air of a poor student, 'And he said to leave Uncle Matty alone.'

The little girl was transparently sincere, as well as guilty for having overheard something that was never meant for her ears. 'Uncle Matty's getting married to Marina and they're busy here.' She shook her head gravely. 'So he wouldn't have time to help Uncle Ed with gardening and stuff.'

Markham's eyes met Noakes's over Giulia's head.

He was willing to be that Vincent had said Ed Frayling needed to *grow a pair* and told Barbara Price to ease off on her plans to get the young waiter down the aisle.

There'd been a row . . .

Barbara Price.

Ed Frayling.

Auntie Barbara and Uncle Ed.

'Thass *champion*, ducks. Reckon we could do with you in CID.' Noakes beamed at Giulia. 'Should've known you'd have your big brother's back.'

With that, Markham's wingman put an arm round the child and shepherded her through to the kitchen. 'Give this lass a hot chocolate with extra marshmallows!' they heard him declare ebulliently. 'By heck she's earned it!'

Returning to the restaurant, Noakes looked Markham straight in the eye.

'You've got to break the girlfriend, boss. She must've given him a false alibi.'

Markham felt a rush of nervous energy so strong that it was as though his whole frame was on fire.

Everything outside the windows of the restaurant had faded to a transparent thinness above the voyaging clouds.

Everything was marvellously light, as though he had received an electric current through his vital powers.

Come on. This is it. Zero hour.

CHAPTER 12

The atmosphere in Markham's office a short time later was tense but energized, the team and Noakes galvanized with fresh hope.

'Thanks for your help with the family, Noakesy,' Markham said. 'It was a great rapport you established back there.'

'Well, they sure ain't buying the idea that poor lad snorted ketamine an' then fell downstairs,' the other said laconically. '*No way.*'

'I think after what Giulia said, that particular theory bites the dust,' Markham replied with no small satisfaction. 'And we now have ourselves a prime suspect.' *At last!*

Doyle was ever ready to play devil's advocate.

'But *Ed Frayling*!' he protested. 'He was never even in the running. Nice laid-back dude . . . easy-going personality . . . girlfriend's a bit boring perhaps . . .' Privately, however, the young DS felt there was something to be said for boring, his helter-skelter romantic history confirming his belief that lookers and livewires were often more trouble than they were worth. 'The pair of them seemed solid,' he continued. 'Frayling doesn't come across like some creepy incel or psycho with a gay backstory.'

'He's in the music business,' Carruthers pointed out. 'Does gigs, remember. So that could be a connection with Parker.'

'That's right,' Burton put in thoughtfully. 'He told us it was *nothing big league*. I remember thinking there was something defeated and disappointed about the way he said that.'

'So you reckon he could've resented George Parker for hitting the big time while he was kind of stuck on the bottom rung?' Carruthers asked her.

'Yes, something like that.' Burton's voice gained in conviction as she continued, 'Look, there he is . . . just a waiter in the local Italian grubbing around to make ends meet, with Parker swanking around giving it the big "I Am" and making Ed feel like he's just small fry . . . clicking his fingers at the staff, with everyone expected to bow and scrape like mad—'

'Jus' cos he's a sleb,' Noakes concluded heavily. 'Mind you, there's nowt wrong with earning an honest living an' being a waiter. He had no call to be ashamed . . . It's better than being a long-haired dropout doing pot an' living off his girlfriend.'

Doyle grinned at the predictable mistrust of artistic types and encomium to traditional values.

'You're right there,' Burton said soothingly, being well versed in the art of managing her former colleague. 'There's nothing wrong with working at Rossi's, and Francesco did say they were lining Ed up for a promotion. But when all's said and done, it's a family business, which means he'd always be playing second fiddle to Marina, Vincent and Matteo . . . never part of the inner circle.' And didn't she know what *that* felt like! Noakes's shrewd piggy eyes were trained on her, but Burton's expression remained bland. 'Then there's his relationship with Barbara,' she continued. 'Maybe the "love's young dream" schtick is a cover for all kinds of problems.'

'Like him fancying blokes?' Carruthers demanded bluntly.

'He wouldn't be the first,' Burton insisted. 'It's quite possible that there's some kind of double life going on.'

'If Barbara was badgering him to get married, that could've brought everything to a head,' Doyle speculated, recalling with an inward shudder what he went through with one-time fiancée Paula on that score.

'*Precisely,*' Burton replied approvingly. 'Put all that suppressed resentment and smouldering jealousy of George Parker into the mix and, well, you could see how the fuse might have been lit.'

'Presumably Vincent Rossi clocked the problems between Ed and Barbara, which is why he told Barbara she should back off,' Doyle picked up the thread. 'But then what was all that about Ed needing to leave Uncle Matty alone?'

'Vincent was observant,' Markham said calmly. 'He must have picked up on sexual vibes that other people hadn't registered.'

'As in Ed having the hots for Matteo?' Doyle's voice shot up an octave. 'But wouldn't we have noticed if there was anything like that going on . . . I mean wouldn't there be tell-tale signs or clues or something?'

'Matteo Bianchi's a strikingly handsome young man,' Markham replied, thinking of the "Italian Stallion". 'And in retrospect, I *do* recall that Ed's eyes seemed to follow him a lot . . .'

'Could just be he was keen to impress the Rossis' future son-in-law,' Doyle suggested. 'You know, get well in with the family . . . feet under the table kind of thing.'

'No, looking back there *was* something else,' the DI demurred. With a grimace, he added, 'Of course, as DCI Sidney is ever wont to remind me, hindsight is a wonderful thing.' Which elicited smirks all round. 'But in this case, I'm inclined to believe there *were* signs that I was slow to pick up on.'

Burton didn't want any self-flagellation by the man she admired above all others (even more than Nathan, if truth be told).

'We don't know when Vincent met up with Barbara,' she began.

'Yeah we do,' Noakes interrupted. 'I checked with Marina an' she said the little lass last had a sleepover with Vincent beginning of June at half term. So that's when the thing with Babs went down.'

'*OK*,' Burton said slowly. 'Nice work, sarge . . . So Vincent cottoned on to signs that things weren't right with Ed and Barbara a couple of months back.'

'An' twigged Ed mebbe had his sights fixed on ole Matty an' wanted to put a stop to any funny business sharpish,' Noakes went on. Turning to Markham, he asked, 'D'you reckon Mister Italian Pinup sussed that Frayling fancied him?'

'Unlikely,' Markham replied. 'But I suspect Vincent was somehow worried about Ed's stability and didn't want any kind of ructions that would upset the commercial applecart.'

'Maybe he wondered whether Ed were doing drugs,' Noakes hypothesized in sepulchral tones that suggested anything was possible when it came to hipsters in the music industry.

'I wouldn't be at all surprised,' the DI concurred. He took a deep breath. 'Look, here we have this young waiter at the local Italian . . . a talented musician who has somehow never fulfilled his early promise, forced to watch moneyed patrons and celebrities like George Parker "flash the cash" in Medway, while he trudges along with unexciting, dependable social worker Barbara, the woman he's settled for but doesn't love.'

'I overheard her at Sheila Craven's wake telling one of the old biddies she didn't want to be a regular social worker cos all that stuff made her depressed.' Noakes sniffed forcefully in disparagement of such pusillanimity. 'She said she planned to get a part-time job with a charity an' take time out to start a family.'

'Quite possibly Frayling's ultimate nightmare,' Markham pointed out. 'If that's right, no doubt he saw the prison gates clanging shut—'

'An' then everything came to the boil,' Noakes finished eagerly.

'*Exactly*,' Markham nodded. 'Dr Patel believes George Parker's murder was pretty much contemporaneous with Stella Fanshaw's but whether it was before or after doesn't really matter ... The thing is, matters came to a head and he somehow *needed* to attack Parker ... *needed* that explosion of rage and tension.'

'Including the, er, sex stuff,' Noakes said awkwardly.

'Well, if there were repressed homosexual impulses towards Matteo and maybe others — who knows, possibly including Parker — that would account for the indications Nathan observed with the forensics.' Markham's features assumed an almost marble rigidity that told Burton he was concentrating hard. 'OK,' he told the team, 'let's just think about Frayling's alibis for the murders.'

'How do we know he ain't out there right now planning who to bump off next?' Noakes challenged.

'I've placed him and Ms Price under twenty-four hour surveillance, Noakesy.' *And to hell with the overtime budget.* 'The Rossis have been asked to toe the official line about Vincent's death being a tragic accident. Obviously they don't believe it for a moment,' he added quickly, forestalling Noakes's objection, 'but it's essential Ed doesn't realize we're on his trail.'

'Fair enough,' Noakes grunted. 'So what about the alibis then?'

A small narrow frown appeared like a half line between Markham's eyes.

'When Sheila Craven died, Ed was apparently doing circuit training in Medway Park followed by coffee with Barbara who gave him a lift into work.' The DI paused. 'It's entirely feasible that Barbara was unaware he made a diversion to the Copse to kill Sheila before joining her.'

Burton took up the narrative. 'But with Norman Collins's murder, she *must* have covered for him, because she said they were at home together all evening — "slobbing in their onesies being couch potatoes" was how she put it.' Ruefully, the DI added, 'I have to say she was totally convincing, she even talked about them having a TV dinner and channel hopping.'

'The vicar was killed around eight o'clock, so Frayling must've slipped out,' Carruthers said. 'And yeah, she *must have known*.'

Doyle moved on to the other victims. 'Then there's Frayling's alibi for Fanshaw and Parker,' he began.

'Don' tell me,' Noakes weighed in with heavy sarcasm, 'the love birds were snuggled up on the sofa again.'

'Apparently they went for a walk on Bromgrove Rise after Sheila Craven's wake. Felt a bit emotional . . . blah blah,' Carruthers informed him. 'Got home around three and decided to veg out.'

'But he nipped out again,' Noakes said cynically, 'by way of Saint Michael's an' the cemetery . . . cos he had unfinished business with Fanshaw an' Parker.'

'If he *did* go out, she wasn't telling us,' Carruthers sighed. 'It'll most likely be the same story for Wednesday night when Vincent was killed.'

The very time he himself was wallowing in self-pity at the Sweepstakes, debating whether or not to drown his sorrows, Markham thought with some compunction.

'Ed no doubt came up with a plausible excuse each time he was absent,' he said. 'And she simply didn't feel able to challenge him . . . or face the truth.'

'She's a decent enough kid, though,' Doyle mused, remembering Barbara Price's kind, plain face and the way she was practically the only person who made any effort with Tricia Dent at Sheila Craven's wake. 'And with working in the care sector, it doesn't seem like she'd be willing to cover for a cold-blooded killer, even if he *was* her fiancé.'

'She's heavily invested in the relationship,' Markham pointed out. 'So I think she would have beaten down any doubts . . . This is the man she wants to marry . . . it *unthinkable* that he could be a killer.'

'But Vincent was on to him, right?' Carruthers was anxious to pin down the rationale behind the final victim's death.

'Presumably he saw something or suspected something . . . coming on top of lurking doubts about Ed, he decided to confront him,' Markham replied.

'But why go it alone, for God's sake?' Carruthers burst out. 'I mean, if he'd got it right, this was a four times killer he was taking on . . .'

'He mightn't have been sure Ed *was* the high street killer,' Doyle offered. 'In which case, he wouldn't want to accuse their potential assistant manager without being a hundred per cent certain . . . I mean, imagine if things kicked off with Ed and they ended up with a truckload of negative publicity.'

'Better than finishing drugged up to the eyeballs with a broken neck,' Carruthers retorted.

'Mebbe he wanted all the glory for being the one to catch a serial killer,' Noakes suggested. 'Best-ever PR for Rossi's . . . *that* would make 'em famous all right.' He made a sour face. 'I c'n jus' see Gavin Conors packaging little Giulia as Bromgrove's answer to Shirley Temple!'

'Hubris could well have been a factor,' Markham agreed, thinking sadly that matters so often ended badly when people overreached themselves. 'Or Doyle could be right about Vincent hesitating . . . unsure whether he wasn't headed down a blind alley.'

Burton nodded vigorously. 'Let's face it, *we're* having a hard enough time getting our heads round the idea of Ed being a killer. And this was someone the Rossis were grooming for promotion . . . someone they relied on. He and Barbara were practically extended family for goodness' sake. '

'Yeah, Barbara still did the odd shift when they needed it,' Doyle pointed out.

'So Vincent could have felt there was a lot at stake,' Markham concluded. 'He'd given Barbara a bit of a heads-up but then decided he needed to clear the air with Ed.' A decision which cost him his life.

Carruthers turned to Markham.

'You said Vincent must've had misgivings about Ed, boss.'

'That's right.'

'Well, what d'you reckon made him start wondering about Ed in the first place?'

The DI smiled wearily. 'Ah, there's the million-dollar question,' he said. After some moments of intense cogitation, he went on, 'Maybe he suspected Ed might have tried to tap Sheila Craven for money or a loan . . . In the beginning, I dismissed this as highly improbable, but now I can see there were undercurrents that Vincent may have cottoned onto.'

Noakes's beady eyes widened at this.

'You reckon Frayling tried buttering her up for dosh . . . like some sort of *gigolo*?'

Markham considered it. 'Well, I remember that Ed said something about wanting to start his own music magazine . . . "when his boat came in or he could find someone to sponsor him".' The DI didn't mention that this was when he and Noakes had dined at Rossi's with Olivia, recalling just in time the hurt look in Burton's eyes as she waited for an invitation that never came.

'Oh yeah.' With unusual tact, Noakes too omitted any reference to that supper with Olivia. 'It seemed like he had big plans.'

'That's right,' the DI concurred. 'Underneath the surface cheerfulness, I had the sense of a young man in the doldrums who was frustrated that he couldn't make his dreams come true . . . forced to wait tables because he couldn't follow his true calling.'

'What about the gigs and stuff?' Doyle asked. 'He had a bit of a sideline going, after all. And he was still young. I mean, it's not like everything was all over for him.'

'Hmm.' The DI shook his head. 'Despite the personableness and breezy manner, I remember thinking there was something hollowed out, almost *withered*, about him, like ungrown despair . . . a young man in a hurry who saw himself going nowhere fast—'

'And headed for marriage, which was the last thing he wanted because it made him feel trapped,' Burton interjected.

'Plus, he'd figured out he were gay,' Noakes grunted. 'So he needed an escape route an' thought he could mebbe get round some old bird who came into the restaurant and fund a new start.'

Burton winced at 'old bird', but the other was oblivious. 'If you're right, guv,' Noakes persisted, 'he could've oiled up to folk who looked like they'd got money to burn an' Vincent *noticed* . . . or p'raps a customer said something.'

'I remember thinking at the wake that Ed was conspicuously charming with the elderly female mourners and parishioners,' Markham replied. 'But of course, there *are* young men, especially in church circles, who always seem comfortable around older women and have the knack of being sweet and attentive. It didn't seem suspicious or sinister but Vincent might have had a very different take on what was happening . . . might have suspected there were mercenary motives at the back of it.'

'If Ed had hopes of Sheila Craven but she dragged her heels or turned him down — maybe even threatened to complain to the Rossis — then it would have been another twist of the rack,' Burton breathed. 'You know, guv, I can see it happening like that. Ed sang in the choir with her . . . she was this elderly widow who came into Rossi's from time to time . . . he counted on lashings of charm getting results—'

'Only she rumbled his game an' didn't like it,' Noakes wound up dourly. 'The woman knew what was what. I remember Matteo saying she didn't like the waitresses making cow eyes at Tom an' all that, so she'd have known what Ginge was after.'

'If he thought it was in the bag and she shot him down in flames, *that's* what might have made him lose control,' Carruthers opined.

'What about the vicar?' Doyle asked. 'Where the heck does *he* fit in?'

'Ed's a churchgoer and member of Saint Michael's choir,' Burton answered. 'So it's more than likely Norman Collins knew him and Barbara pretty well . . . I'm pretty sure I overheard Barbara telling someone at the wake that they had been following some sort of marriage schedule with the vicar.'

'*Marriage schedule*?' Doyle asked, thinking that it sounded like a train timetable.

'Pre-marriage instruction . . . sessions with the priest to prepare them,' Burton explained, thinking that this was something she and Nathan would no doubt have to navigate in due course if they opted for a church wedding.

Doyle's expression suggested he shared her apprehension about the nuptial "Ball and Chain".

'Anyway,' she went on hastily, 'Mr Collins could have realized something was very wrong with Ed . . . Maybe, like Vincent, he had suspicions and challenged Ed—'

'If Collins worried about Ed being gay or bi or whatever, he could've been encouraging Barbara to tie the knot as soon as possible,' Carruthers suggested, 'and him interfering was like a red rag to a bull.'

'That too,' Burton agreed.

'But if he thought Ed was screwy or promiscuous, surely Collins wouldn't have wanted Barbara to hitch up with him? I mean, sealing the deal with a *killer!*' Doyle objected.

'I doubt it was as clear-cut as that,' Markham pointed out. 'More like this tiny cloud on the horizon . . . the vicar feeling somehow vaguely uneasy about Ed without being able to put a name to his fears. Perhaps, like Barbara, he didn't care to examine his misgivings too closely.'

'Mebbe Sheila Craven said summat about Frayling hitting on her . . . pestering her for help, that kind of thing,' Noakes volunteered.

'Eminently feasible, Noakesy. As I say, Mr Collins may have instinctively sensed an aura of danger around Ed and somehow betrayed his fears so that it became too big a risk to let him live.'

Doyle was still struggling with the notion of Ed Frayling as their prime suspect.

'There *is* something about him,' he mused. Quickly he added, 'It's not the fact that he's gay . . . more that he just doesn't look like he's got it in him to go round strangling and coshing . . . doesn't have the brawn for one thing.'

Markham came to the youngster's rescue.

'I know what you mean, Sergeant,' he said, thinking of the slim young man with his charming diffidence, melodious voice and sleek complexion. 'But remember his circuit training? And even the unlikeliest of candidates can be tiger-cats ready to spring . . . Besides, what Giulia told us makes Mr Frayling a promising lead.'

'Yeah, but she's just a kid,' Doyle came back. 'Who's to say she didn't get the wrong end of the stick . . .? Had a nightmare and then convinced herself she'd heard Barbara and Vincent arguing?'

'*Nah.*' Noakes was staunch in his support of Giulia. 'She heard them all right.' His face clouded over. 'When Serena told her that Vincent was dead, the poor kid came straight out with it cos she thought it were somehow all her fault for being naughty an' earwigging.'

'I agree.' Markham's tone was decisive. 'What Giulia said had the ring of authenticity. She didn't come across as showboating or attention-seeking . . . I'd say, a credible little character.'

'OK. So where do we go from here, boss?' Doyle asked. 'So far it's just the word of a kid.'

The CPS would make mincemeat of us, was his subtext.

'I want to bring Barbara Price in,' Markham said calmly. 'But *discreetly*, without Ed knowing anything about it . . . ideally when he's on shift at the restaurant.'

'I can sort that,' Burton responded promptly.

'It would be good to dig into Ed's antecedents at Saint Michael's too,' the DI continued. 'I have a *hunch*,' he made a wry expression as he used Sidney's least favourite epithet, 'that we may find a connection to some kind of sodality associated with Saint Joseph . . . youth club, junior music group, altar servers' guild — something on those lines.'

'You reckon there could've been abuse going on, guv?' Noakes demanded bluntly. 'Some holy joe taking advantage?'

Well aware that such a conjecture was very little to Kate Burton's taste — her solidly Anglican upbringing equating to an intrinsic respect for authority whereas Noakes's Methodism made him generally less reverential towards the clergy — Markham steadily replied, 'I think it's possible there was some formative experience that may have resulted in a disordered sexuality along with suppressed resentment of religious officialdom and older people.'

Kate Burton was too professional ever to allow personal prejudice or distaste to obstruct an investigation. Scribbling busily in her little notebook, she concentrated on updating her *To Do* list.

Doyle's thoughts turned to their third victim. 'What about Stella Fanshaw then?' he asked. 'Did Frayling try to get money out of her as well, only she said no and then he flipped?'

'Perhaps Sheila had said something to Stella about Ed that niggled — that he'd pestered her for money or she thought he might be using the church to target vulnerable women,' Carruthers suggested. 'And Frayling was afraid she might blab.'

Burton tapped the gold-topped pen against her teeth. 'Or the vicar might've shared his concerns with Stella and then Frayling somehow found out about it.'

'Entirely possible,' Markham concurred. 'The Good Book tells us the root of all evil is money, and I think it's likely Ed's obsession with financial gain was a major factor behind these killings. Taken with a confused sexuality and triggers from adolescence, you might say he was a time bomb waiting to go off.'

They were interrupted by the telephone on Markham's desk.

At the conclusion of the short call, he turned to the team, his expression unreadable.

'Well, that's an intriguing development,' he said.

'What is?' Noakes demanded impatiently.

'Henry Morland is downstairs asking to see me.'

His colleagues looked blank.

'I'd forgotten all about Grigory's Boy,' Noakes said at last, the two sergeants groaning at the feeble pun.

'It always seemed like *Morland* was a good bet,' Doyle mused. 'Religious maniac,' he caught Burton's gimlet eye, 'er, I mean, *scholar*. Iffy past . . . *controversial* . . . mixed up in scandal.'

Carruthers grinned as though to say, *Stop digging!*

'Seemed like a stronger prospect than Frayling,' he offered as his colleague shot him a grateful glance. 'I mean, you could imagine *him* throttling and clobbering people whereas the other looks well, I dunno, too feminine somehow.'

'Very effective camouflage in the circumstances,' Markham observed with some asperity. He turned to Burton. 'Bring Nathan up to speed will you, Kate. See what he thinks about Ed Frayling as our number one suspect . . . then we're going to need a strategy for nailing him—'

'Assuming Babs agrees to play ball,' Noakes finished grimly.

'Maybe whatever Morland gives us will provide leverage,' Carruthers said.

'Indeed.'

Markham's ears began to sing a little.

They were so near to a breakthrough, he told himself. *So near.*

'I'll see Morland in the interview suite in twenty minutes, which gives Kate time to brief Nathan and alert the top brass,' he said. 'I want the whole team there.'

'In for the kill,' Doyle said looking satisfied before blushing violently as he realized what he had said.

Noakes pulled out his mobile. 'I'll jus' check in with Rosemount . . . Got a deputy now,' he told them proudly. 'Young lad on an apprenticeship, coming along nicely an' dead keen to learn.'

Markham regarded his friend affectionately. God only knew what some wet-behind-the-ears novice made of the old warhorse, but his traineeship was likely to prove one hell of a ride.

'Twenty minutes tops,' he told them soberly. 'The clock's ticking.'

* * *

If Henry Morland was taken aback to be confronted with Markham's entire team in an atmosphere that fairly vibrated with tension, he showed no sign of it.

'Would I be right in assuming that there's been a development?' he asked looking, as Doyle said afterwards, like *he* was the one in charge.

'You give us a name, Dr Morland, and we'll tell you if you're right,' Markham said without preamble. 'The investigation has reached a critical juncture, so we will be very grateful for any information you can provide. Whatever you tell us remains within these four walls.'

'There was a rather intense young man who came to the Healing Centre a year or so ago,' Morland replied. 'As I recall, he had something of a fixation with Rasputin. He fairly peppered me with questions about how he used hypnotism to win over older women in particular . . . devout types and churchgoers . . . Finally, he asked about courses in hypnotherapy for the elderly — said he was a music student and fancied a change of direction because his girlfriend worked in social services or something like that. I'd seen him round and about, he mentioned having to wait tables in Rossi's while he tried to make it as a musician. Seemed decent enough, though one had a sense of troubled waters. The centre didn't offer the type of course he was after, but I gave him the name of a few places he could check out.'

'An' you've only remembered all this *now?*'

Noakes's tone was pugnacious, but it didn't appear to bother their interviewee.

'It was a somewhat unusual encounter, but there was no reason why it should have stuck in my mind.' With a sardonic gleam, he added, 'After all, Rasputinists come in all shapes and guises.'

Touché, Markham thought in amusement.

'It was only when I saw him wandering round Saint Michael's cemetery that I recalled our meeting . . . Something about the way he looked bothered me . . .'

'When was this, sir?' Burton asked quickly.

'Sunday evening . . . about eight o'clock. It was still fairly light, so I got a good look at him.'

'What were you doing in the graveyard at that time of night?' Noakes demanded before anyone else could jump in. 'Strange place for a stroll.'

'The parish council wants to commission an antiquarian history of the church and its grounds. They've asked if I might be interested.' Again, that glint in his eye. 'My interest is purely academic, as opposed to vampiric.'

Collapse of stout party. Markham mentally awarded Morland points for his easy sang-froid.

'What was it that troubled you?' the DI asked quietly.

'The look of concentrated hatred in his face,' came the prompt reply. 'He was standing where the oldest graves are . . . I was over to the right, looking at a little portico structure that used to be a columbarium before it fell into disrepair. You can still see some inscriptions to various archangels on the cremation niches.'

'Presumably he didn't notice you?' Markham remarked.

'No. To be honest, it looked like he was in a world of his own . . . and judging by his expression, his thoughts were none of the pleasantest.'

'And you recognized him as the young man you'd spoken to before?'

'Oh yes. But it was odd . . . he'd, well, *gone off* somehow . . .'

'You make him sound like mouldy cheese,' Noakes growled.

Morland's expression was suddenly bleak. 'It's difficult to explain, but the youth I met had come across as quite personable . . . slight and not very tall, but frank-looking with an engaging manner . . .'

'And you felt there'd been some sort of deterioration?' Markham prompted, remembering his own sense of some hidden deformity — something gnawing at Ed Frayling that he hadn't been able to articulate at the time.

'He just stood there with a strange, contorted expression — almost as though another entity had taken over . . .

Frankenstein's monster or something equally sinister.' Morland exhaled as though to steady himself. 'No doubt this all sounds terribly far-fetched, but I had a real sense of evil.'

'You didn't come to us, though,' Carruthers pointed out. 'And more people died,' he added ruthlessly.

'All I had was intuition . . . *guesswork*,' Morland replied composedly, though he had turned very pale. 'Can you honestly say you would've taken me seriously?'

'We'll never know now, will we?' Noakes said with brutal emphasis.

'It's all too easy to take someone's name away,' their interviewee told them. '*Calumny and detraction*,' he enunciated stonily, like the Catholic priest he had once been. 'Moreover,' with a curl of the lip, 'I was aware my reputation had gone before me, so any talk of psychic insights wouldn't necessarily be well received . . . and you'd most probably assume I was trying to deflect suspicion elsewhere.'

The tone of voice showed that Morland knew all too well he had himself been a strong contender for prime suspect.

'You ain't said who it is yet,' Noakes pointed out with his customary bulldog tenacity.

'After seeing him in the cemetery, I checked my records. The young man's name is Ed Frayling and I think he may be . . . a person of interest.'

'Yes,' Markham confirmed. 'We're very interested in him in connection to the murders.'

A spasm of shock rippled across Morland's face before he managed: 'Thinking about the murders, something crystallized in my mind and I knew I had to come to you.'

'We're glad that you did, sir,' Markham said simply. 'Thank you.'

After Morland had been shown out, Noakes muttered. 'Fanshaw, Parker an' Rossi all dead cos Mister Hocus Pocus were worried about "calumny an' detraction" . . . You couldn't make it up!'

'He has to live with that for the rest of his life, Noakesy,' the DI said gravely. 'And remorse is a terrible thing.' Still haunted by fear that he hadn't done enough to rescue his own dead brother from spiralling into drink and drugs as a result of the abuse that had scarred their childhood, Markham knew this better than most, clamping down on the familiar dull ache of regret as Jonathan's face momentarily swam before his eyes. If, as he suspected, it was the case that Ed Frayling's fiancée had closed her eyes to multiple murder, then Henry Morland's anguish would be as nothing compared to what lay in store for the social worker.

'Morland said Frayling wanted to know all about how Rasputin put women into a trance or what have you,' Carruthers recalled, 'and he was asking about hypnotherapy courses.'

Doyle was forcefully struck by this observation. '*Hey*, d'you reckon he tried any of that mind-control malarkey with Sheila Craven?'

'He'd have had a job getting Mrs C under,' Noakes spluttered.

'Maybe so,' Markham said slowly. 'But an interest in psychic manipulation appears significant in the circumstances.' *Not to say malign.* 'If Ed attempted anything of the kind and it backfired or he was challenged about it, that might have provoked a violent reaction.'

At any rate, said Noakes's grim expression, such shaman-like propensities constituted another nail in Ed Frayling's coffin.

'Right,' Markham called them to order, 'enough of the speculation. Let's see about getting Frayling's other half in. She'll be the key to it all.'

* * *

It was evening by the time Kate Burton arrived at the station with Barbara Price, installing her in the interview suite before reporting to Markham.

Fortuitously, with Price's fiancé doing the evening shift at Rossi's, there was no risk of their prime suspect being alerted to the fact that the police were closing in. Markham could not begin to imagine how Vincent Rossi's devastated family would manage to behave as normal, but Burton had assured him they were cooperative. 'I've briefed them, guv. They're an incredibly tight unit . . . putting the grieving on hold till we've got Frayling. They know if he gets a whiff of our interest, it's game over. Believe me, they'll do this for Vincent. They want his killer banged up for life.'

'We need a confession from Frayling,' the DI said. 'So our best option is to have Barbara confront him somewhere that we can stake out beforehand.'

'Groundhog Day,' she quipped, thinking with a sense of déjà vu that it always came down to this. *The cornered rat with nowhere left to hide*.

'Indeed.' He gestured to the papers that he had been studying. 'Please thank Nathan for his pointers. I'm just going to run through the prompt sheet one more time.'

His colleague took this as her cue to leave the office and head downstairs. But after she had gone, Markham made no effort to examine the notes, moving across to the window.

Outside, the sunlit clouds that had earlier scudded across the tops of leylandii in the station carpark were slowly turning teal-grey and sinking below the skyline. The DI's thoughts, however, were anything but sluggish.

He knew now that Ed Frayling was their man. Standing there, Doggie Dickerson's pungent criticism of his nephew-in-law, the would-be rock star, came back to him: 'An ego the size of St Mary's Cathedral . . . reckons the promoters are tossers for not seeing that he's the Next Big Thing.'

The youngster who Doggie had told him was under pressure from a nice steady girlfriend panting to get him to the altar.

Ungratified vanity and disappointed ambition had undoubtedly warped Frayling and set him on the road to murder. And it was likely a partner anxious for commitment had brought all his sexual insecurities bubbling to the surface.

Research by Doyle and Carruthers had established that the musician was both an altar server and attendee of

St Joseph's Youth Club until he suddenly dropped out in his teens, reappearing after a gap of some years to swell the church choir. Markham thought it probable there was more to Frayling's abrupt departure than mere teenage disaffection; some trauma or emotional dislocation whose origin was as yet obscure . . .

The cheery voices of uniforms in the carpark going off shift recalled him to the present.

There was a narrow window of opportunity for them to bring Barbara Price onside. She had to be back home before Frayling clocked off work, so they would need to work fast.

Swiftly, he scanned Finlayson's notes, relieved to have his endorsement for focusing on Frayling. The psychologist advised that when dealing with Barbara Price they should play down Ed's financial and sexual motivation for murder, on the basis that such ugly truths would disable the internal defences she had erected and in all likelihood cause her to shut down completely. Instead, they should frame what had happened as a case of mental breakdown leading to the attack on Sheila Craven, with the other murders part of a chain reaction when Frayling desperately tried to cover up what he had done, not least from panic lest he lose the life he had built with Barbara.

I am in blood stepp'd in so far that, should I wade no more, Returning were as tedious as go o'er.

Noakes, in particular, was unlikely to look favourably on the notion of Frayling as some kind of tragic hero, but Markham saw Finlayson's logic. Whatever Barbara Price did or didn't suspect about his murderous activities, non-judgmental sympathy was undoubtedly the best approach to take.

As, indeed, it proved.

With Noakes, Doyle and Carruthers watching from behind the one-way mirror, Kate Burton gently dismantled the false alibis, having first told the woman they knew that Vincent Rossi had raised concerns about Ed's mental health (keeping Giulia's name out of it) and there was significant evidence which pointed to his being under severe emotional strain.

'She jumped at the whole nervous breakdown scenario,' Doyle said wonderingly afterwards.

'Like a drowning woman,' Carruthers agreed.

''Course she did,' Noakes grunted. 'Means she don' have to face up to her part in it.'

Watching the slack-jawed, weepy social worker, he had detected more distress at the disintegration of her romantic idyll than pity for her fiancé's victims.

'We can't establish that she knew what he was up to, Noakesy,' Markham said quietly. 'It's reasonable for her to say she had no idea he was capable of anything like that and she only kept quiet about him going out from fear the police might fit him up — there were so many stories about innocent men being wrongly accused — and anyway, he often went out on his own because he found solitary rambles helped with his music . . . any number of excuses.'

'It's all bollocks, guv,' his friend said stubbornly. 'An' she's gonna get off scot-free.'

'More than likely. But the main thing is, we know Ed's booked a studio for some solo practice at the Music Factory tomorrow afternoon . . . We've got tomorrow morning while he's at work to stake it out. Now that Barbara's agreed to cooperate, there's every chance we'll get a confession.' With steely deliberation, Markham added, 'I want justice for Sheila Craven, Norman Collins, Stella Fanshaw, George Parker and Vincent Rossi.'

The roll call had its impact.

'Yeah, me an' all, guv,' Noakes mumbled.

'All right, back here six o'clock sharp tomorrow morning and we'll divvy up the tasks.'

'What if Price decides to tell Frayling that we're on to him?' Doyle asked. 'She's pretty nuts about him, after all.'

'It's a risk,' Markham agreed. 'But Nathan believes deep down she'll want to have it out with Ed. Judging by the snatches of conversation Giulia overheard, she needs to know if he ever slept with anyone else, including men, while they were together.'

'I thought Shippers said she couldn't face up to the sex stuff,' Noakes objected, 'an' thass why we had to spout all the crip crap about Frayling having a nervous breakdown.'

'He felt it would be counterproductive in terms of the initial interview,' Markham replied steadily. 'But he's fairly certain it's been preying on her mind for some while and now it's crunch time, she'll be desperate to find out one way or another.'

'D'you reckon she knew about the extortion, guv,' Carruthers asked. 'assuming Frayling was tapping folk for money?'

'Hard to say. Maybe once he's confessed, she'll be more forthcoming.'

'Wouldn't count on it,' Noakes muttered.

The DI noticed that his fellow DI looked very wan.

'Well done, all,' he said. 'especially you, Kate. Now go and get some sleep, ready for tomorrow.'

Noakes lingered in the doorway shuffling his feet.

'Yes, Noakesy. You too.'

His friend beamed. 'I'll square it with work,' he said happily.

After they had all gone, the DI made his way back upstairs.

It was quite dark now and the wind was getting up.

Ed Frayling would be arriving home shortly, unaware that the last act of the drama was imminent.

Markham seemed to feel unseen presences waiting invisibly in the wings.

The souls of the dead, demanding justice.

CHAPTER 13

'*Phew*, this place stinks of weed,' Noakes said early the next morning, wrinkling his nose as they stood in cannabis-scented studio 4 of the Music Factory, a collective which operated under the auspices of Bromgrove Council's Youth Enterprise Trust. Situated at the bottom of Porlock Mews, a narrow street lined with poky offices and garages, the property had been derelict for many years before the council took it over.

Markham had been determined to keep the entire operation low-key, but since it was indispensable to get the frowsy janitor onside, they had given him the impression this was CID reconnaissance for a drugs operation with 'all assistance gratefully received'. The odour that Noakes had detected made the drugs connection entirely feasible.

'Never fear, Worzel Gummidge's bound to call in the favour,' Noakes observed grumpily. 'He's even more decrepit than Doggie Dickerson.' And no doubt just as dodgy.

'Looks ideal for surveillance,' Carruthers murmured appreciatively as they wandered past the soundproof recording booths which served studios 4 to 6 on the second floor of the down-at-heel building.

'I've arranged with "Worzel" to tell Ed that the booths are temporarily out of bounds due to maintenance work,' Markham said. 'Rewiring or some excuse like that.'

'D'you reckon he'll buy it?' Doyle asked dubiously. 'I mean, this dump ain't exactly Abbey Road,' he said looking round at the peeling paint and scuffed lino. 'It doesn't seem like the council or whoever owns it gives a flying fajita about DIY or looking after the place.'

'We'll put up standard health and safety signage to give the impression that everything's official,' Markham replied easily. 'In Ed's overwrought state, I doubt he'll query it. And anyway, according to Barbara, he's only bothered about having a practice room — somewhere he can improvise and all the rest of it in private.'

'Is it just him?' Carruthers enquired. 'Or does he plan on bringing other people along for a jam session?'

'Barbara was positive he'll be alone,' Burton replied. 'He likes to unwind by himself.'

'After killing folk,' Noakes rumbled.

'Is Barbara really up for this, ma'am?' Doyle asked, echoing his concerns of the previous day. 'I mean, she looked pretty flaky from where I was standing . . . like she could easily blow our cover—'

'For *lurve*,' Carruthers cut in sardonically before adding, 'It's a good point. What's to say she won't warn him? She knows we need a confession to make this stand up in court . . . As things are, it's all pretty much circumstantial, so she might decide to come the sacrificial heroine and try to get him off.'

'True,' Burton replied soberly. 'But in my experience of women who've been strung along, there's usually a huge amount of bitterness and hurt when their world is turned upside down and they find out they've been taken for fools . . . Barbara will want to hear from Ed's own lips if he ever betrayed her. Given the way she's been deceived, vengefulness is almost certain to kick in.'

'What if he jus' lies his head off . . . swears blind he loves her an' there's never been anyone else blah di blah?' Noakes demanded. 'Then we're stuffed.'

'Nathan thinks an emotive challenge about Ed's sexual proclivities coming out of left field will unbalance him, so that he opens up about everything including the murders,' Burton rejoined. 'He more than likely has an overpowering need to talk about it and unburden himself. If he feels sure enough of her ultimate dependence on him — and all the indications are that he does — then he'll succumb to that impulse.'

'As in he's gonna cough to five murders cos she pulls some agony aunt routine?' Noakes looked as though he wished he could believe it would be that easy.

'Nathan's over with Barbara, priming her to talk about the sex side of things, because it's almost certain the question of Ed's true nature has been preying heavily on her mind ever since that confrontation with Vincent Rossi.'

Noakes looked as though he'd learned as much as he ever cared to know about Ed Frayling's sex life but conceded, 'If the lad's as screwed up as Shippers seems to think, then mebbe we're on to a winner.'

Burton's chin lifted. Doyle whistled a few bars of 'Stand By Your Man' before she quelled him with a stern glare.

'What time is Ed due here?' Carruthers asked.

'Four o'clock,' she said. 'After he's done the lunchtime shift at Rossi's.'

Markham scanned their surroundings. 'DI Carstairs is sending over some plain clothes officers to sort H&S props and get the techies to rig up what we need in the booth for studio 4.'

'Camera feed?' Doyle asked.

'The works,' the DI confirmed. 'All anyone will see round the place is a few guys in overalls who look like workmen. The objective is to ensure we have eyes and ears trained on studio 4 from the moment Ed Frayling arrives.'

Carruthers frowned. 'What about the other studios?' he enquired. 'Won't it look odd if Frayling's the only one allowed in and there's no other musicians around?'

'Not a problem,' Burton said briskly. 'Our janitor friend can say he cancelled bookings for the other studios but somehow mislaid Ed's contact details. He'll make it sound like he's sneaking Ed in as a special favour . . . all on the q.t. so to speak.'

'D'you reckon Worzel can pull it off?' Carruthers sounded dubious. 'He's not exactly RADA material.'

'He'll be fine,' Burton snapped repressively. 'At least he will be after I've gone through it with him a few times. I guarantee he'll be word perfect by this afternoon.'

Doyle grimaced. God help the poor sod once Burton started channelling her inner Professor Higgins.

'Who's bringing Barbara across?' Carruthers asked.

'Undercovers,' Markham instructed, 'once Nathan's satisfied she's good to go.'

The rundown, squalid premises depressed him, but there was no denying the location was perfect for the climax of their investigation. He only hoped that Barbara Price would come through and give them enough to put Frayling where he belonged. At a level, Markham was angry with himself for being taken in by the young waiter's convincing mask of sanity and smokescreen of settled domesticity. But in truth, had Giulia Rossi not set the ball rolling, he doubted whether they would ever have rumbled the man who he now realized was dangerously disturbed and a conniving predator to boot.

Emerging onto the pavement outside, the DI was grateful for a freshening breeze that stirred the overhanging plane trees and sycamores. 'Carstairs is organizing a discreet exclusion zone monitored by plain clothes,' he said. 'Everything as unobtrusive as possible so nothing leaks out.'

'What next?' Noakes wanted to know.

'I do a last-minute briefing for Sidney and Ebury-Clarke,' aka toad-face, 'then it's all systems go.'

The little group, watched from inside the building's peeling stucco facade by its Dickensian guardian, turned the corner of Porlock Mews and was gone.

* * *

Shortly after half past four their prime suspect entered the building and, after some desultory chat with (word perfect) Worzel, let himself into studio 4. Squeezed into the adjacent recording booth, Markham's team waited, observing silently as the young musician clattered about, arranging things to his satisfaction.

Ed Frayling proceeded with what Markham recognized as some classic Carole King, accompanying his pleasant tenor on guitar. Listening as the strains of 'You've Got A Friend' floated through the CCTV microphone transmitter, Markham was struck by the horrible irony of hearing a serial killer voice such tender, poignant lyrics. Noakes meanwhile mimed being violently sick.

A quarter of an hour followed in which Frayling tried out some other well-known ballads before moving on to riffs, completely oblivious to everything but his own enjoyment.

Suddenly feet clattered up the stairs and Barbara Price burst into the studio, looking dowdy as usual in a long shapeless cardigan over black leggings.

She was unexpectedly convincing, Markham decided, hardly breathing as she blindsided her astonished fiancé with an emotional account of the visit to Vincent Rossi. As she spat accusations that he had never loved her and deceived her with men, it seemed to the DI almost as if the doubts Frayling's partner had successfully repressed for so long were at last emerging from her subconscious mind like slithering reptiles.

Burton was tense, worried that the woman had gone from zero to 100 mph in a matter of minutes.

Don't lose it. We need him to confess.

Almost as though Barbara had heard the unspoken plea, she sank down on a rickety school bench which ran along one wall together with a motley assortment of music stands, synthesisers, keyboards and other equipment. They could see the hands in her pockets were clenched fists.

Her voice was hoarse. 'Look, Ed. If you've lied to me about this, then who's to say you haven't lied about . . . other stuff. I told the police we were at home those evenings when Norman, Stella and that DJ were murdered. But we weren't together the whole time . . . I didn't say anything about it to the police in case it looked bad. And anyway, I trusted you . . . up till now.'

Frayling's complexion now showed patches of pale pink and dead white but he said nothing, just sat rooted to his chair, the guitar on his lap.

'*Please,* Ed. You can see where I'm coming from.' Her tone was just on the verge of getting nasty. 'And now Vincent Rossi is dead . . . and I'm wondering if you had anything to do with it, seeing as he warned me about you.'

Frayling bent down and carefully, lovingly, returned the guitar to its battered black case.

Then, in an eerily mechanical tone, strikingly at variance with the harmonious crooning of his practice session, the young musician spoke, his gaze empty and totally devoid of expression.

'I never really loved you, Barb. At least not in the way you wanted. Yeah, I did the murders, but who's going to believe you . . . a failed social worker trying to get her own back because her boyfriend prefers blokes—'

He broke off as dumpy, bovine Barbara Price launched herself at him with something sharp glinting in her hand, moving as Doyle said afterwards, like greased lightening.

The detectives crashed into the room to see arterial blood spurting from Frayling's neck, Price's precision tweezers having found their mark.

'I hope I've severed his fucking voice box,' she shrieked as the two sergeants pinioned and subdued her, her chest heaving as though she had run a race.

Markham and Burton dropped to their knees by the crumpled figure on the floor.

As his fellow DI frantically tried to staunch the bleeding with tissues, Markham could see Frayling was trying to speak.

Gurgling and writhing, he somehow got the words out: 'He said it was all right and that God forgave.'

Then the terrible noises ceased and bloodshot eyes rolled back in his head.

Doyle and Carruthers had hauled the dead man's screaming partner out of the room, her maniacal cries echoing down the corridor, and now the two DIs contemplated each other across Frayling's corpse.

'I gave instructions for the undercovers to check Barbara over before sending her in,' Burton said white-lipped. 'Visual only, though, in case she was spooked . . . I was thinking more about self-harm than . . .'

'Don't blame yourself, Kate. I didn't foresee this outcome any more than you did. The sexual insult that made her snap.' Not the admission of multiple murder.

'There'll be an internal inquiry.'

'Which you'll pass with flying colours.' He laid a hand on her arm which would not stop shaking. 'We've solved the case and arguably done both society and Frayling a favour. He'd never have seen the light of day again, fed and watered at vast public expense . . . At least this way justice is done without the families facing the ordeal of a trial where some smart-alec brief drags people's reputations through the mud.'

'You heard what he said at the end, guv?'

'Yes, I heard.'

'You know what it could mean?'

'That too.'

He helped Burton up, her smart fawn trouser suit covered in Frayling's blood.

'You're in shock, Kate,' he said gently. 'Let's get you checked over. Analysis can wait.'

* * *

Unusually for the team, which usually repaired to the Grapes pub for post-investigation drinks, 'Markham's Gang' met at the Sweepstakes on the Saturday after wrapping up the high street case.

This was the first visit of Doyle and Carruthers to Markham's apartment, and they were awkward and diffident to start with. The DI was vastly amused by the manner in which Noakes virtually assumed the duties of host, installing the other two in comfortable armchairs and sorting out beers and snacks (he knew exactly where Markham kept the Kettle crisps, Pringles and 'cheesy bits') while telling them sternly 'not to make a mess cos that carpet cost a bomb'.

Since he normally guarded his privacy with ferocious determination, Markham was in fact surprised how comfortable it felt to see them there. But the truth was, they were essentially his surrogate family, the two sergeants somehow recalling the high spirits (and occasional bumptiousness) of Jonathan in those rare carefree times when he sloughed off his demons. Even Carruthers, whose wariness and watchfulness had gradually dissolved under the influence of the others, now felt like a comrade-in-arms, so that he felt confident there was no risk of their conversation being reported to Sidney or Ebury-Clarke.

Watching the two young men, he allowed himself to wonder what Jonathan might have become . . . what he might have achieved if he had ever been able to escape the shadow of abuse. The note he had left before hanging himself was so defeated, so *flat* . . . even the burning anger towards their mother (also now dead) for looking the other way had sunk to pale embers. Just a simple goodbye and 'See you soon, Gil' . . .

Markham forced down the memory of his brother's elongated corpse twitching in the stairwell of that filthy squat, his toes unnaturally pointed like a ballet dancer's, and poured himself and Kate glasses of the ever-ready Châteauneuf-du-Pape, noting that she attacked her drink with some gusto before plonking herself down cross-legged on the floor next to his own particular armchair (Noakes having told the others, 'That's the guvnor's'). He felt an almost painful twist of the stomach seeing her in Olivia's accustomed spot, but trusted the red wine to work its usual magic.

The Grapes, with its old-fashioned nineteen-seventies decor, quirky furnishings and hotchpotch layout, was their resort of choice for councils of war, its bosomy landlady Denise being a huge fan of the handsome inspector who treated her 'like she was one of the nobs'. Markham knew that he had only to ask and she would have made over the back parlour entirely for their use, banishing less favoured patrons to the main lounge. But the sensitivity of this case was such, that he felt the need to keep it safely within his own four walls.

The day was bright with mild, soft sunlight pouring in, bringing out the rich sheen of the baroque red and gold vintage wallpaper Olivia had chosen when they got the living room redecorated shortly before she and Markham broke up. Doyle took in his surroundings with considerable interest (for girlfriend Kelly's better information), while trying not to be too obvious about it. The ballet prints and figurines were not to his taste, but that was the guvnor all over — arty farty with a capital 'A'. Like Noakes, however, he felt proud to have a boss out of the common way. I mean, you couldn't imagine anyone else in CID having a pad like this.

Carruthers felt the flat possessed the ambience of a private club, its balletic accents merely enhancing the sense of civilized connoisseurship. He'd heard that the DI's study overlooked the neighbouring municipal cemetery but knew there was no chance of being admitted to Markham's personal sanctum. As his gaze fell on Noakes wolfing down Pringles, salted peanuts and cheese straws — from a bowl, no doubt out of a desire to maintain standards in front of the two sergeants (whereas if alone with Markham, it was probably a case of straight from the packet) — he grinned at the contrast between their elegant surroundings and such unabashed plebeianism. He wasn't sure he understood the bond between the guvnor and his oldest friend (talk about the attraction of opposites!), but there was something about it that touched him nonetheless and made him wonder if *he* would ever inspire such dogged loyalty.

Kate Burton steadily drank her wine, while reminding herself to slow down since it wouldn't do to get too tipsy. Things were better these days between herself and Nathan, her partner notably more tender and patient whenever she reminisced about her dead father or wandered down nostalgic byways in a manner that must be trying to someone of his cooler, more prosaic temperament. It was only occasionally that she felt a vague unhappy loss or want of something over-shadow her like a cloud. Aware of Noakes's gaze shifting between herself and Markham (like he was refereeing a ping pong match, she thought exasperatedly), she took a firm grip on her emotions and resolved that from now on she would exercise the greatest possible circumspection when it came to the guvnor. It was clear — not least from his haggard appearance and the way he was downing the red wine almost as rapidly as herself — that he was missing Olivia badly. If there was a chance that things could come right between them, she wasn't going to queer anyone's pitch.

'OK.' With heroic restraint and contrary to his general practice, having finished his bowl of snacks and by way of oblique tribute to the guvnor, Noakes neither licked his fin-gers nor wiped them on the mismatched mushroom-coloured cords and yellow sweater that were his choice for weekend casual wear. 'How'd it go with Sidney an' Ebury-Clarke, boss?'

'Oh, I'm afraid they weren't having any of it, Noakesy. I've been advised in no uncertain terms that Henry Morland Ph.D. is strictly off limits.'

Burton's face was troubled.

'Even though we reckon it was Morland that Ed Frayling was talking about?' she said.

There was silence as the dead man's final cryptic utter-ance seemed to fill the room.

He said it was all right and that God forgave.

'It was straight out of Morland's playbook,' Noakes insisted. 'Cos of being on matey terms with the Almighty, giving absolution an' all that . . . like RCs do when folk go to confession in the tardis.'

Markham smiled at his friend's unconquerable preju-dice against the "black box" and said mildly, 'Confession isn't unique to Catholics, Noakes. It's practised in the Anglican church too . . . remember those confessionals in Saint Michael's.'

His friend was in disputatious mode.

'With Proddies it's more about the sky pilot giving *advice* an' jus' kind of being there to *listen*, but Morland's and *your* lot say priests c'n wipe the slate clean an' cancel the bad stuff, so if anyone's made a mess it's OK an' they get to start over.'

'I take your point, but as you can imagine, the canonical niceties hardly cut much ice with Sidney and the chief super,' was Markham's wry response. 'Moreover, they didn't regard Ed's last words as some kind of dying declaration or having any legal weight whatsoever. As far as *they* were concerned, he was *in extremis* and babbling.'

'But *you* don't think so, guv?' Carruthers said shrewdly.

'No . . . It seemed to me that Ed must have been referring to a third party — a male — who knew he was our killer.'

'But it was *Morland* who dobbed Frayling in, remember?' Doyle protested. 'Told us all that stuff about running into him in the graveyard and realizing it was the same guy who'd asked a load of questions about Rasputin and hypnosis.'

'I suspect that may have been a very polished performance,' Markham replied slowly and shook his head. 'It certainly took me in.'

'Me and all,' Doyle admitted. 'But maybe Frayling *was* rambling, boss . . . with him being religious and churchy, p'raps at the end he was thinking back to what some priest said — wanted to make an act of contrition thingy before he snuffed it.' The DS was quite proud of himself for being able to remember the technical term.

'I'd be more willing to accept that hypothesis were it not for my having found a connection between Morland and Ed Frayling,' Markham said gravely.

'You mean they didn't just run into each other at Morland's creepy Rasputin shrine?' Carruthers asked eagerly. 'They knew each other before that?'

The room seemed to hold its breath.

'I did some digging in Catholic diocesan records . . . just on a hunch,' Markham told them, with an ironical inflexion on the last word, 'and eventually discovered that in 2015 Ed Frayling was briefly a student at St Peter's Seminary out in Calder Vale.'

'*Oh no.*' Oblivious of grease, Noakes rumpled his hair into agitated prongs. 'You don' mean to say Morland was there too.'

Markham nodded grimly. 'He was a pastoral tutor there from 2015 to 2016, not long before he left the priesthood . . . It's a small theological college, only a hundred or so students, so their paths *had* to have crossed.'

'Thinking back, Morland never actually said whether he knew Frayling from before,' Doyle mused. 'He just kind of implied their first meeting happened when Ed rocked up at the centre.'

'It was very skilfully done,' Markham agreed. 'But that omission raised a red flag with me.'

'Mind you,' Carruthers interjected, 'you've got to look at it from *his* point of view . . . He was handing us a serial killer . . . maybe even a student of his. Stands to reason he wouldn't want to bring up that they knew each other in case we got the idea they were *accomplices* or something like that.'

'Or maybe Frayling only confessed to Morland right at the end when he felt he was really losing it big time,' Doyle suggested. 'And *that's* when Morland decided he had to turn him in.'

'But Ed had already killed to cover his tracks,' Burton objected. 'Why would he suddenly tell Morland and risk him going to the police?'

'Who knew what was going on in the sick twist's mind,' Doyle retorted smartly. 'He could've subconsciously *wanted* Morland to stop him.'

'You've been reading too many of them psychology text-books,' Noakes grunted. 'I reckon ole Ed were on a roll . . . got a taste for it with Parker. No way did he want some ex-padre spoiling his fun.'

'My point is, that if Henry Morland was innocent of any wrongdoing and had a clear conscience, then there was nothing for him to worry about,' Markham countered. 'Honesty required that he should be completely frank. That evasion bothered me.'

'*Yeah*,' Noakes declared emphatically. '*Tell the truth and shame the devil.*' Then, catching sight of Markham's expression, he continued, 'Carruthers said "accomplices". Is that what you think, boss . . . that they were *in it together*?'

Markham took his time about answering, straight dark brows contracted in thought and the finely drawn mouth tightly compressed.

'Something tells me there was complicity,' he said at last. 'But I don't believe we could ever prove it.'

'What about Babs?' Noakes hazarded. 'Mebbe *she* saw 'em together.' With a grim expression, he added, 'That one's looking at life inside, an' I reckon social workers are about as popular as bent coppers. If she's got owt on Voldemort, then now's the time to lean on her . . . offer a cushy berth in the loony bin or some Disneyland prison.'

'I don't see us getting anywhere with that, Noakesy, even if I approved of that kind of wheeler dealing. It didn't sound like Barbara had a notion that anyone else was involved.'

'But for God's sake, *why*?' Carruthers burst out. 'I mean, what motive would Morland have for wanting all those people dead?'

'Greed, if he were hoping to help Frayling stiff old ladies,' Noakes intoned. 'Or mebbe jus' downright badness.'

'There's something else,' Markham said quietly.

They stared at him.

'You mean, you've got *more* on Mister Creepy?' Noakes asked. 'As in he had a grudge against the vicar an' the rest of 'em?'

'Norman Collins apparently made representations to Bishop Buckley about Morland,' Markham told them.

'*Representations*?' Doyle echoed stupidly.

'That was His Lordship's typically weasel word for it,' Markham explained. 'But when pushed, he admitted that the vicar had expressed reservations about "unorthodox practices" including repressed memory therapy.'

Carruthers whistled a long note. '*Blimey*,' he said. 'Maybe Morland was treating Frayling and it somehow led back to Collins—'

'Cos Collins or someone he knew had done something to Frayling,' Doyle interrupted excitedly. '*Hurt him* . . . sexual abuse or something and Morland knew all about it . . . wanted to help Frayling get his revenge.'

'What's to say Morland *himself* hadn't abused Frayling in some way — got a hold over him — at that seminary place or in therapy?' Carruthers shot back. 'Could've been sexual or just sicko mind games. And then he somehow programmed Frayling to kill Norman Collins cos the vicar was trying to get the centre shut down . . . Maybe it was *Collins* who was behind those allegations that ended up in the *Gazette*.'

'The thing is, it looks as though we'll never know,' Markham said bleakly.

So many unanswered questions.

'Maybe Morland's just a sadist,' Burton said tonelessly. 'Maybe he enjoyed playing a vicarious part in the whole thing? Seeing how far Ed was prepared to go . . . just plain evil . . . *amoral*.'

Noakes looked complacent at this, since it was rare for him and Burton to be on the same page. 'Yeah,' he nodded vigorously. 'Thass what I said . . . downright badness.' He rumpled the stiff little quills some more, looking comically like an overweight, paunchy Teddy Boy. '*Hey boss*,' he tackled Markham, 'are you *sure* there's no way we can get him?'

'It's all too tenuous,' his friend replied wearily. 'Purely circumstantial. And I think Morland would easily bat away any accusation that he hadn't been frank. He'd say that he had completely forgotten about the seminary . . . came across so many people in his career . . . the forgetfulness of age, memory not what it was. And anyway Frayling was very different these days — reinvented himself as this hipster musician — so he hadn't made the connection with St Peter's etcetera etcetera. The DCI and Chief Super would be putty in his hands.'

'Yeah, I s'pose he'd wrap Sidney an' toad-face round his little finger with that whole slimy mind-control thing he's got going . . . jus' like Rasputin,' Noakes opined gloomily, less inclined than formerly to take the view that the Russian mystic had some redeeming features.

'D'you think there was any reason why Morland might have wanted to harm Sheila, Stella and George Parker?' Burton asked meditatively. 'Apart from greed or getting his thrills by proxy?'

'Not that I've been able to uncover, Kate,' Markham shrugged, 'but who knows . . .'

He let the chilling possibility hang in the air before adding, 'Morland could have harboured some hidden enmity towards *all* the victims, given that Medway is such an insular little community, but so far I haven't been able to trace the connections . . . If there *was* complicity between him and Frayling, he's covered his tracks well.'

'Why d'you think he came to us in the end, guv?' Doyle asked.

'I remember he talked about Frankenstein's monster,' Markham said after a pause of some moments. 'Perhaps he felt he could no longer control his creature . . . That Ed was spiralling towards self-destruction—'

'An' it jus' weren't fun no more,' Noakes finished morosely.

'Or perhaps he'd settled old scores and Ed was expendable,' was Burton's verdict.

Markham knocked back the rest of his glass before helping himself and Burton to more from the sideboard, watched with some concern by Noakes. The guvnor was by no means a reckless drinker, but him and Miz Sobersides almost looked like they were trying to outdo each other. The situation needed watching . . . Mind you, having to give up on nailing Morland would drive a saint to the hard stuff . . .

He tried a last throw of the dice. 'You *sure* there's no way round the high-ups, boss? Covert obs? I've got time owing from Rosemount an' the new lad's shaping up nicely.'

Markham smiled in a way that made Kate Burton's heart turn over, the chiselled features softening marvellously as he contemplated his former wingman.

'Don't even go there, Noakesy,' he warned. 'God knows, I hate to think of Morland getting away with it, but there are possibly ways of making Medway uncomfortable for him.' Noakes smiled knowingly at these words. 'The best I can do for now is put the word out with regional squads and ask them to keep a watching brief . . . Otherwise, I believe on this occasion we'll have to trust to Karma,' Markham continued. 'Don't forget how Rasputin met his end.'

'Yeah, got hisself murdered by some aristo who fed him buns laced with cyanide,' Noakes said eagerly. 'An' they shot him and threw him in the river when he wouldn't stay dead.'

'*Nosferatu* meets *Fatal Attraction*,' Doyle said with a shudder.

Noakes was on a roll. 'When the commies dug him up, they chucked him on a bonfire, but his chest wouldn't burn an'—'

Doyle baulked at hearing about botched cremations. 'You're putting us off our crisps, sarge,' he protested.

'It's *history* innit.' Noakes's tone was reproachful, as of one casting pearls before swine.

'Well, my point is that if Rasputin was a charlatan, his sins found him out in the end. God is not to be mocked, you know,' Markham said quietly.

'Galatians six,' the other said approvingly to theatrical eyerolls from the younger men.

'He had a wild time before checking out, though,' Burton said unexpectedly. 'Women couldn't get enough of him . . . ate the scraps from his plate and kissed the hem of his shirt like he was a reincarnation of the Sun King or some kind of sex god.' She hiccoughed. 'They even cut his fingernails and sewed them into their dresses like they were holy relics.'

'*Eeugh!*' from Doyle.

Burton looked she was enjoyed the reaction she was getting. 'The peasants joked that instead of the royal flag they should have flown a pair of his trousers over the palace.'

Noakes looked po-faced at this.

'He may have looked all gaunt and goaty — a sort of Russian Fagin — but he just had this colossal vitality and confidence.' She had clearly been reading up on the subject. 'People compared him to a gorilla . . . like he was Siberia's answer to King Kong.'

Carruthers was surprised to find that starchy Burton could be quite amusing when she put her mind to it. *You ought to get sloshed more often, ma'am*, he thought.

'A perv with some sort of genuine psychic gift?' he hazarded.

'Yeah, jus' like Morland,' Noakes grunted. 'Too bad we can't lay a finger on the bastard.'

'I think we can find a way of making the neighbourhood too hot for him,' Markham repeated. More soberly he added, 'If he pulled Ed Frayling's strings . . . or worse . . . then he's a dangerous man. You can be assured, I'll make it my business to monitor his movements.'

They had no doubt he meant it.

With a visible effort, Markham turned the conversation away from Henry Morland.

'So your new trainee at Rosemount is shaping up well?' he enquired of Noakes.

'Oh aye. A history buff an' all.'

'An admirer of General Gordon perchance?'

'He's more for Nelson . . . wants us to get a picture for the residents' lounge.'

'Admirably patriotic.'

'Well, dunno about that . . . I were never sure about all that "Kiss me Hardy" stuff.'

Burton brightened.

'There's a debate about that, sarge,' she piped up. 'Some people think it was *Kismet, Hardy* . . . that's Turkish for Fate.'

'Like Karma,' Noakes said, clearly pleased at the coincidence, to say nothing of his preference for a scenario that didn't hint at any funny business on the high seas.

Markham chuckled. 'There's a story about Auberon Waugh, the satirist — you know, the son of Evelyn Waugh who wrote *Brideshead Revisited*,' he added seeing that the other looked mystified.

'Oh aye, the bloke who wrote about poncey types who went round carrying teddy bears.' Noakes didn't look as if he thought such antecedents promised much in the way of entertainment.

'The very same. Well, he was shot while serving in India I believe . . . and he thought he was going to die and said to some infantryman "Kiss me Hardy". Obviously he was quoting Nelson. Only in the end he *didn't* die, and most of the soldiers gave him a wide berth after that because they misunderstood his meaning.'

Noakes looked happy to know the army at least knew what was what.

Carruthers grinned. 'Nelson had a mistress — Lady Hamilton — so that gets him off the hook.'

'Happen it's only fair we should have something that shows Trafalgar,' Noakes said magnanimously. 'Summat *tasteful*, mind . . . The lad told me they stuck Nelson's body in a cask of brandy so it didn't go off. I don' think old folk want to know about stuff like that.'

Not long afterwards, the team dispersed, Noakes accompanying Doyle and Carruthers to enjoy the footie and a take-away at the latter's flat (it being Muriel's Bridge Night). Then Nathan Finlayson called to collect Kate and whisk her off for an evening of culture at the Bromgrove Playhouse which was showing the South Korean thriller *Parasite* ('Rather you than me, mate,' Doyle thought when he heard their plans).

Markham was alone but didn't mind the solitude, sipping his wine as the flush of the day gradually declined and shadows filled the room. He thought of all the players in this latest case, wondering how they had reacted to the news that Ed Frayling was the high street killer . . .

The buzzer sounded unnaturally shrill in the stillness.

His heart gave a great lurch,

It could only be Olivia.

Seeing her in the doorway with swollen panda eyes and mascara-streaked cheeks, he simply drew her inside.

'Hello, Liv,' he said.

THE END

THE JOFFE BOOKS STORY

We began in 2014 when Jasper agreed to publish his mum's much-rejected romance novel and it became a bestseller.

Since then we've grown into the largest independent publisher in the UK. We're extremely proud to publish some of the very best writers in the world, including Joy Ellis, Faith Martin, Caro Ramsay, Helen Forrester, Simon Brett and Robert Goddard. Everyone at Joffe Books loves reading and we never forget that it all begins with the magic of an author telling a story.

We are proud to publish talented first-time authors, as well as established writers whose books we love introducing to a new generation of readers.

We have been shortlisted for Independent Publisher of the Year at the British Book Awards three times, in 2020, 2021 and 2022, and for the Diversity and Inclusivity Award at the Independent Publishing Awards in 2022.

We built this company with your help, and we love to hear from you, so please email us about absolutely anything bookish at feedback@joffebooks.com

If you want to receive free books every Friday and hear about all our new releases, join our mailing list: www.joffebooks.com/contact

And when you tell your friends about us, just remember: it's pronounced Joffe as in coffee or toffee!

ALSO BY CATHERINE MOLONEY

THE DI GILBERT MARKHAM SERIES

www.ingramcontent.com/pod-product-compliance
Ingram Content Group UK Ltd.
Pitfield, Milton Keynes, MK11 3LW, UK
UKHW041526160425
5499UKWH00035B/554